THE VULTURE

GIL SCOTT-HERON

THE VULTURE

Grove Press
New York

First published in the United States in 1970 by
The World Publishing Company

First published in Great Britain in 1996 by the Payback Press
an imprint of Canongate Books Ltd, Edinburgh

This edition originally published in 2010 in Great Britain
by Canongate Books

Printed in the United States of America

ISBN: 978-0-8021-2058-8

Grove Press
an imprint of Grove/Atlantic, Inc.
841 Broadway
New York, NY 10003

Distributed by Publishers Group West

www.groveatlantic.com

12 13 14 15   10 9 8 7 6 5 4 3 2 1

To Mr Jerome Baron
without whom the 'bird'
would never have gotten
off the ground.

Standing in the ruins of another black man's life.
Or flying through the valley separating day and night.
'I am Death,' cried the vulture. 'For the people of
   the light.'

Charon brought his raft from the sea that sails on souls,
And saw the scavenger departing, taking warm hearts to
   the cold.
He knew the ghetto was a haven for the meanest
   creature ever known.

In a wilderness of heartbreak and a desert of despair,
Evil's clarion of justice shrieks a cry of naked terror.
Taking babies from their mamas and leaving grief beyond
   compare.

So if you see the vulture coming, flying circles in
   your mind.
Remember there is no escaping, for he will follow close
   behind.
Only promise me a battle; battle for your soul and
   mine.

The Bird is Back

It would not be much of an exaggeration to say that my life depended on completing *The Vulture* and having it accepted for publication. Not just because it placed more money in my feverish hands than I thought I might ever see at one time, but also because I had bet more than I had a right to on that happening and it was such a long shot.

In 1968 I was a second-year college student at Lincoln University in Oxford, Pennsylvania. I had put up all the money I had earned plus a small grant from the school to follow up what had been a less than scintillating freshman year.

Six weeks after school opened I quit. I dropped out. The reason was the same one that had brought my first year crashing down around my ears. I had an idea for a novel and wanted to write it. I thought I could find the proper rhythm and could balance my schedule between class-work and work on the story, but there was no way. I was getting nothing done. There's a story I heard once about a jackass that was set down squarely between two bales of hay and starved to death. I was just like Jack. When I opened a textbook I saw my characters and when I sat at the typewriter I saw my ass getting kicked out of school for failing all my subjects.

What I asked the school for was similar to leave of absence. I would remain on the campus for the rest of the semester since I had paid for room and board, but I would be at work on the novel and would receive **I** (Incomplete) for all my final grades. The advantage was that when I finished the book and if I wanted to apply for re-admission to Lincoln or elsewhere, I would not have a complete set of failures to overcome.

The Dean reacted as though I had taken leave of my senses

and asked me to get the school psychiatrist to approve. That read like a challenge and perhaps a bit of 'C.H.A.' by the Dean. (In traditional institutions when someone makes a request for extraordinary consideration the person responsible for approval likes to 'cover his ass'.) The Dean must have thought I was crazy. It certainly seemed crazy that someone as poor as I would bet his last money on a first novel.

My plan was to finish the book before the second semester began in February. That showed how little I knew about what I was doing. By January I had little more (that I felt good about) than I had when I saw the psychiatrist in October and gained his approval. And I still had no ending for the damn thing.

January brought me the idea for the ending I needed and a method of connecting the four separate narratives to the book's opening. Now all I needed was a chair and my typewriter.

That was damn near all I had. Over the next two months I worked in a dry-cleaners about a quarter-mile from the school. The owner and his wife both needed to work elsewhere and wanted someone to mind their property. I slept in the back and took meal money from the small income generated by the students.

The miracle that got *The Vulture* accepted by a publisher, along with *Small Talk at 125th and Lenox* (a volume of poetry published simultaneously), consisted of a series of cosmic coincidences and intervention by 'the spirits' on my behalf. Let it suffice to say that the interest in the book of three brothers at Lincoln I will never forget; Eddie 'Adenola' Knowles (a percussionist on four of our first six albums and founding member of The Midnight Band), Lincoln 'Mfuasi' Trower (Eddie's roommate, who also missed a good deal of sleep as they sat up reading the manuscript instead of doing their school work), and Lynden 'Toogaloo' Plummer (my best customer at the cleaners who never failed to sit down and read a few pages when he came in with his things). Those three friends probably have no idea that they were the barrier that saved me from being pulled into the discouraging blank pages that I faced occasionally when a scene or an idea about the plot, the characters, the connections, something, would not work. I will always owe them.

I must also say here that I came from a family that zipped through college much like high school and kindergarten. My mother and her two sisters and brother all graduated from college with honors, literally at the top of their respective classes. I set quite another precedent by being the first one of their line to ('Ahem') 'take a sabbatical'.

To say the least it was not a popular decision but my mother had faith. In a telephone conversation we had after the deed had been 'undone' she said that she *didn't think it was the best idea I'd ever had* but to *go ahead and finish it and promise that, whether it was published or not, I would go back to school somewhere afterwards and get my degree.* She finished by saying that *I would always have a home with her and that she loved me.*

I did not dedicate *The Vulture* to my mother. I dedicated *Small Talk at 125th and Lenox* to her instead because she always appreciated the poetry so much and helped me with lines and ideas (including the punch line for *Whitey on the Moon*). And there was a special man, a very gentle man, the father of a high-school classmate of mine, who was the person I believe 'the spirits' helped me connect with somehow.

I did go back to school. I have a Master's degree from Johns Hopkins University in Baltimore that was sent, sight unseen, to my mother upon my completion of the work, and I have since dedicated many accomplishments in my career to the person who brought me no further grief at that time of stress and need for a kind word, Mrs Bobbie Scott Heron. She is a helluva person and a good friend.

I hope you enjoy *The Vulture* as much as I enjoyed the thrill of writing it. My experience of putting it together was my way of doing the high-wire act blindfolded, knowing that if it didn't work, if it wasn't published, there was no safety net that I could land on and no hole that I could crawl into, no way to face the other folks at Lincoln and no money to go anywhere else. In retrospect, I think it has held up remarkably well.

The major task of a murder mystery writer is to conceal the identity of the perpetrator while not getting caught yourself. It's a bit like a puppet master who must not be seen pulling the strings.

I admit that as a 19-year-old I had never put on a puppet show in my life. I knew that I was controlling the characters connected to each other. I knew that as the story progressed I had to advance the reader toward the identity of the killer(s), but not that each revelation had to shed new light on all of the suspects.

I was also caught in a language and culture trap. I was writing a story for anyone/everyone to enjoy and guess about as they read, but my characters and their way of speaking and language had to be true to the neighborhood and the murder had to be true to the underworld culture and its symbols.

The Vulture might work as well (or better!) on film as it does on the page. My biggest problem setting it up was how *to show you* the murder of John Lee without showing you the murderer. Hence, the autopsy report in the opening section.

Some people accused me of using that and a half dozen other devices as 'red herons'. Why they are so adamant about that is 'a mystery to me'.

I do hope you enjoy 'bird watching'.

Gil Scott-Heron
New York, September 1996

Phase One

John Lee is dead
July 12, 1969 / 11:40 P.M.

Behind the twenty-five-story apartment building that faces 17th Street between Ninth and Tenth avenues, the crowd of onlookers stared with eyes wide at the bespectacled photographer firing flashbulbs at the prone body. The hum of conversation and the shadows of the rotating red lights cast an eerie glow and kept the smaller children tugging at their mothers' cotton dresses.

From the apartment windows high above the ground, faces with no visible bodies scanned the darkness and listened to the miniature confusion below.

A young white policeman stood next to the curb leaning into the patrol car, ear to the receiver, listening to the drone of the dispatcher. Suddenly he placed the receiver down and yelled something to the photographer, who cursed and yelled that he *was* hurrying.

The police ambulance driver stood next to his wagon and chatted with a second officer, a kinky-haired black, waving occasionally at the body. The two ambulance attendants, both in their early twenties, sat on the hood of the prowl car smoking cigarettes.

'You through, Dan?' the white officer asked the photographer.

'Keep your shirt on,' came the irritated reply.

The crowd of passersby inched closer to the corpse, trying to get a better look. Here and there women turned their heads and shielded their children's eyes as they noticed for the first time the red ooze that trickled from the base of the skull.

The photographer limped away muttering, and the wagon attendants moved in with a flexible stretcher. With some difficulty they hoisted the bulky frame of the deceased onto a hammock-style death rest and pulled a sheet over his head. Then they loaded their cargo into the van, and within seconds they were whistling down the block toward Eighth Avenue.

The black policeman was asking questions of the group of pedestrians and receiving negative replies to all of his inquiries. He walked back to the patrol car and slid in under the wheel.

'What do we have?' his partner asked.

'Nothing but the wallet.'

'What about the woman who found the body?'

'Nowhere to be seen. She's prob'ly somewhere pukin' her guts out.'

The prowl car lurched toward Ninth Avenue. The whine of the siren bit into the heavy silence of the night. The neon midnight beacons summoned the restless for beer and whiskey. The youngsters, knowing the Man as they do, followed the prowl car's progress up the avenue with suspicious stares.

'Does the name John Lee mean anything to you?' the black finally asked.

'No,' the rookie replied. 'I donno what to think.'

'I know what you mean. At first I thought some junky had taken another overdose, but when I saw that blood comin' out the back of his head, I figured somebody did him in ... But he wuzn't robbed.'

'Shit!' the rookie exclaimed. 'I don' give a damn. It's outta our hands now. Let the others worry about it.'

'Yeah. But these Puerto Ricans piss me off.'

'What?'

'Talk a mile a minute all day an' cain' answer one simple question for me.'

'They got so many junkies they probably identify.'

'We oughta bury 'um all in the gutter.'

'Can't.' The young white laughed. 'Against the law to bury a man at home.'

In accordance with the Act of April 16, 1907, P.L. 62, as amended by the Act of July 12, 1935, P.L. 710, 16 P.S. Sec. 9521, and on section 503 of the Vital Statistics Act of June 29, 1953, P.L. 304, 35 P.S. sec. 450, 503, I hereby request that an autopsy be performed on

the body of _____ John Lee _____ at the expense of the County of New York and send a report to me or the coroner of the County of New York.

                    Melvin A. Diggs
                              Deputy Coroner

Date: July 13, 1969
Witness(es): Arthur T. Randall

CERTIFICATE OF DEATH

DEPARTMENT OF PUBLIC HEALTH

FILE NO.

DIVISION OF VITAL STATISTICS

BIRTH NO. 46703171

DECEASED — NAME				
1.	FIRST John	MIDDLE	LAST Lee	DATE OF DEATH (MONTH, DAY, YEAR) 2. 7/12/69

RACE WHITE, NEGRO, AMERICAN INDIAN, ETC. (SPECIFY) 3. Negro	SEX 4. Male	AGE — LAST BIRTHDAY (YEARS) 5a. 18	UNDER 1 YEAR MOS.	DAYS	UNDER 1 DAY HOURS	MIN.	DATE OF BIRTH (MONTH, DAY, YEAR) 6. 5/8/51

COUNTY OF DEATH 7a. New York	CITY, TOWN, OR LOCATION OF DEATH Manhattan	INSIDE CITY LIMITS (SPECIFY YES OR NO) 7c. Yes	HOSPITAL OR OTHER INSTITUTION — NAME (IF NOT IN EITHER, GIVE STREET AND NUMBER) 7d. 427 W. 16th St. (Rear)

STATE OF BIRTH (IF NOT IN U.S.A., NAME COUNTRY) 8. New York	CITIZEN OF WHAT COUNTRY 9. U.S.A.	MARRIED, NEVER MARRIED, WIDOWED, DIVORCED (SPECIFY) 10. Never Married	SURVIVING SPOUSE (IF WIFE, GIVE MAIDEN NAME) 11. None

SOCIAL SECURITY NUMBER 12. 154-30-6657	USUAL OCCUPATION (GIVE KIND OF WORK DONE DURING MOST OF WORKING LIFE, EVEN IF RETIRED) 13a. Student	KIND OF BUSINESS OR INDUSTRY 13b.

RESIDENCE — STATE 14a. New York	COUNTY 14b. New York	CITY, TOWN, OR LOCATION 14c. Manhattan	INSIDE CITY LIMITS (SPECIFY YES OR NO) 14d. Yes	STREET AND NUMBER 14e. 306 W. 15th St.

FATHER — NAME 15. Hamilton Lee	MOTHER — MAIDEN NAME 16. Cassie Johnson	INFORMANT — NAME 17. None	MAILING ADDRESS

18. PART I. DEATH WAS CAUSED BY:	[ENTER ONLY ONE CAUSE PER LINE FOR (a), (b), and (c)]	APPROXIMATE INTERVAL BETWEEN ONSET AND DEATH
IMMEDIATE CAUSE (a) Overdose of Heroin		None
CONDITIONS, IF ANY, WHICH GAVE RISE TO IMMEDIATE CAUSE (a), STATING THE UNDERLYING CAUSE LAST DUE TO, OR AS A CONSEQUENCE OF: (b) Inflicted blow to the skull base		2 min.
DUE TO, OR AS A CONSEQUENCE OF: (c)		

PART II. OTHER SIGNIFICANT CONDITIONS: CONDITIONS CONTRIBUTING TO DEATH BUT NOT RELATED TO CAUSE GIVEN IN PART I (a)	AUTOPSY (YES OR NO) 19a. Yes	IF YES WERE FINDINGS CONSIDERED IN DETERMINING CAUSE OF DEATH 19b. Yes

ACCIDENT, SUICIDE, HOMICIDE, OR UNDETERMINED (SPECIFY) 20a. Homicide	DATE OF INJURY (MONTH, DAY, YEAR) 20b. 7/12/69	HOUR 11:30 P.M. 20c.	HOW INJURY OCCURRED (ENTER NATURE OF INJURY IN PART I OR PART II, ITEM NO) 20d. Inflicted by unknown party

INJURY AT WORK (SPECIFY YES OR NO) 20e. No	PLACE OF INJURY AT HOME, FARM, STREET, FACTORY, OFFICE BLDG., ETC. (SPECIFY) 20f. Street	LOCATION (STREET OR R.F.D. NO., CITY OR TOWN, STATE) 20g. 427 W. 16th St.

PHYSICIAN — CERTIFICATION I ATTENDED THE DECEASED AND DEATH OCCURRED AT THE PLACE, ON THE DATE, AND, TO THE BEST OF MY KNOWLEDGE, DUE TO THE CAUSE(S) STATED. 21a.	SIGNATURE Hollis Farmer M.D.	DATE SIGNED (MONTH, DAY, YEAR) 21b. 7/13/69
MEDICAL EXAMINER — CERTIFICATION ON THE BASIS OF THE EXAMINATION OF THE BODY AND/OR THE INVESTIGATION, IN MY OPINION, DEATH OCCURRED ON THE DATE AND DUE TO THE CAUSE(S) STATED. 22a.	SIGNATURE Fortis Billings Coroner	TITLE	DATE SIGNED (MONTH, DAY, YEAR) 22b. 7/13/69
CERTIFIER — NAME (TYPE OR PRINT) 23a.	MAILING ADDRESS STREET OR R.F.D. NO. 23b.	CITY OR TOWN	STATE	ZIP

BURIAL, CREMATION, REMOVAL (SPECIFY) 24a. Burial	DATE (MONTH, DAY, YEAR) 24b. 7/16/69	CEMETERY OR CREMATORY — NAME 24c. Woodlawn	LOCATION 24d. Woodlawn Road, Bx., N.Y.	CITY OR TOWN	STATE

FUNERAL HOME — NAME AND ADDRESS (STREET OR R.F.D. NO., CITY OR TOWN, STATE, ZIP) 25. Calton Funeral Home / Bx.	REGISTRAR — SIGNATURE 26. Carol Dollars	DATE RECEIVED BY LOCAL REGISTRAR 26b. 7/18/69

Spade

'Name: Edward Percy Shannon; age: eighteen. Nickname: Spade. Born on October 6, 1949, in Cambridge, Maryland. Mother and father died last year in auto accident. May 19, 1967. Lives with cousin named Calvin Shannon. High-school grad, George Washington High School in Manhattan. Swimming team. Fourth in class at Osaka-Kyoto School of Defense and received green belt, ninth degree. Has broken toe, left foot. Broken rib, left side. Shall I go on?'

'I know it all,' I said.

'Ha! That's good! You know, of course, what all of that was about. That was a little demonstration as to how thorough I am. That's exactly how thorough I demand my men to be.' He paused long enough to offer me a cigarette from a gold case. I accepted. 'Drugs is a very serious topic around here . . . I see that you have no previous police record. That's another essential. An ex-convict is a constantly hounded man. I need nothing that can tie me to illegal activities.'

He looked up from the paper he had been reading about my life.

'Have a seat,' he suggested.

I sat down and watched him go over the typed papers from his filing cabinet. This was the first moment of quiet in the room. There had been the initial darkness when I entered, during the showing of a home movie. Then there was a brief conversation between my host and my friend Smoky. A minute later the projector was switched off, and the lights switched on, revealing the den, a working office for the man who controlled a major part of the drug traffic in the city.

'Tell me. You smoke reefers?' he asked.

'Yeah, I . . .'

'Snort?'

'No.'

'Skin pop?'

'No.'

'Good,' he said, adding that information to the sheet. 'I don't mind my men getting their kicks. In fact, I sponsor a thing or two now and then, but a man who takes drugs regularly is unpredictable . . . You know any junkies?'

'A few.'

'What do you think of them?'

'I don't know jus' what you mean.'

'They're animals!' he said. 'All of them. I know that you're probably fed up with that term, as much as a man's exposed to it nowadays, but I'm damned if it's not adequate. The men and women you'll be dealing with are desperate sometimes.'

I could tell that he was really gone now. His hands were waving in the air, and his eyes took on the deep concentration of a man who's really enjoying his own rap. I wasn't really interested in what he was saying as much as the way he said it.

Frank Zinari was his name. From all indications, he was one of the top men in the drug game in the Bronx and Manhattan. Of course, I knew that there might easily be a hundred or more top men, but this guy really lived the part. Smoky, an old high-school friend of mine, who had dropped out in his junior year, had seen me one night and through the conversation asked me how I would like to make some easy money. I said I'd like it fine. He told me that his boss, a man named Zinari, was looking for a man; and now I sat in a fabulous crib drinking Johnny Black from a swing-out mahogany bar and sitting on clouds that some furniture maker had captured and shaped like chairs.

'. . . the women will offer you sex, and the men will try to cheat you or rob you or maybe even kill you . . . Now, I've been having trouble with Sullivan charges.' I frowned, not understanding. 'I mean that some of my men have been bothered about carrying concealed weapons. That's why I was particularly interested when Smoky brought your name up. You know a type of self-defense, and there's no telling when you might be called on to use it. If at all possible, avoid this type of confrontation, but if not, do your best to teach the motherless bastards a lesson.'

He was grinning a bit. Proud of his colloquialism, I guess. I looked past him through the glass doors that led to the indoor swimming pool and recreation room. The man himself, Zinari, sat before me with bulging cheeks, struggling with the wrapper of an expensive cigar.

'So what do you say, Spade?' he asked without looking up.

'Sure,' I replied.

'Good,' he said, removing the cigar from rubbery lips. 'Now, I want to make sure that you and Smoky are together on everything.' He paused and beckoned Smoky from his vigil by the door. 'Each night except Sunday and Thursday you will meet these people at these places.' He handed me a sheet with fifteen names on it. 'They are all in the same area, but they don't know each other, so don't try to make any adjustments that might be easier for you. I have it the way it should be. You and Smoky get together on a meeting place where you will turn over to him what you collect from the pushers. Now, the people you work with know better than to be late, but the schedule allows for you to wait twelve minutes. After that, move on to the next spot. Clear?'

'Sure.'

'Oh, one more thing. You will see me only when I send for you. Our only contact will be Smoky. He will pay you each week on Friday. Naturally, he'll see you every night and relay any messages that we have for each other.' He stood and offered me his hand. I shook it.

'What about bread?' I asked.

'Two hundred per week.'

Zinari turned toward the projector and started rewinding his film. I took that to mean that our business was finished. I followed Smoky through the den door, still watching Zinari out of the corner of my eye. I hoped that he would not disappear and I wake up thinking of the money I might have had.

'yeah man! zinari iz aw ri'; no trubble at all. less you try in mess wit' hiz dus'. you know, dat cat iz allatime uptight 'cauz a purty boy muthuhfuckuh think he kin git away stealin' from the man. try if'n you wanna, but if he ketch you, yo' ass iz grass.'

'Two hundred a week,' I said, thinking out loud.

Smoky and I were cruising down the West Side Highway, caught in a mild stream of rush-hour New York traffic. The real crush was opposite us, where motorists were sardined together trying to escape uptown to the suburbs and to Jersey by way of the George Washington Bridge. Smoky handled the big black Cadillac easily, weaving in and out of traffic like a puppet master with the huge car as a mechanical extension of himself. His eyes, hidden behind thick sunglasses, and his hunched posture as he sort of drooped over the steering wheel, displayed his relaxation. He muttered again. His language was a combination of street slang and high-school intellect that he seemed to whistle through a LeRoi Jones beard. Having been a friend of his for so long, I had learned to interpret it.

'yeah, man,' he said, 'thass a good pil a dus' you makin'. i'ss s'pose t'keep you from gittin' greedy ... look, fergit that animal shit! jus' deal wit' de muthuhfuckuhs when you have to, an' don' git involved, ya see? all whi' people think nigguhs iz animals anyway. he didn' say dat shit jus' 'cauz these iz takin' a l'il hoss ... anyway, you meetin' a lotta fine street foxes an' dey gon' promise you a l'il dis if dey kin git a l'il dat, primarily dey gon' be after dat green stuff you be carryin'. all you needa do iz lean wrong one time an' nex' thing you know, you all fucked up.'

'Where are we gonna meet?' I asked Smoky.

'what time you say you gon' be through?'

''Bout twelve.'

'i be near harvey's on 129th street.'

'Good. I'll meet you there.'

Smoky swung the big Caddy down the narrow runway that the city calls the 19th Street exit from the highway. He let me off on 17th Street and Eighth Avenue, pointed back uptown. I waved as he swung back into the six-o'clock Friday horde.

As you approach 17th Street on Eighth Avenue you pass the pizza shop, the staple company that went out of business, other abandoned storefronts, a grimy brownstone, and a corner group who stand in the same spot every evening whistling at the secretaries who wouldn't spit on them. It was quite a change from Zinari's Riverdale paradise. It meant I was almost home.

Midway between Eighth and Ninth avenues on 17th Street there is a park on the south side. There are blue park benches to the left and right of the entrance and a small courtyard with blue picnic tables. To the far right as you enter there is a blacktopped basketball court where teenaged Puerto Ricans run, soaked in perspiration, and call each other various varieties of bastards. In late June, just after the New York schools call it a year, the park is as crowded and lively as a small Mardi Gras.

The sun was setting when Smoky let me out in front of the park. The men of the neighborhood sat and played dominoes and twenty-card poker.

I took a seat on top of one of the picnic tables and watched the basketball game in progress.

'Hi, Spade,' someone called from behind me. I turned, to see

Spade | 11

the approaching figure of John Lee, smiling and clad in khakis and a T-shirt.

'Whuss happnin'?' I asked.

'I need to talk t'you for a second, man.'

'Do it.'

'You int'rested in some good Red?' he asked.

'Can a fish dig water?'

'I got some,' he said in a low voice.

'Come on stronger.'

'Panamanian Red.'

'You dealin'?'

'Yeah. You down?'

'You got trey bags?' I asked.

'Treys *an'* nickels.'

'Whuss a trey countin' for?'

'Ten or 'leven joints.'

I thought about that for a minute. Panamanian Red is one of the more rare variations of marijuana. Also generally much more expensive. Along with Colombian Gold, Acapulco, and the powerful Black smoke from Vietnam, it is very hard to come by in the city. At least, an amount large enough to start dealing.

John sat down next to me on the table. The sight of the Spanish boys running, naked to the waist, with handkerchiefs tied around their sparkling hair and sweat marks staining their crotches, was enough to give me hallucinations of a great waterfall of beer.

'Ten joints?' I asked, to be sure I had heard right.

'Well, the way you roll 'um, prob'ly six. Goddamn Pall Malls.'

'Lemme have a trey bag, then,' I said, sliding him three bills. 'I got to check up on Red an' find out what happened, so I can roll six joints for three dollars.'

John had on a pair of knee-length athletic socks under his

khaki trousers. He slid down the rubber band that held the socks up and found a small manila envelope in the folds of the sock. The envelope was half full, folded over and glued to the opposite side, forming a neat square. He handed it to me and smiled a bit.

'Thass some good shit,' he said.

'I don' need no goddamn commercial. I already bought the shit.'

John was a pretty nice guy, on the whole. He had worked at the food market on 28th Street all through high school and was the man responsible for many highs when the neighborhood was low on green. He was a dark, baked-bean-colored guy with a round, close haircut and a pimply face. He was heavy and slow, not much athletically, but his bulky frame indicated a physical strength.

'How long you been dealin'?' I asked him.

'Jus' a coupla days,' he said.

'Red all you got?'

'Naw. I got some straight smoke too. It's Cuban.'

'I bet it's sweet as hell,' I commented. 'All that Cuban smoke been comin' over in them sugar barrels.'

John, I noticed, was lost in thought. I had gotten interested in the action on the basketball court. Two of the Puerto Ricans had gotten into a heated argument that resulted in one of the guys banging his nose into the other guy's balled-up hand. I lit a smoke.

'You comin' t'night?' Lee asked me.

'Yeah. I'll be there, but I donno if I'd cut them niggers loose in my crib on a Friday night. School jus' gettin' out, too. You know they gon' wanna be high.'

'It'll be all right,' John said.

'Yo' folks still gone?' I asked.

'Another week. Ha! I bet my ol' man wishes ta hell he wuz havin' hiz vacation in town. Aunt Agnes, thass my mother's sister, she's a cold pain in the ass. I couldn' go see her every year. Ha! 'Bout once every ten years'd do me fine.'

I tapped the envelope on my nose.

'Ten joints regular?' I asked.

'Gar-An-Teed!' Lee declared.

John moved on toward the 16th Street side of the park. I saw Game and Nissy, two of the neighborhood characters, having a heated discussion about something. They were just outside the perimeter of a circle of crapshooters. Game was probably laying odds on Lew Alcindor scoring a hundred in one game or something. John got into the conversation, whatever it was. His wide ass was almost laughable from where I sat. I couldn't help but dig him, however, because his attitude was always: 'Spade!' – and I dug that. I suppose he was really afraid of me, but a lot of people on the block steer clear of a man they're scared of. John was one of the few who had decided it would be better to get in tight.

The basketball game was picked up again. There was a replacement for the guy with the bent beak. He sat on the side-lines with tears in his eyes and a wet T-shirt across his nose.

There was a different type of noise filling the park now. The cry of various numbers from the crapshooters as they risked their hard-earned pussy-bait on a flick of the wrist. There were shrieks as mothers decided it was time for dinner, and the traffic of small children turned toward the exit and the apartment buildings as the thought of another meal of rice and beans beckoned.

The small girls still wandered here and there with jump ropes and hula hoops, but now the night people were coming. There were the winos and phony subway blind men who had escaped the crush and the Man with enough bread to appease their Jones for one more day. The calls for Angela and Maria became more insistent as the sun slid toward the other side of the world. The victims of the street were not particular if other younger ones were fascinated by their activities and decided to give it a try. They were not crusaders for or against anything. If someone thought that they were cool because they were high all the time or trying to be, let's go and get high. Otherwise, what the hell? They had decided long ago that the game of life really was not worth playing, because the inventor of the game kept most of the rules a secret. Mothers' shrieks subsided, and those who had not responded were being yanked by the hair away from the park to safety; away from the grown animals in the playground zoo. Mother always knows best.

The name on the small label read 'Bambú,' and under that was: 'Sobrinos de R-Abad Santonja. Alcoy.'

I lifted the protective flap and read the inscription.

'El papel marca Bambú es el mejor – fino y mas aromático.'

I hadn't had any Panamanian Red in a long time. It had given me sort of a festive idea, and instead of the Top brand of paper that I usually rolled with, I skirted the neighborhood to 23rd Street to secure some of the stronger, more expensive Bambú. I tore open the small manila folder and peeped in at the red and green leaf mixture. I took a good lungful and then poured it all into an ashtray to separate the seeds from the grain. These are the seeds that pop from the heat in the middle of your smoke and scare the hell out of you.

I pulled out two sheets of Bambú and folded them, forming a neat trench. Then I tapped the fine powdery grains into the paper and leveled it off. I licked the glue on the corner and stuck the sides together. Then, using my key chain, I sealed the ends of the paper off. Presto! A perfect joint. It took a lot of practice to roll a joint like that every time.

I rolled the entire bag and marveled. Six joints, and any one of them could get a man high. No wonder all the cats quit drinking once they got hip to smoke. I looked at my watch. Eight-thirty already? Time to take a shower and shave before I got dressed to go to John's party. I knew that the niggers would be out in full force. Gig time on a Friday night!

John Lee's Party / 10:15 P.M.

There's something about Friday night that reminds me of a starter's pistol. It seems to release everybody from their week-long hangups. They feel a freedom that they wish they could feel all the time. Stay up all night and get high if they want to. Stay up all day the next day and get higher if they want to. Go and praise God on Sunday if they see fit. Or ignore Him if that's what they feel like doing. You can see a whole lot in seventy-two hours in New York City. All you have to do is know what you're looking for.

Friday night in the neighborhood has always been a gas. There is always somebody throwing a private gig, or some organization willing to inhibit your delinquency for a dollar. These groups had started to flourish once it was no longer the thing to run the block with your main men and roll over anybody who didn't dig what you were into.

The parties in our area, the Chelsea district, are notoriously wild. When we had all been fifteen or sixteen, there had been a gang for every block and a chick for every gang member. The big gang fights had been often and bloody, but rarely fatal. It was a chance for every cat to go out and swing a chain with little chance of being the major concern at a Sunday funeral. That was a passing fad. As the gang members grew older, their turf and their women became more and more a part of their pride and what they symbolized. It was a *something* to hold on to. That was when the knives, razors, and guns turned up on the weekend and people started searching you at the door when you came to a dance. All of a sudden the fun of ambushing a whitey became a serious topic. Most of the gangs started to dissolve when killing became reality, but the ones who decided to stick it out were hell. Everything was for keeps. The whiteys battled the P.R.'s and the blacks, and it went the other ways around too. The gangs all wore their jackets and insignias. The Easter suits stayed in the closet. They were reserved for your burial.

The Dock Battle of 1966

I had made my reputation early. At sixteen, I was already out in the street by myself. Spade, gravedigger for all bad niggers *and* spics. I wasn't a gang member, and I fought anybody I had to. In doing a thing like that, you set yourself up as a quick target the minute you beat up a gang member. Even a punk will try to back you up if he knows he has a follow-up and you don't. It just so happened that before I became a serious problem I had a break. A friend of mine from school named Hicks, who was the leader of a Chelsea Houses group called the Berets, called on me one evening to invite me to a party. He had been trying to convince me that I should hook up with his gang for protection. They were supposed to throw this beer-and-reefer gig on the docks at 20th Street on a Friday night. I took myself for a look-see.

I went to the party, and there were perhaps thirty of us, girls and guys drinking beer and roasting hot dogs over an open fire. The girls that the Berets had invited were primarily Puerto Rican chicks. This was a guarantee that everybody would get some leg, even if a few trains had to be engineered. All of these babes were notorious for drinking like fish and screwing everything that wasn't nailed down.

Out of the darkness behind us we were attacked, caught completely by surprise. I was sitting on the edge of the rotting dock with my feet hanging over the water. Before I could even turn around, I was pushed or kicked and was plunging into the murk that lapped up around the decaying columns.

I went under immediately, taking in a great mouthful of the slimy water. The shock of the cold blasted my brain, and tears stung my eyes. As I went under, I could hear the foghorns from the drifting barges of garbage farther up the filthy Hudson. As I came to the top, I could see a fire starting to grow on the dock about twelve feet above me, and I could hear all the broads screaming and the yells of surprise and pain coming from the other Berets.

My blue jeans felt like weights around my thighs. They had somehow come loose during my fall and now were binding my legs together and hindering my attempts to tread water. I went under once more and struck my head against something. Pain flashed across the length of my mind. I grabbed out in front of me and managed to get a hold on one of the pillars that supported the dock. All of the noises that had previously been so frightening to me now attracted me. I wanted to see someone and be with some people. The wet, mossy wood felt like a snake's belly, cold and alive. The knit sweater that had been my pride and joy was ripped open, exposing my quivering skin to the snake's bosom. I started to cry, I know, but at the same time I started climbing, hoisting myself up the column.

The scum and murk of the water irritated my eyes, but still I could see the smoke rising above me in great balls. The sweet odor of the reefers had been replaced by the stink of burning wood. When I peeped over the platform, I could see the battle. My man Hicks, the leader of the Berets, was on his knees trying to fight off an attacker. He was dressed only in his bathing suit, and blood poured from a slashing razor cut on his shoulder. The towel he was kneeling on was dripping with the fluid from the head of the Puerto Rican girl who had been in his arms short minutes ago. Without really being aware of what I was doing, I seized a beer bottle and began to raise and lower it on the head of the fallen leader's attacker's skull: over and over I hit him until I felt his blood splatter against my chest and I was sure he was dead.

Hicks's eyes sought mine, but I was dazed and unsure of reality. Everything had happened so fast. The Beret that Hicks held in his hand was soaked with blood too. I watched without moving as he rolled the distorted figure of his woman over and pulled a revolver from beneath the towel.

'BAM! BAM! BAM!' Three times the sound of dynamite split the night in half. Twice it seemed that the noise had been the gun's greatest effect, but the third time Hicks had aimed at the body I had beaten into a pulpy mass. The form jerked, hung on the edge of the pier, and then dropped into a coffin of water.

The sound of sirens registered for the first time. Much of the screaming had subsided. There were no enemies left; few of the Berets remained. They had either chased the P.R.'s back toward Tenth Avenue or fled from the Man. Hicks collapsed back onto the towel with the revolver curled under him.

I touched the girl next to him. She was barely breathing, and the warmth that her body had seemed to possess before had faded as she lost more and more blood. Hicks too was in trouble. I ignored the girl completely and lifted Hicks over my shoulder. I threw the gun, which dangled from his limp fingers, over my head into the river. Blindly I started trotting, running, stumbling toward Chelsea. I was familiar with many of the back alleyways that made up the neighborhood. We would be safe if I made it east of Tenth Avenue.

I turned under the West Side Highway exit ramp at 20th Street. It seemed that the sirens were coming from every direction at once. I started thinking that Hicks and I would never make it out of there alive. The cops would beat us and say that we died in the gang fight. I thought we had escaped death, only to find it all over again.

'Hey, kid! Kid! C'mere!'

The words came out of the shadows of the storefront next

to me. It was an old black man, nearly invisible in the inky darkness of the entrance to the shoddy store.

'I wuz lookin' atcha comin' down the street,' he croaked. 'C'min an' I'll hidja.'

I didn't raise any objection at the time, but I wondered why he would do this. All of the old people I knew wanted the hoods dead and all gang members lined up against a wall and shot. I got to the partially open doorway, and the old man lifted Hicks from my shoulders. His strength amazed me. I started to protest that I could make it, but I wasn't really sure that I could.

'Close de do',' he said back over his shoulder.

I reached back for the door, but the sound of the sirens drove me to the threshold again for a final look. Fire engines and prowl cars and ambulances made red a dominant color beneath the shadows of the highway overpass. The acrid smell of the flaming pier was still wedged in my nostrils, painting my mind ugly.

'Jus' hi' long you think you kin stan' inna do' lookin' like de wrong enda hell?' the old man asked.

'I'm sorry, pop . . .'

'I ain'cha pop . . . wouldn't be pop fo' no young hoods an' thugs like you.'

He was shuffling around in the darkness with a clarity of movement. I couldn't even begin to recognize any of the hazy forms that presented themselves in the no-light of the store.

'How's my man?' I asked.

'Thass whut I'z 'bout to concern myse'f wit ni,' was the reply. 'I'm tryin' t'fin some dry close fo' you so you kin go git whut I need. He done los' a lotta blud, joo know.'

I knew. Blood had poured from the wound on Hicks's arm, all down his chest and into the waistband of his swimming trunks. A crimson blotch covered the damp knit on my back.

The old man raised from his slumped position long enough

to hand me a stiff flannel shirt and a pair of paint-stained overalls.

'This all I got,' he said.

'Thass all right,' I told him.

'Gotta be . . . you got any money?'

'Naw. I ain' got nuthin' but a wet ass.'

'. . . an' a dyin' frien'. Mebbe we bettuh take 'im to the hospital.'

'We can't!' I shouted.

His old eyes regarded me with annoyance from their sunken caves. He shrugged and reached into the front pocket of his own tattered overalls and came up with a ten-dollar bill.

'You go an' git me a big box a gauze an' some cotton swabbin' things an' some adhesive tape. I need some a them ice packets too. Evything else I need, I got . . . an' git what-evuh you need fo' yo' own patchin's. You don' look like you 'bout to fall out dead to me.'

I had been changing into the dry clothes, waiting for the instructions. The thought of Hicks laying in that back room was scaring me. More than the gang leader's death was at stake. What to do about the old man would be a problem if Hicks died. Maybe he was willing to help me as long as Hicks lived, but death would change all that. What would I do with the body? What would I do to silence the old grocer? I was thinking that I would definitely be forced to kill my good Samaritan if Hicks couldn't make it. I broke into a cold sweat and started running toward the drugstore.

The old man's ten spot was squeezed tightly in my hand. Even the dampness of my body could not overcome the warmth that came with the fear that was now a part of me. Inside my head I was reviewing the store's layout and making plans. There had to be a back way out. I had to convince Hicks when and if he recovered that he had been responsible for the death of the boy whose body the police had probably already seen floating in the river. Once I had made Hicks believe he was the killer, and not me, I wouldn't have to worry about any pressure that the Man would apply to Hicks when they caught him.

I played the part at the drugstore, listening to the druggist's jokes about winos burning the docks down while high on Robutussin Cough Syrup. I bought the articles the old man had listed and started back down Eleventh Avenue. The commotion that had been in the streets fifteen minutes before was fading. Firemen remained to hose down the blaze, but ambulances were speeding away behind patrol cars. I returned to the store.

The old grocer was waiting quietly when I returned. He had left the door unlocked for me, and I went straight through to the back room, where he sat with a wet towel across Hicks's forehead. He had ripped another towel into strips and was using it as a tourniquet. Hicks was twisting and moaning in a semicoma.

Without a word the weatherbeaten hands took the package from me and set things in order on a scratched nightstand next to the cot. A dim light cast shadows around the cubicle and distorted the crow's feet about the eyes.

'I useda be a medic back in prehist'ry times far as you concerned. I wuz a man noted fo' steady han's an' allat.' He was talking for me, not to me.

'Why you doin' this, old man?' I asked him suddenly.

'I dunno why,' he said, without looking up. 'I wuz jus' askin' me why I wuz doin' it.' He took a needle and thread from a pan of hot water on the nightstand. 'I guess it's cuz I knew them whitey police wuz gon' ketch yawl an' whup yo' po' l'il asses. I didn' wanna see no white man beatin' yawl.'

'One cop like another,' I said.

'I wanned t'see yo' poppas beatin' yawl, not no cop,' he said.

That was the last thing I remember hearing. He told me the next morning that I had passed out.

The thoughts of the Dock Battle party entered my mind as I hiked the three flights of stairs to John's apartment. Four people had been killed that night, and no telling how many beaten or cut. As Hicks got better, I began to fill in the missing details in his mind, making sure he considered himself a killer. We stayed in the back of the old man's store for almost five days recuperating, so that we would be ready when we hit the street again. The P.R.'s had been bragging that they had gotten rid of Hicks and me. When we came out on the block together almost a week later, all the black people in the area knew it within minutes.

I could hear the sound of light laughter as I approached John's door; a good time being had by all. I entered without knocking and was greeted by a startled smile from Debbie Clark.

'Hi, baby,' I greeted.

'Everything's all right,' she said. 'But you're late.'

'Thass impossible, hon. The ball don't really ball till I show.'

'Yeah, but one night you're gonna come in drag-assin' an' we all gonna be gone.'

'Aw, you sweet young thing. If I hadda known you wuz gonna be here early, I woulda been here all day.'

'Bullshit!' she said, smiling.

I chucked her chin lightly. 'Where's John L.?' I asked.

'He's further on in. I'm the hostess.' She struck a pose. 'Look for him at the bar.'

'Why don't you hostess me on back, so I can see what I can get into.'

'Wow! You do move fast!'

'I wuz jus' thinkin' over what you said, an' decided I might be a little late.'

'You ain't *that* late.'

'An' my rap ain' that good?'

'No comment.'

Someone knocked on the door, and Debbie pushed by me, muttering about leaving the door open. Her nicely built chocolate frame rubbed a part of me that I liked to have rubbed, and I plunged into the darkness looking for a drink.

Already passed out was one nigger who had had a little too much of whatever it was he had had. That was one of the good things about our neighborhood, however, among the booze brothers, anyway. When a man had too much to drink, he didn't cramp, he camped until he and the room got back on friendly terms. There was very little wine in the air, and less liquor. John had everything under control. It seemed that the people were content to sip beer and do some dancing.

I walked through the small hallway toward the living room and the two back bedrooms, where the people were doing their thing. The people were spread along the walls and jamming the middle of the floor with some wild dancing. There was only one red bulb lighting the room with the bar in it, and that was where I knew I'd be operating from. I sensed rather than saw people. I checked for a path by looking for a silhouette and then blundering forward until I hit something.

'So Debbie is hostessin' John L.'s gig, huh? Another innovation on the block.' I was thinking out loud. John had been after Deb for almost a year, but she would never give him a play. I had always told him that it was because she didn't want to be tied down to any one man, but I really thought that it was because everybody believed that John was a nowhere cat.

My eyes started focusing, getting accustomed to the light. Bodies took on form, and faces had names. I was hailed from several parts of the room, and I waved and shook hands like a politician.

My main record started spinning, and I caught a glimpse of a mini-skirt that revealed a fine pair of legs. So I said to myself: Why not? I touched her hand with mine, and she grasped my fingers firmly and followed me onto the dance floor. Somewhere out of the walls Smoky Robinson was crying '*Ooo Baby Baby.*' Our bodies touched, lightly at first, a gentle probe on my part. You can never tell when you've got somebody's Cousin Minnie from Over the Ridge, Ohio, who's going to scream bloody murder and go home telling everybody that she was raped on a dance floor in New York. This was nobody's Cousin Minnie.

'I thought I knew every fine chick on this side of the Mason-Dixon Line, but I seem to have missed someone. Who are you?' She took the compliment with a smile. I knew that at best it was only a variation on a theme she probably knew by heart.

'I'm Crystal Amos,' she said. 'Who are you?'

In truth I was Humphrey Bogart, romancing a good-looking young woman in a darkened, secluded hideaway. My voice was noticeably deeper as I went into my thing.

'Eddie Shannon,' I bassed. 'Some folks call me Spade.'

She stopped dancing. 'Eddie Shannon?'

'Yeah. Is it *that* bad?'

She relaxed in my arms again. Our bodies began to touch, rhythmically, more firmly with each beat of the song.

'No, it's not bad, but I've heard the name.' Her smile was genuine.

I let it drop and pulled her closer to me. The song was coming to its climax, Smoky begging and pleading for the woman to give him that chance he needed. Crystal flattened her hips against me, and we touched completely. The record ended, and I took her arm.

'I'm afraid you lost your seat,' I said, indicating the fact that a woozy cornerboy had fallen in her spot.

'That's all right. I was tired of sitting anyway.'

'You been sitting? What's wrong with these niggers, anyway?' I asked. 'They blind?'

She smiled a warm, shy smile. She had a cute face that a smile did things for. Her eyes were light brown, and everything was complemented by her caramel complexion and soft brown hair.

'Can I get you a drink?' I asked, discovering the makeshift bar abandoned behind us.

'No . . . I don't drink. It, uh, tastes like medicine.'

I smiled. 'I'm gonna have one,' was all that I said. I poured a shot of Scotch and threw in two ice cubes and lit a smoke. As I leaned back against the wall, I struck another pose and maintained my scowl as much as possible.

In Chelsea, Spade was supposed to be the closest you could come to witnessing a walking death mask. I had picked up the tag 'Angry Man' because I seldom decorated my looks with a grin. I thought about that and chuckled. It was just another part of being onstage twenty-five hours a day.

My thoughts shifted to the little thing next to me. She had turned down a brother's invitation to dance while I was pouring my drink. I saw her now looking up trying to catch my eye. I just wouldn't give her the satisfaction of acknowledging her attention. I was actually trying to figure her out. It had been a long time since a young lady in my neighborhood had said that liquor tasted like anything but a good time. Most of the chicks were so hung out on acting grown that they fell into the parties in worse shape than the cats. They were buying their own Bacardi Light and really struggling into gigs with too much drink and too little coherence to offer any kind of companionship. Most of the time they weren't even good for screwing, because they passed out or threw up all over everything.

'I didn't expect you to be a gentleman,' I heard Crystal say.

'What?'

'You know what I mean. Like not drinking when the young lady that you're with refuses.'

'You can only refuse for you. You can't refuse for me. What I think you're talkin' about iz some real phony shit,' I said. 'All it really turns out to be iz coppin' out on yo' manhood. What do you care if I drink or not? I'm gonna enjoy it, an' it won't get you high . . . Excuse me if I don't make a big deal out of it.'

She looked a bit deflated. I didn't know if it was because I had been so blunt with my disdain for manners that she appreciated, or because I hadn't gone out of my way to get in tight with her. She turned her head, so that only her profile was visible. She started to pay a lot of attention to the dancers.

'By the way, was I a good guy or a bad guy?' I asked.

'Nothing like that,' she said. 'My cousin Delores mentioned your name a few times during our gossip. You know how girls talk.'

'And you remembered me from that?'

'. . . And the way you came in tonight, with everybody calling you and speaking to you. I couldn't help but notice how well known you are.'

'Well, to tell the truth, I don't know yo' cousin too well. I guess she's mostly into a younger thing.'

There is a social caste system in the neighborhood. Since the Dock Battle I had been accepted anywhere I wanted to go. My running men during the corner years, fourteen to seventeen, were always all at least two years my senior. The legend reads that after you go through the corner stage you evolve into a lounge-and-bar man. That was the period I was entering now. When I hit eighteen, I went straight to the Man and got my card. I had been drinking and buying taste in the neighborhood for a few years, but that was simply because my reputation told the liquor-store man that if he didn't sell to me he might have some repairs to make on his store when he showed up the next day. Immediately after my signing to go to war if my number came up, I started hanging out at places like the Cobra on Tenth Avenue. The customers were generally bigshot whiteys. Businessmen, tourists, career women, and entertainers all flocked to the joint because it had a write-up in *Playboy* and a few other magazines that said it was 'in.'

'Delores is seventeen,' Crystal said. 'How old are you?'

'Eighteen.'

'What's one year? A lot of girls have boyfriends older than themselves. Most girls feel like they need it.'

'I can unnestan' all that, but what I mean is that she ain't trav'lin' in the same circles that I am.'

'Which means that she's too young for you?'

'It simply means I ain't got time for no lead weights aroun' my legs right now.'

'Few people can stand lead weights around their legs.'

Somehow Crystal and I had gotten into this tug-of-war thing, each of us trying to make a point.

'Yeah, but a lot of people don't see the situation as I do. To me, you're either a girl or a woman, a boy or a man. I'm not really speakin' now only in terms of age. I mean the way you dig life.'

'What decides which?' Crystal asked.

'You either live life or you don't. You either get out an' go for what you're after, or you watch the world drift away from you.'

'And?'

'And if you know what you want when you're twelve, you're grown.'

She was watching me drink, and I had a sneaking suspicion that she wanted a drink. I thought she was about to show me a little independent action to show me that she was mature. I was reaching for the bottle.

'I still don't want a drink,' she said.

I stopped in midair and smiled at her. She was watching the couples in the middle of the floor dancing and weaving in time to the beat.

In the distance, Derek Martin was singing a song called 'You'd Better Go,' and an angel soprano accompanied him, telling him that his time had run out, but he kept on rapping strong. I watched a few couples appear from the shadows and cling to each other. I wrapped an arm around Crys and led her onto the dance floor.

By eleven o'clock John's party had turned into a downhome 'sweat box,' with barely enough room between people for a man to know what in the crowd was his and what belonged to someone else. The fast records were for breathers and time-outs. All of the windows were open, but late June is no time to be looking for a breeze in Manhattan. Crystal and I were sitting on the stairs even with the next floor. I was smoking one of the joints I had rolled from John's bag, and Crys was holding a cigarette to camouflage the sweet aromatic drug.

'Take a drag,' I coaxed.

'I don't want any, Eddie.'

'Look here. I ain' tryin' to turn you into no junky or get you high so I can screw you. You ain' gonna get high the first time you smoke anyway.'

'So why should I do it?'

''Cause damn holy rollers iz always preachin' 'bout the evil a this an' the evil a that an' come to fin' out they wouldn't know a joint an' couldn't identify one if they got bit on the ass.'

'Have I been criticizing you or what you do?' she asked slowly.

'That's not the point,' I said. 'Look, what am I s'posed to be? A pusher or what? Like, I want you to start smokin' to add to my income, right?'

The effect of the liquor and the Novocain reaction that comes with marijuana had me talking and listening in slow motion. I was starting to ramble about nothing. Behind the lenses of the reflector sunglasses, tears were welling up in the corners of my eyes as I began to nod and lean on the stairs and lose parts of the conversation.

'All right,' Crystal agreed.

She took the stick from me and tried to imitate the way I had inhaled it, taking it straight down to my lungs. She only succeeded in damn near choking herself to death. I couldn't help but laugh, and in spite of everything. Crystal fell all over me, laughing at her own ineptitude.

She looked at me carefully when the laughter subsided and took the sunglasses from my eyes.

'Do you always wear these?' she asked me.

'Yeah. I wear them most of the time, anyway.'

'Why?'

'To be cool, I guess.' I started laughing again.

'I can never really see a person who wears these things. People just aren't the same when their eyes are hidden.'

Softly she wiped the tears from my eyes, tears that had been uncontrollably released when I became temporarily hysterical at her attempts to get high. Everything always seems to be a million times funnier when you're high, and I was sorry that I couldn't stop. I could nearly feel the embarrassment that Crys felt.

'I'm too young for you too, aren't I?' she asked.

'Well ... aren't you? You claim seventeen, but how old are you really? How long have you been livin' insteada just watchin'?' My eyes weren't focusing properly. I took another drag from the bush and then stubbed it out and put the roach in my shirt pocket. I felt as though Crys and I were caught somewhere in a mist between life and reality.

Her face was very close to mine. I felt very masculine and in control of everything that happened between us; lord and master of a slow-motion jungle. I draped an arm around her and looked away. The dim lights flickered at the bottom of the stairs, and the smoke fought its way across the ceiling. I turned her face to mine and kissed her very gently. I felt her lips parting under mine. Very tenderly I touched the fabric covering her breasts, and her sighs began, her breathing ragged in my ear. I touched the cloth of her skirt just above the knee. She gasped for air and clung to me. The drowsiness that had grabbed me blunted my senses and kept my mind away from her small sobs.

'No, Eddie. Please, no . . . Will that prove that I'm a woman?'

I removed my hand and touched her face softly. She kissed my cheek and mouth as I struggled to light a cigarette. There was nothing I could say.

August 3, 1968 / 4:00 P.M.

Memories of the party faded. I started working for Zinari on the Monday following John's gig, and I was raking in more money than I had planned to see for quite some time. I got involved with the job and lost sight of friends from the block. I was determined to do a good job.

At the same time, John Lee had become very involved with his job too. I heard about one narrow escape he made from the Man because Junior Jones burned up the patrol car. I knew that I wouldn't want to have my business balanced on anything as dangerous as that. I tried to act as though it was just a part of life. I told myself that it was no concern of mine, because I wasn't on the corner anymore. I still heard the news, though, and it was very strange to hear one of your basketball teammates referred to as a twenty-dollar Jones. The mainline train to hell was collecting passengers at a rapid clip. The older cornerboys had gone the way of the needle, and all I could do was shake my head and swear that it wouldn't happen to me. Sometimes in the middle of the night I saw myself in a dream world of rubber walls and straitjackets, crying and trying to free myself from insects that crawled all over me and nibbled at my privates. My hands would be so covered with ants and spiders that I couldn't determine the fingers. My hair was infested with lice and leeches. I would wake up screaming and run to the liquor cabinet, where I sat up for the remainder of the night with a drink in my hand, trembling.

It was a Thursday in August. I had worked for fifteen straight nights, and Zinari sent Smoky with a message to take a four-day weekend. He also sent a fifty-dollar bonus.

That's how I happened to be in the coffee shop on Ninth Avenue when John Lee came in. There had been very few words between us since the party. There was no static in the air. It was just that our new roles seldom crossed paths. We both mingled with the night people in different sections of town. When I was off, John was working, and vice versa.

Hot days like this gave a man an idea of what life in hell itself would be like, and made a lot of wishy-washy people think seriously about trying to find God. Inside, the air-conditioner was keeping everything together, and I kept the jukebox playing, so Tommy, the owner, said next to nothing to me.

My job had been running as Smoky predicted. The pushers I met nightly were no trouble. They were people of darkness who wanted to spend very little of their time under the streetlights where I met them. There was seldom any conversation. Maybe once in a while they would try a 'Whuss happnin'?' But after a while they saw that my answer would be 'You,' and no more. Our relationship was entirely business. I wasn't really as cold as all that, but in the eyes of the junkies there were always too many things being reflected. The death of men and women without a burial. It was as though death had paid his call and left without stamping his usual notice on the forehead of his victim. He took the heart and soul, but he left the shell of the listless survivor, discarded as worthless. The bulging facial expression, bloated features, and shaggy clothes that often disguised blue veins filled with pus in scrawny arms. The silly smiles that met your inquiring stare when they snapped out of a nod leaning on an impossible angle. All of these things were a part of the cats I had been with and of. There was no running away from the faces that were often transformed into familiarity by the dim light. There was no denying that this was an old friend with a different name and a different reason for dying before his time.

'ain' nothin' persnal 'bout nothin',' Smoky whistled through his beard.

There were often evenings when I came through the door at Harvey's near the witching hour and saw Smoky rapping with the women who frequented the place in the late evening. They were all nurses and librarians and social workers, lonely women in general who knew that respectable men often came in to eat at Harvey's because it was the nicest cafe in Harlem.

I would fall in about ten of twelve or so, and more often than not the game between Smoky and the women was already under way. I would come over, be introduced, and then lay and listen through the hum-and-giggle conversation. Smoky would say things like, 'yeah, well dadadadada,' and the chicks would 'Hee Hee!' Harvey would come out of the kitchen in the back occasionally and make up fantastic tales about the service, where he always turned out to be at least the indirect hero by pulling a fast one on some white officer. Harvey's wife would look out from behind her perch in the kitchen and wink at me as her mate rambled on.

The women who sat with us always seemed to strike a chord somewhere in the back of my mind. They were always reasonably intelligent women, with a secret storm boiling between their legs, but too much pride to get into a thing with the first man who came along with the equipment to extinguish it. The eternal longing in their eyes was for some man to make a positive effort to seduce them, so that they could momentarily imagine themselves in love and discredit the evil thought that their actions were only the timeless, rhythmic movements of a woman in heat, a woman being destroyed from within because her physical needs fought the constant battle with her mind to control the countless caresses that she eventually would succumb to and the many orgasms that she desired.

Smoky would sometimes forget that we were supposed to be working. We would be joined in the small dining area by two women, and he would nudge me in the side as though my own eyes were failing me.

'look, man! two birds come in lookin' for a play. les play.'

'What about Zinari?' I would ask.

'zinari got miz zinari an' any else he want. i wan' some too.'

Anything that would resemble a difference of opinion on my part would never be considered. He would always call the women as though he knew them and invite them to join us. If they balked, he would go over and sit with them, assuring them that we weren't drunk and that our only desire was for a little freshness to decorate our table, a little female company.

I must admit that Smoky was generally a winner. He was an ideal man to double-date with. Whereas I was a bit picky, he would rap to the girl that I paid least attention to.

'nuthin' but some leg,' he would say.

He would always bill us as clerks in the real-estate business. This is a business with a future. With determination and a few breaks, there were tremendous advances to be made by Negroes. This was all a part of Smoky's initial approach. He explained it to me very simply one night.

'wimmin in harlem jus' like whi' wimmin. they movin' becuz uv two things. firs' thing iz the body. mos' a them out that time a night cauz they can' sleep. they cain' sleep cauz they wan' a man. the secon' thing iz that they alwaze thinkin' 'bout tomorrow even if t'night iz mo' important. they ezier an' mo' quick to the sack if they think the cat iz ejucated an' got a l'il money. they know they takin' a chance they never see 'im agin, but they need a l'il romance an' all that shit they read 'bout in the movie magazines. they wanna be wined an' dined, but a cupa coffee an' a charmin' rap will do jus' as good.'

I saw the whole point. We all used each other. The women used us for sex, and we used them the same way. A double cross with no winner, because all the participants were aware of the swindle.

I was injecting my third quarter into Tommy's jukebox when John came in. His huge bulk obliterated a customer's view of the steam that rose from the smoldering concrete. I waved and indicated the booth I was parking in. He returned the wave and plopped, mopping sweat from his fat cheeks.

'Whuss been happnin', man?' I asked, sitting opposite him.

'You know how it iz, man. Same old same o.'

'Yeah, but I think this heat is some new shit.'

'That motherfuckuh is fryin' brains.'

James Brown came on doing 'Cold Sweat,' and John and I grinned. The smiles were forced, and I thought about that. It was odd that we would be forcing grins for each other. Things were changing, I had to admit. John was into his dope thing, and I was into mine. I looked back at him with renewed interest. The youth was gone, and he looked like an old man, freshness erased by some unknown blackboard cleaner. It was a new day for John Lee. There had always been a smile on his lips and a chuckle rolling over his vocal cords, ready to be exposed with only the slightest provocation. The daytime was gone from his eyes. All that remained was the night. He was dressed in a good Italian knit shirt, double-breasted, and silk pants. He was the corner fashion post. The blue jeans and T-shirt were gone, but so was the sunshine. Along with the height of fashion had come the alleys of the neighborhood and the shadows of buildings that purged the air of theater cops who would inform you of your constitutional rights. John knew all of this stuff the same as I did, but nevertheless the fame and fortune that was his as the dealer was not something that could be easily dismissed like a T-shirt. It was a type of recognition, perhaps not the applause given to a movie star, but the sort of praise you dream about. It was attention, and that was what John wanted. He wanted it badly enough to live near the junkies, who would kill him for a dollar. He wanted it badly enough to take the chance of being dimed on by some punk who would never reveal himself. Somehow I saw all of these things in the lines in Lee's forehead, and I slowly turned to face my own crumbling mask in the mirror over the booth.

I took a swipe at my hair. There were dark, curly waves that I brushed carefully in place every afternoon before going out. My nose was flat and wide, but it went with the lips and eyes that mirrored my father's Latin ancestry. I breathed on the reflector sunglasses, wiped them, and put them back across my view.

'Whuss gonna happen when you git busted, man?' I asked Lee.

'I ain' gonna git busted. What are you, Mother Nature?'

He was irritated. I took another swallow of the soda before me.

'Yeah, I am,' I said. 'How's things wit' you an' yours?'

'Who?'

'You an' Debbie.'

'We all right. I bought her a leather coat, three quarters, and a watch. One a them wide square watches with 'bout half a dozen different bands. She digs them things.'

John yelled back to the kitchen for some food, and Tommy scurried out, wiping his hands on his apron and muttering some nonsense about the Mets.

John ordered, and I got up and put another quarter in the

jukebox. A group of five girls came in and took the booth opposite John and me. One or two of them timidly faked conversation while the others watched us out of the corners of their eyes.

For the first time since I started working for Zinari there were questions rolling around in my head – questions that were important to my work and to John's. Until I looked at John and saw the circles under his eyes and the lines in his forehead, I had been unaware of everything except two yards a week. Now there were images of the things that were really involved. I was running up and down on a felt cushion with lime stripes. Next to me was James Bond and Our Man Flint and Bill Cosby. We were all wearing Dracula capes and laughing at each other but not at ourselves. In the corner was Rod Serling, watching us and speaking into a microphone. He was talking German, and the whole audience was Crystal, and she was crying because of what was being said about me. Behind me were Oddjob and Smoky – the hired killers. But I was the only one who didn't know that the play was fiction.

I saw a picture of white Narcotics detectives with powdery faces falling on Lee from a rooftop and beating his knotty head with billy clubs as long as firemen's hoses. They beat him until the shape of his head was no longer familiar and blood ran down Ninth Avenue and small children came out to sail their boats in the crimson river.

The chatter from the girls in the booth across from Lee and me became more bold as we ignored them and made small talk. They began to speak of us in the third person, just loud enough for us to hear the compliments over the din of the records.

'Goddamn teeny-boppers!' I snorted.

'Not the one in the red shell blouse,' John said without looking up. 'I saw a pair of legs on her that could wrap around a man's waist and have him begging for mercy.'

'Bet she couldn't get 'um aroun' yo' waist,' I said, eyeing John's middle.

The conversation reminded me of Crystal. I was still with her on and off, and everyone in the neighborhood thought that I was taking her down. The truth was that I had been afraid. I hadn't known quite how to deal with her freshness, her smile, her warmth, or her obvious affection for me that went beyond that idolizing that a lot of chicks had. I didn't want to lose her.

I was shaving when she knocked lightly on the door. I had opened the apartment to her, expecting my older Cousin Calvin. Calvin and I shared the apartment, and he had left only minutes before to see his girl. I thought he might have left his keys. Crystal came in, and I complimented her light blue skirt and blouse. She smiled as I ducked back into the bathroom with lather all over my face. She rambled through the stacks of old forty-five rock-'n'-roll records and through my cousin's jazz LP's and then called me. 'Can I put on some music?'

'Sure.'

Lou Rawls came on nice and easy. I could hear her humming and singing the blues rendition as I wiped the remaining foam from my face. It was inspection time. I actually needed a haircut, but Crys said that she liked long hair, so I submitted to a bit of henpecking. Also it made me look older to some of the women that Smoky and I talked to. There were chocolate half-moons under my eyes. I hadn't really been getting a lot of sleep. I got home about one-thirty most of the time, but when Smoky and I had some women, I was crawling into the sack with the sun and the big trucks, and Con Edison men were starting their noise. I just sat in the kitchen and watched TV. There was no sleep. I tilted the sunglasses over my eyes and went back to the living room.

'Hey, girl.' I smiled. 'Lemme have a kiss.' She pecked me on the cheek. 'I thought I was coming to get you at Delores' house at eight,' I said.

'I wanted to come,' she said. She pulled me to her when I was back within arm's reach. Her lips found mine, and I was taken over by the fire within her body, the sheerness of the silk blouse, and the perfume that blew my mind.

She ran her fingers through my hair and under my T-shirt. The cool touch of her palms across my stomach and chest made me gasp and crush her to me. Her breasts flattened against my chest, and I ran my tongue across her lips until they parted and gave me entrance. I began to touch her everywhere as our tongues fought each other. Her breasts, arms, and hips were all targets for my hands, and the sudden desire that I had for her alarmed me. Already I could feel myself swelling and yearning to enter her.

I began to undress her. I shed her clothes and threw them in the direction of the easy chair behind us. The couch sighed as I lay next to her and wrenched my pants down over my knees. With tenderness and all the restraint I could manage, I guided her hand to me, and she was released by her desire to touch me as she was being touched.

The ribbon that had held back her brown locks became tangled and fell to the floor beside us. Her face was framed by the curls, and I saw her more as an angel than ever. I bent to kiss her breasts.

Somewhere on the other side of the world I heard her voice break through the fog in my mind.

'Eddie,' she called. 'I'm not . . . this isn't the first time.'

I heard her and understood all of the things that the statement implied, but I couldn't stop to analyze. There was a naked woman next to me. Without thinking of what I was doing, I was on top of her. With one smooth movement we were one. She shook momentarily and then bucked under me. Our chests flattened against each other, and I could hear through my own body her rapid heartbeat as we began to match our rhythm and response. Then as quickly as I began, it was over. She shook spasmodically, and her nails dug furrows deep into my shoulderblades. I could feel the onrushing end and fought it until it all but overcame me, and I sent the messengers of my virility hurtling through her body.

I rolled off onto the floor and lay quietly. I could hear Crys trying to retain a normal breathing pattern. She was the first to move. My eyes were closed, but I saw everything clearly. She stepped over me and padded to the closet, hesitated, and then went into the bathroom. I heard the sound of running water, a splash, and then nothing.

When she emerged from the bathroom, she was wearing a pink towel around her neck and one of my bathrobes. I had put on my pants, but I still lay in the middle of the floor, smoking a cigarette.

She sat on the couch behind me as the seconds ticked away.

'What's wrong, Eddie?' she asked softly.

'Nothin', hon.'

'This *is* what you've wanted, isn't it?'

Now there was a question. My jaws started to tighten, and I could feel the blood rushing to my head. What in the hell do you think? What does a man want except to lie next to a woman and embed himself in her loins and feel her shudder? What does a man need except to know that somewhere in the world he is still the master? That nothing can take the place of the power he possesses between his legs? What is the supreme prize but the treasure that a woman carries at the base of her stomach? What is life all about except fucking?

All at once I realized that this did not answer the question.

'I don' know,' I told Crystal.

She didn't look surprised. There was neither anger nor disappointment in her eyes. The brown stare that I loved so much had clouded to a noncommittal gray.

'Is the game all over?' she asked no one in particular. 'Now that the hunter has captured the game . . . and found out that it will not go down in history as a singular accomplishment?'

'That's not the point!' I yelled.

'Then what is the point? What have I done today except the thing that you've wanted since the night we met? . . . Now I want to know if that's all you want? You've had me! Is it over? Do you want me to go?'

There was a blazing fire in her face. The smile that I wanted to see was gone, replaced with bitter disappointment. I knew then that our first act of love had been a failure. My own ego had eaten up the happiness that she should have returned to. My pride was ruined because I was supposed to dance a victory dance after breaking down all of the girl's defenses; but all I had was, at best, more empty, pointless exploitation. I was not the conquering hero. I was the runnerup. I was not Leif Ericson. I was Christopher Columbus. I had been deceived.

No! I had deceived myself. She had never told me that she was a virgin. I felt like banging my head against the wall, but instead I extended a hand to Crystal, and she lay next to me crying in my arms.

'Spade! What the hell's wrong wit' you, man?' It was John Lee.

'Oh, wow! I wuz daydreamin', man.'

'Thinkin' 'bout tryin' to git to that broad over there?' His eyes slanted toward the red-bloused teeny-bopper.

'Naw,' I said quickly. 'Thinkin' 'bout callin' Crys an' tellin' her to come over an' watch us smoke some a that mean bush you got. How 'bout a nickel bag?'

'Sounds hip to me.'

'Tell me somethin', man. Whut wuz that shit you came up with las' week about the Juneyuhs shootin' up?'

'Wuzn't what I thought,' Lee said. 'They been shootin' wine in their legs.'

'Wine?'

'In their legs,' said Lee.

January 4, 1969

When January comes to New York City, she brings traveling companions – dirty snow, forty-mile-an-hour winds, jackets, earmuffs, and scarves. As the weather grew colder in the city, I totally lost contact with everyone who had been a part of my life except Crys. She and I constantly saw each other, but everyone else was just a part of the gossip I heard about when I stopped into Tommy's for a cup of coffee. Once baseball season ended, Tommy became a radio who broadcast all of the neighborhood's misfortunes.

Usually, come winter, I make the Cobra my home. It features a three-piece jazz group on the weekends and tasty soul food all of the time.

I visited the bar on the Saturday night following New Year's Day. The collecting had been light, and neither Smoky nor I had seen any reason to sit and chit-chat in Harvey's. Fortunately, he gave me a lift down the West Side Highway and then plowed off through the slush.

I was dipping into a Jack Daniels as the group came on. The pianist did a few light chords and the group swung into Cannonball's 'Mercy.' The crowd began to warm to the strokes from the bass, and the rendition brought out the soul in the audience. Here and there you could hear a 'Git it, baby!' or 'Do it jus' one time!' The waiters and waitresses waded through the crowd serving food and drinks from trays balanced on one practiced hand.

From the dimness behind my corner table an arm reached over and tapped me on the shoulder. It was Howie, the head waiter.

'Nissy wants to see you, man. Sez it's urgent,' he whispered.

'What the hell about?' I asked.

'Man, I don' know. Might be jus' another excuse to try an' git the hell in here, but I ain' havin' none a that shit.'

I got up from the corner of the bar and waded through customers and candlelight atmosphere. Through the door that led to the small alcove I could see two struggling figures.

My mind went out to meet them. Nissy? What the hell would he want with me? He could possibly want some wine money, but he knew better than to bother me about something like that.

Nissy was a wino, a man dedicated to the pursuit of the grape. He was always either drunk or trying to get drunk. His whole hustle was shining shoes when somebody set him up with the equipment. And as soon as he had enough for a quart, he would be gone to get high, and a little kid would cop his polish and box and be gone. Occasionally he could get a job running messages for the numbers man or something, but once he got high, he'd quit. Money was only important because it furnished wine for today. To hell with tomorrow. His bloated face gave me a wild stare as I came through the frosted glass.

'I gotta see ya, Spade,' he squeaked breathlessly.

'Thass what I hear. Cool it!' I commanded, dropping the sarcasm. 'Let 'im go, Hemp.' Hemp was one of the Cobra bouncers. He was holding Nissy at arm's length by the front of his filthy overcoat, the smaller man's feet practically off the floor.

'I gotta see you, Spade,' he repeated.

I waited until Hemp had disappeared back inside. I turned and faced Nissy with contempt in my eyes.

'How menny times I tol' you not to hussle this place?' I asked. 'You gon' come by here one night when I ain' here an' Howie ain' gonna be for no bullshit, an' he gonna have Hemp an' Jason throw yo' ass in the river. You need a cold bath?'

'Naw, Spade . . . Lemme tell yeh. Then we see who's right.' I nodded. 'Somebody got to Isidro t'night. They put a bullet in between his eyes. I swear! Paco an' Jessie went to fin' Slothead, an' they gonna get John Lee. They said they gon' cut his dick off!' Nissy was panting, and his eyes were rolling in his head.

'You drunk!' I yelled.

'No! Man, I seen Seedy dead wit' my own eyes! I swear!'

I looked him over for a second and then nodded.

'Wait a second. I'll be right back.' I turned and went inside. Howie was standing in the corner I had occupied: his face wrinkled when I reached for my coat. I picked up my topcoat and scarf and swung over the bar and grabbed a bottle of Jack Daniels Black.

'I'm goin',' I told Howie. 'I'll pay you later.'

'In the street,' Howie whispered. 'Please don' start no shit in here t'night.'

'I ain' startin nuthin',' I told him.

I slid back into the lobby and found Nissy regaining his cool, leaning against the outer door smoking a stogie. I handed him the bottle and started squeezing into my coat. I waited until he took a shot.

'I need all the details you have, man,' I told him.

'Okay. Fifteen minnits ago the cops pull up at Seedy's pad an' jump out, runnin' upstairs. You dig? Then a ammalance come an' they haul his ass away. It's Seedy. They got 'im covuhud but I know who it iz. There wuz a hole in the mid of hiz head, a small 'un. Not too much blood. The cops come out an' they ast a few questions an' then they haul ass. That's when I hear Paco an' Jessie say then gon' get Lee.'

'How you know I wuz in here? Where's Lee?' I couldn't ask the questions fast enough. Nissy was still pulling at the mash.

'I jus' took a chance. You know, Saturday night. Where *you* gon' be? I donno where Lee iz at. Home?'

I was already preparing myself to deal with the Hawk. My gloves were on, and the scarf was around my neck.

'Somebody hadda hep Lee. I donno who else would hep the cat, considerin' heppin' him agains' who. Them spic mothuhs gon' tear him a bran' new one.' Nissy was starting to ramble.

'What makes Paco think that Lee did it?' I asked.

'I donno. No sign I could see. Look like a clean hit. Guess he put one an' one togethuh an' got Lee.' Nissy fell out laughing at his joke.

I came out of my pocket with a bill. The little wino's eye caught the picture of Hamilton and nodded.

'You haven't seen me in a week,' I said. 'You know nothin' 'bout Seedy an' John an' none a that shit. Right?'

'You goin', huh?' he asked, pocketing the bill.

'Ain't rilly got no choice,' I said.

'Damn! Gon' be mo' killin' t'night. Wish all this could happen in the summer when it ain' too cold to go an' watch. . . . Who you wan' me to see if they git you?' Nissy asked.

'I don't give a fuck,' I snorted.

I went through the last set of doors on that note and out into the early-morning chill. My watch read one-thirty. The wind blew grains of snow up against my sunglasses, and the swirling flakes began to crust on my eyebrows and in my hair. At my feet, along the sidewalks, were stains where dogs had come along escorted by frozen masters and done their thing to help keep New York beautiful.

From the high-rise apartments that faced 17th between Ninth and Tenth avenues, there were still millions of lights hanging in the windows, fighting to aid the streetlights illuminate the corners and save travelers from muggers.

A sudden thought crossed my mind. Where in the hell could Lee be at this time of night? The answer was home, but if he was there, what would the P.R. boys do to get him out of the house? Even they weren't so bad that they were going to bust in to the man's crib and take the whole family off. That was Roaring Twenties action. I checked for cars and crossed Ninth Avenue. I was tired, hungry, and needed a drink. I should have taken that Jack Daniels away from Nissy. A wino couldn't even begin to appreciate a mellow thing like that. It was almost like handing a grade-A-1 steak to a vegetarian and watching him throw the choice meat to the dog.

I headed downtown on Ninth Avenue. John lived at 306 West 15th Street. I passed the four-hundred block between Ninth and Tenth. John lived between Seventh and Eighth.

Cars and trucks struggled through the foot-high slush with fog beams that simply flashed everywhere except through the dirty mess that children wake and marvel at. No school tomorrow, and a million games to play. Building snowmen and castles and hitting the fat bully across the street with snowballs would be the order of the day. With a little luck, the pony-tail girl from the next building would be out, and she would either be impressed by his sled and marksmanship with snowballs, or be pushed in the drifts with the other creepy things.

I ran up the stairs to John's apartment. The dim light in the hallway added to the shivers. Inside my fur-lined gloves my hands felt like icicles that couldn't be flexed. I took off my sunglasses to wipe away the haze. That was when I saw the figure standing in the corner of the hall, wrapped in a shadow and smoking a cigarette. As the smoke was inhaled, the corner was illuminated.

'Whuss happin', Paco?' I asked the Puerto Rican.

'I theen' you know whuss happnin',' he said slowly.

'No, I don', bruthuh. Thass whut I'm askin' you. You know I don't go through no bullshit thing, right?' I stopped about five feet from him. He remained in the corner dragging on the weed. I removed my gloves and slid them into my coat pocket along with the sunglasses. I pulled out a cigarette and in so doing made sure that my coat was unbuttoned and would not restrain my arms.

'Seedy iz dead, man. You know that?' Paco asked me.

'Yeah, I jus' heard. Thass a shame. You got any ideas?'

'One.' Paco grinned. 'Yo' amigo John Lee.'

'Why you think that?' I quizzed.

Paco shook his head, and a small smile took over his face. He was convinced that I was playing a game with him.

'If I gotta tell you, man, I will. John an' Seedy in the same job, an' if Seedy ain' in the job, then John get alla business. Izzit right, o' what?'

'Whuss John gotta say?' I asked.

'He ain' in here,' Paco said. 'He be here soon or late, but he gon' be here. You see what I mean?'

'I see yo' point. But how you know John did it? How cum somebody else didn't do it?'

'I know he is the one,' Paco flashed. 'He could win mos'!'

'There ain' nuthin' I can say, huh?'

Paco giggled and tossed his cigarette down. I tossed mine down too.

'You can say adios to John Lee.' He giggled. I could see now that he was high. He scratched the side of his face softly, and his head swung out of the corner darkness. His eyes were half-closed, and his teeth were bared.

'John ain' goin' nowhere, Paco. You are. You leavin' here, an' if I ever hear about yo' hangin' out near this place, I'll kill you.' I was moving in on him. All at once I realized that

Paco was not the real danger. His eyes opened at the sight of something behind me, and I had only a second to duck as Jessie's arm swung by neck-high. I caught the startled P.R. near the elbow and turned it until I heard the straight-edge clatter to the floor. I hiked the arm another notch and was satisfied by the bone-cracking snap that answered me. Rushing up from the lower landing, I heard the hurried stumbling of Slothead, so I reversed my position and flipped Jessie back down the flight, where the sounds told me he had met his bald brother head-on. There was a collision, and I heard them tumble back to the landing below.

I turned around and stooped for the razor, but it was gone. Paco had it clutched tightly in his left hand. His high had evidently deserted him as he scanned the darkness for an angle on my body. I backed up a couple of paces and lowered my arms, allowing the heavy coat to drop to the floor.

'I'm gonna kill you, Paco,' I breathed. 'I'm gonna grab you by you' neck and choke you till the blood comes through your teeth, an' then I'm gonna drag you to the Man an' swear you committed suicide.' I was almost screaming, and the echo of my shouts came back at us again and again.

'D'you hear me, Paco? I'm gon' kill you!'

He was standing there unsure of what his next move should be. Sweat materialized over his top lip. I blocked his exit to the stairs, and I didn't know if I was glad of that or not. Any man is dangerous when he's in a corner. I knew just how good Paco was with a razor, too. I had seen the chicken fights in the park on 17th Street. Paco was seldom beaten, but I wasn't bluffing at all. I had every intention of taking the razor and choking the scrawny bastard until life was only a memory.

Without the slightest warning, however, the door behind the Puerto Rican opened, and John's father was standing there with a .45 pressed against the base of my enemy's skull. Paco dropped the razor and waited for instructions. The straight-edge hit the floor.

'Go on and move!' Mr Lee said.

Paco walked slowly past me, not looking to the right or to the left. His eyes were wide open. He disappeared down the stairs, and I heard him fussing with his two brothers, who made no reply. Seconds later the echo of their slow departure faded. I exhaled.

'Goddamn spics!' Mr Lee cursed. 'Alla time with a lotta crap, even at this time in the morning. What the hell wuz that all about?'

'Oh, they followed me here,' I lied. 'Something about me not covering a bet that their brother was supposed to collect on. I told them that I paid him this morning, but I didn't have any proof.'

'Goddamn spics,' Mr Lee said. 'It's a good thing Cassie's not here. She would have had eight heart attacks.'

I was waiting for him to hint about how he was glad nothing like that ever happened to John. I wanted to hear a few words about good ol' John Lee who never did anything except pull a pigtail or two. I needed to hear Mr Lee say that John was a fine boy on his way to college and all that. I wondered silently how John had so easily blown his parents' minds.

'Come on in,' Mr Lee said. 'I bet you could use a drink.'

'Or two,' I admitted.

'Were you on your way up here?'

'Yeah,' I said. 'I got locked out, and the Hawk was howling so tough that I wuz gonna lay here for the night.'

'John's somewhere with his girl,' the big man said, pouring me a drink.

'That's good,' I said.

'What?'

'Make that drink a double,' I said.

April 17, 1969

The days seemed to disappear. Before their arrival could be announced, their departure was already a matter of fact. I saw pictures of Santa Claus on a broomstick. George Washington and Abe Lincoln rode in on a one-horse open sleigh. Suddenly, before you could say April Fool, spring was back. Small girls appeared with ropes to jump and colorful hula hoops to spin around nothing waists. Little boys popped up with new skates and bicycles to ride. The grass sent up tiny buds, like periscopes, to scout around for Jack Frost and see if he had really gone back north. Before the arrival of the scouts, everything was only an underground rumor.

I was returning home on a Thursday, trying to beat what seemed to be an oncoming spring rainstorm. The skies were just beginning to tune up for a good cry when I met Debbie Clark. She was sitting under the mezzanine in front of my apartment building.

'Where is everybody?' I asked.

'On a Thursday? Who knows? It's hard enough to find any real people around here on the weekends.'

'An' whuss L'il Miss Happiness doin' spreadin' so much sunshine?'

'Nuthin' at all,' Debbie said.

'Where's I.Q. and Websta an' all them othuh triflin' niggers?'

'Websta's workin' his ass off prob'ly, an' I.Q. is bookin'. . . . You know, thass a real oddball.'

'Wuzn't he some kind of good-student-list man or somthin'?'

'He got that college scholarship he was after,' she replied. 'An' he's a regular guy, too.'

'You find that odd?'

'Well, he's the only guy I know who quotes Shakespeare an' smokes pot,' she said.

'The pot is the regular part?'

'What I mean is that he's not . . . well, he's smart but he hangs out.'

'I see what you mean,' I said.

'And then again, he's odd. I think he's girl-shy or somethin'.' Debbie wandered back and forth between I.Q. being regular and odd. 'I mean, he's okay, but he's not like you.'

'How's John?' I asked.

She blew up.

'Why does everyone expect me to know? Am I some kinda radar, or do I have the *fat freak* in my pocket? I don' know where he is, an' I rilly don' care!'

'All right! All right! What did I do wrong today, Lord?'

'I'm sorry,' she said, like a river changing course. 'I know what you think, but I don' know where John iz, an' I don' go with him, so I get tired of folks askin' me about him like I've got him tied to a tree somewhere.'

'I didn' . . .'

'I know you didn't. That's what makes me mad. Did you ever try to find out? Everybody in this neighborhood is into the same bag. I go out with him a few times, and right away, no matter what, I'm eternally hooked to him.' She paused. Her anger faded and then rekindled. 'What kind of spell does he have on you all? Are you afraid of him?'

I laughed out loud.

'Me? Afraid of Lee?'

'That's not funny. You never asked me out, an' Delores told me that you don't go with Crystal . . . Am I that ugly?'

I had nothing else to say. I sat back and lit a cigarette. Debbie held out her index and middle finger, forming a V. and I filled it with a smoke.

'Well, I'll tell you this. I'll never go out on another date with that fat ass, if I'm in the house forever!'

'He'll still ask you,' I said.

'I jus' won't go.'

'So why did you ever go with him?'

'I never *went* with him. We dated. I like to go out. I didn't realize a date was a marriage license.'

'Okay,' I breathed.

'I had always kinda hoped that you *would* ask me out,' Debbie said suddenly.

'You always been a fine thing, Deb, but I guess I wuz jus' one a the ignorant multitude.'

'Well, you know how it is. You've always been sort of the man around here. Spade this an' Spade that. I had heard of you a long time before I met you. An' when you were nice an' everything, I had to get a crush on you.'

'John is the man aroun' here now,' I reminded her.

'Yeah, and Johnny used to be a lot of fun. I was never really strung out on him, but he was a good time, an' he was good to me. Now he doesn't have time for this an' that. Sometimes he sleeps all day an' runs all night. He was lonely before, but you know there ain't nobody aroun' here lonely with money.'

I paused and thought about that. I thought about the lines I had seen in Lee's face. The lines that were in my face. I knew that the Puerto Ricans would still kill John if they thought they could do it somewhere that I wouldn't find out. I knew that Lee must have dreams about the Narco men catchin' him with a whole bag of smoke. There was no more nice-guy John Lee that was my friend. He was dead. All that remained was for the new John Lee, the new street man, to remember the sleep he used to get, and to see clearly that the next time he closed his eyes they just might not open, or the ushers could lower him into the ground. The sad thing was that I was not much better off. I never touched the skag that the junkies were ridin' on, but I touched the money that they got together by mugging and stealing and selling their women's bodies. I did a harmless thing when taken literally, but right over my shoulder was Smoky counting the bullets he would fire into disagreeing heads at the first sign of trouble. I was just another link in the chain that was wrapped around the body of so many slaves who would soon be cast into the slimy Hudson or dumped into a niche at Potter's Field. All I had was Crystal. As long as I had her to pull me back into the good world from time to time, I would make it. I wondered at times like these why I didn't just crush her to me and say, 'Girl, you are all in the world I have, and I can't lose you.' I knew that this was the only thing that was missing from our relationship that could make her happy. I knew that as long as I played all of the hands with icy fingers, her heart would carry a section of the chill.

'So we'll go out sometimes,' I told Debbie.

'Why not tonight?' she asked.

'You got school tomorrow,' I said quickly.

'Ain't no problem.'

'All right,' I agreed weakly. 'What time?'

'Eight-thirty?' she asked.

'Punctuality is my middle name,' I said, forcing a smile.

I sat there with a lead weight in my stomach. There was a size-ten shoe in my mouth. Already, however, in the back of my mind a plan was forming to keep my candle burning at both ends. If I could get Debbie to and fro on a date, and John Lee didn't find out, I was straight both ways. The thing to do would be to take a cab up Tenth Avenue, since the gang would be on Ninth, and then come back the same way about midnight, when most of the younger cats and chicks would be in the house. I would be a two-way loser if I got caught, but a helluva winner if I got over. I cursed my ego as I realized how I had done myself in. It had all come to a head when she hinted that I might be afraid of John Lee. It had been a subtle dare, and I was always a man to accept a challenge. I had always needed to prove my bravery. Not to reinforce the image that was handed out, but for myself.

'Bye.' Debbie pecked me lightly on the cheek and skipped off through the light rain. I sat there dreaming up a device with several size-twenty boots on a rotating wheel so that I could plug it in and kick my own ass.

April 17 / 8:35 P.M.

Debbie wasn't ready when I arrived at her apartment. The rain had stopped, leaving the evening overcast, and birds returned to waterlogged trees: but they had had their audience chased. I was wearing silk pants and a Nehru shirt-jacket with my raincoat tossed over my arm.

Debbie met me at the door with her housecoat on, and I thought for a moment that our date might be off.

'I'm sorry I'm not ready, but Mom was going to a P.T.A. meeting with Dad, so I had to fix her hair and everything before I could get myself together. They didn't really want me to go.'

'But it's okay?' I asked.

'I told them it was something special, so they agreed,' she said.

'Good.' I smiled.

The thought occurred to me that Debbie and John might not have such a hot thing in bed. That just might be her reason for playing with me.

Debbie was whistling something. She asked me if I wanted a drink, and when I accepted, she came out with a bottle of Dunhill. I poured myself a small hit and threw in a couple of ice cubes. I was back in my profile bag. I leaned back against the couch and dug the furniture and interior decorating. Nice upholstery and covers for all the chairs and sofa. Some sort of thick drapes blocking out the night, and pole lamps that looked like lanterns.

'I thought we might hit a place uptown called the Night Owl,' I called in to Debbie. 'It's a totally new thing. I've only been there once.'

'What's it like?' she asked.

'Wait and see.'

'I hope I like it.'

'Oh, I'm . . .'

I was interrupted by a knock on the door.

'Could you get that?' Debbie called.

I opened the door. It was John Lee.

'Spade, what are you . . .' John began his question and then put a spot on Debbie over my shoulder, clad in only her slip. His mouth clamped shut, and he yanked the door from me and slammed it in my face.

I turned to face Debbie with shock. I found it impossible to change expressions. I don't know how, but at that second I saw through Debbie's whole facade, as easily as I saw through the sheer slip that she wore.

'You black bitch!' I screamed. 'You set that up! You called Lee and made sure that he'd catch me, didn't you? You knew he'd be working ordinarily, didn't you?'

My right hand shot out with cannon force and slapped the girl into a sitting position halfway across the room.

'You black bitch!' I repeated.

'At least he won't bother me now!' Debbie cried.

I grabbed my coat from the couch and lunged out into the empty hall. My own stupidity was blinding me, and the walls seemed to be closing in on me. I punched angrily at the button that summoned the elevator. I needed a drink.

I stepped into the trap. She wanted me. She wanted a man. She needed someone to caress her and do the thing to her she had been trying to get all that liquor to do. She wanted me to do what the fat boy couldn't do for her, if he did anything at all. Cool Spade, I thought. The man has done it again. His program is so together that not only is he getting the leg that he's after, but stuff that he didn't even know he was in line for. The main man is pulling another fast one on the world. Poor silly bitch can't resist the reputation and the coolness that this nigger wears like another vine. Goddamn! Goddamn a silly-ass Spade and all the idiocy that it represents! Goddamn motherfuckin' make-believe people! They ain' out here and they wouldn't dare try to pull all that cool shit in the middle of 17th Street with the P.R.'s on one corner and the whiteys on another and them right in the motherfuckin' middle! Goddamn! There was no point in getting into a thing about saving the princess from the fat ogre. All I had really been doing was trying to screw John's piece of tail. I had needed that just for myself to prove to me that I was the MAN, while John was just another two-bit dealer. He would never be another Spade. All Debbie had been was just another piece of ass!

I sat in the corner of the Cobra and drank a Jack D. and listened to Ray Charles sing about crying. Listen to the blind man see.

Time. The word comes through the turnstiles of your mind, ringing that bell that attracts your attention like the warning bell near the end of a line on a typewriter. Time is here; then it is gone. I remember the first day I learned the meaning of the word *gone.* I had found my grandmother dead. *Gone* meant no tomorrow. *Gone* meant over. Dead meant that you, who had been *something,* were now nothing. That was the first time I saw a body lowered into the ground while people cried. I cried too, because I realized that I would someday die, and I was afraid of death. No longer was death a shootout in a cowboy movie or Christians being eaten alive in a Roman arena by toothless lions. It was the end of everything.

Time is also supposed to be the great healer. In the weeks

that followed, I knew that John Lee would give me a chance to explain to him. I was sure that John would be man enough to sit down and listen to what I had to say, but he seemed to avoid me as though he knew that talking with me would be fatal for his ideals. It never occurred to me that he might sense the truth and just not want to hear. I never thought that he would rather believe something that was wrong than to find out the truth about the woman he called 'love,' but I was no student of the mind. John held Debbie the way I held Crystal, free of blame. To find out that Debbie never really wanted him would have been to discover that the solid ground he walked on was really only sand.

July 9, 1969 / 8:29 P.M.

I didn't travel the same roads I had once traveled. The corner Spade had become the missing link, and instead of greetings on the block, I heard whispers being thrown past, talk of my former deeds, as though I were a ghost instead of a man. I was looking down on the corner from my window when the phone rang.

'Eddie?'

'Yeah, Crys.' Her voice was shaking.

'I've got to see you,' she said.

'Yeah, baby, tomorrow, jus' like we planned.'

'Now! . . . Not tomorrow or next week or whenever. Now!'

'All right,' I said. 'I'll be right there.' I dropped the receiver and then picked it up again. I dialed Smoky, hoping that he wasn't gone for the rounds. I told Smoky that there was a family emergency and asked him if he could make my rounds for me. He said that he would, and I thanked him.

I ran out into the street dressed as I was. Blue jeans and a sweatshirt was all that I wore. Not my general street thing at all. I hailed a cab as it rolled down Ninth Avenue. All sorts of things grabbed my middle as I remembered the urgent, pleading tone in Crystal's voice. I had never heard anything like that from her, even during our infrequent arguments.

The cab made fairly good time, but nothing like the instant teleportation that I wanted. We were going down-town on Avenue D just off 14th Street when I told him to halt. I tossed him two bucks for the dollar-and-a-half lift and made it inside. In the elevator I lit a cigarette and wiped my sunglasses clean.

Progress was slow in the elevator. Riis projects had been around a long time, and the elevator was a part of the history it represented. I thought about what it would be like inside with Crystal. I'd try a 'Hey, baby,' and see how that got over.

As I knocked at the door, a flash of fear shot through me. In spite of the exterior thing that I was trying to get together, I was nervous. I could feel cold drops of sweat forming in my armpits and trickling down my side. I shivered involuntarily.

Crystal opened the door, and I stepped in, false smile in place. I stooped to peck her on the cheek, but she moved out of range. It was only ten before nine, but the house was silent and empty, like a tomb.

Crystal had been crying. The attempt she had made to straighten herself out had not been worth the effort. Her eyes were puffed and red, and the little lipstick that she used was uneven. I had been shocked to see her looking like that. I forgot the part I was supposed to be playing. She handed me a letter as we walked through the hall to the living room. I reopened it where the seal had been originally broken and read it.

I pretended to keep reading even after I had finished. My mind was gone. I couldn't even stop and focus on the written words in order to salvage the deeper meaning. Surely this was not what the author had been trying to say. It was some sort of code, some kind of trick. This was a lie!

'You believe this?' I asked Crystal.

'Why would she lie?'

'Do you believe it? That's what I'm asking you,' I yelled.

'Yes, I do. I believe every word of it.' Crystal's eyes clouded, and she started sobbing again. She stretched out on the sofa and turned her back on me. I wanted to lean over and hold her and comfort her, but my feet were embedded in rock. I couldn't pull them free of their position.

I looked around the dimly lit room. The only light was the one directly behind me that I had used to read the letter. I wanted Crystal's mother and little brother there. The only jury I had before me were the silent furniture sentinels, who could only observe. I needed people.

I saw Mrs Amos sitting in the corner easy chair where she usually sat during my visits, making small talk and waiting for Crystal to come out and entertain her guest.

'Mrs Amos,' I was saying. 'You know me. This is Eddie. Remember Christmas when we all went shopping together and I bought you the house shoes and the sweater? Don't you remember me?' Mrs Amos sat unmoving in the corner. Unmoving and unblinking and unbreathing. 'Why in the hell don't you say something, Mrs Amos? God, what's wrong with you?'

Crystal's little brother, Mack, was sitting at his mother's feet playing with a section of an electric train.

'Hey! Mack! This is Eddie. I'm like a big brother to you, Mack. I took you to the movies and the zoo, and I gave you that train. I'm yo' boy! Mack? Well, at least look up at me and act like you know me. Doesn't anybody here know me?'

I glanced down at the letter again and looked to the crying girl on the couch. I realized with a start that there was no one else in the room.

Dear Crystal,

How are you? Perhaps you are wondering already about this letter. Perhaps I should not be telling you this. Most likely the letter will make you absolutely no difference. I am writing because you need to know that the man you are probably sleeping with, Eddie Shannon, is going to be the father of my child. When I told him this, he laughed and said 'So what?' In a few times that I saw you, you struck me as a very nice girl who would probably fall for a guy like Eddie, just as I did. You raised questions in my mind very often, but Eddie assured me that you and he were just good friends. It was only recently that I learned that he was using both of us for play toys. I am telling you all of this because you probably think that Eddie will marry you if something goes wrong. That's what I thought. My life is all messed up as a result of this. I will have to raise a child without a father. I have moved away from home. I could never live with my family after this. Please do as you see fit, but remember that I warned you of it all for your own good.

Debbie Clark

Crystal continued to lie on the sofa, sniffing. Some sort of wall had sprung up between us. I could only shake my head silently. My mind would not permit my body to do the things I needed to do. I was helpless and hopeless. I balled up the letter and tossed it to the floor. I took the envelope and put it in my pocket, and without so much as a good-bye, I went through the door and down to the street below. I cast one single glance back to her window as I started uptown on foot. The lights were out in the apartment. It was all over.

I was back on the block in twenty minutes with my head still spinning and the atmosphere of the world pressing down on me like a bleak moment in one of Edgar Allan Poe's nightmare classics.

I stopped at Delores' house on 13th Street and Eighth Avenue. Delores was Crystal's cousin, but she was also Debbie's best friend. There was another mystery involved with everything now. Delores met me at the door and ushered me through to the living room with a smile that I quickly erased.

'Where's Debbie?' I asked point blank.

'How should I know? At home, I guess.'

'Look, Delores,' I was speaking with my teeth clenched and my voice barely above a whisper. 'I'm gonna find her if it takes me the rest of my life. You had damn well better tell me if you know anything 'cause if I should ever find out you knew an' sent me huntin' turkey, I'll beat you until yo' own mama wouldn't recognize you. An' yo' boyfrien' ain't bad enough to stop me.'

'She's in Baltimore,' Delores said.

I knew that to be true. I had taken the letter envelope and seen: 'Baltimore, Maryland July 8, 1969.' I needed an address in Baltimore.

'Where?' I asked.

'I don't know.'

'Look here,' I said. 'Yo' bes' frien' gits knocked up, an' I ask you where she's at, an' you say you don' know. Girl, you mus' think I'm crazy!'

'She has friends,' Delores said. Her eyes were pleading with me not to ask her any more questions, but I didn't care.

'And that's where she's havin' the kid?'

'She's gonna have an abortion.'

I was completely out of everything. I needed a drink, but I didn't trust Delores out of my sight. I could hear her parents running off at the mouth about some TV show they must have been watching in the next room. I could barely see the girl through the sunglasses. I took them off.

'That cost money,' I breathed.

'She had almost five hundred dollars when she left.'

I whistled out loud. 'Is that enough?'

'I don't know,' was the reply.

'Who's she stayin' with?' I asked.

'She's stayin' with Faye Garrison.' The conversation was

becoming thick and weighted. Delores kept throwing suspicious stares back over her shoulder toward the door that separated us from her parents.

'Where do . . .' I began.

'Spade, stop!' For the first time Delores raised her voice, and I looked to the door. 'I don't know everything! I've already told you more than I should have. That wasn't really any of my business! I don't know how you're mixed up in any of this, but anything you're involved in is always bad and ugly. I told Crystal to leave you alone! You know how tight Crys and I are . . . Now you come in here askin' me about Debbie when I've just seen Debbie leave here four days ago with more money than I've ever seen in my life. You're a rotten bastard, Spade. I wish you were dead!' She ran from the room and slammed the door behind her. Her father looked out into the living room and saw me.

'You know how women are,' I grinned.

He didn't say anything at all. He simply sat looking through the wedge he had made until I closed the door behind me. At the corner store I bought another pack of cigarettes, a paper, and a sports book. Once inside my apartment, I showered and shaved, then donned new clothes. I checked myself out in the mirror as I made the front door. New shirt and silk pants, plus a white raincoat and alligator shoes that started at sixty-five bucks. I caught a cab to the Port Authority at 41st Street and was entering the terminal when they announced my bus; 10:15 P.M. to Baltimore.

Baltimore, Maryland / July 10 / 2:30 A.M.

Nine o'clock hits Baltimore like a nightstick. All of the facilities of the central nervous system go immediately off duty. I arrived during the time each day when morning and night are colliding just offstage. The lords of the night are not yet fully prepared to relinquish their confiscated territory. The night people on the planet Earth are sullenly aroused by a knock at the door atop the solar system. It is the sun. Several stars are involved in a mutiny, and little by little the sun robs the moon of all his subjects. The moon dreams of recapturing the stray night lights, and he fades either east or west to recall them. It is daybreak.

I stood in the Baltimore bus terminal watching the beginning of the fray near the other side of heaven. I checked the city phone book looking for the name I knew would connect me with Faye Garrison. There was only one such name, and I prayed that I could find it.

Garrison, Odom 216 N Chas	BI 6–0907
Garrison, Oliver 37 Aztec Dr	KL 8–6472
Garrison, O.T. 995 Royal St	TA 4–7299

I stopped at the name O.T. That had been Oscar Taylor Garrison's initials. Faye had been a go-go girl at a dive called El Sombrero on 20th Street and Eighth Avenue. The owner had been O. T. (On Time) Garrison, who bought another place in Baltimore, where he and Faye moved. All of this came back to me when I saw his name and address listed.

I jumped into a cab outside the terminal. The warm air assaulted me after my sit in the air-conditioned coolness of the bus. I gave the driver the address on Royal Street and then settled back, watching the sleeping city flash past the windows. Sleep was closing in on me. Lights changed: Red-yellow-green-yellow-red. The initial anxiety I had had was wearing off. The tense feeling that had choked at my bowels was releasing me to the warm womb of drowsiness and ease. I thought I might need to see Debbie because I had lost Crystal, and there was no doubt in my mind that Crystal was lost to me. Crystal had been a great part of me. She had replaced the love I lost when my mother died. My father and I had been enemies. We stood opposite in terms of everything. My mother had been sort of like a mediator who struck agreements for us, so that it was possible for us to live together under the same roof. Crystal had been my love. She gave me the kind of love that cannot be measured in the amount of fear you command, because fear cannot be a mother for true love. The love that supplements reality when your goals become hazy and obscure.

I got a tremendous surprise when I knocked at the door. I could see the whole situation turning around in my hands. Debbie did not seem surprised to see me. I was a bit let down.

'I'm watchin' a late-late-late,' she said. 'C'mon in.'

I followed her. The door opened onto a wide red carpet that needed a vacuum cleaner's services.

'I came about the letter you wrote Crystal,' I said.

'I know,' she admitted, looking back. She plopped down on the couch in front of the idiot box and stared at Humphrey Bogart, my man. She was eating an apple.

'I want to know why you did it?' I asked.

'I needed the money.'

'Well, just how much was my soul worth?'

'Tsk. Tsk. Let's not be like that. Five hundred.'

'From who?'

'John Lee.'

Of course. Why in the hell? What in the world? Why in the devil hadn't the image of that fat idiot appeared on my screen. Of course. What had I been thinking of?

'I went to John and told him that I needed money. He said he would give it to me if I wrote the letter. It's that simple.'

'You have the abortion yet?'

'Day after tomorrow.'

'Did you tell dear John I wuzn' sleepin' with you?'

'No . . . Would you believe that?'

She was perfectly in control of everything, at ease with the world. I was the one who wasn't sure what was going on. I could not even look at her.

'Pardon me,' she said in Spanish. 'Have a drink?' I nodded.

She nodded in return and went off behind me somewhere in the kitchen, coming back with Old Grand-Dad, two glasses, and ice.

'You want to mix?' she asked. I shook my head no.

'How you gon' make out?' I asked.

'Okay,' she said.

'Five hundred ain' a whole lotta bread.'

'It'll do. When I'm well I'm gonna dance with Faye down at their club. That's where they're at now.'

How much she had changed since I had last seen her. She had aged so much that she hardly seemed like the same girl. She had decided just what she was going to do, and she was making the most of it. I wondered how many girls I had known who came up pregnant and decided that life was over and started screwing for a living?

'You know,' I said, 'You're carryin' my kid, an' I never went to bed with you.'

'So?' She smiled.

'I wuz wondrin' if I gave it to you by proxy or somethin'.'

'No. Nuthin' like that.'

We both had a good laugh at that. The drinks I had originally poured were now warming our midsections and loosening the initial discomfort. I dished out refills.

'You sold me out,' I told her.

'I had no choice,' she said softly.

'You're the one who had this crush on me . . . and you sold me out twice. Once to get rid of Lee. Once to get money from Lee.'

'Don't act hurt, Spade,' she said. 'Nothin' ever really hurt you. You came to my house with one thought. That was getting into bed with me. I got you into a corner before you got me on the sheets. You know how the game is played.'

I lit another cigarette. She was so right and so wrong at once. I wanted to scream and break the silence that surrounded us. Yes! We were out to use each other the first time, and you won, but not the second time. You were wrong the second time. You swung a long way below the belt when you took Crystal from me. I noticed that Debbie wasn't kidding me. She hadn't known how much Crys meant to me. It was all part of being Spade, the man with a death mask for a face. The man with a tombstone for a heart. The man without a solitary soul who knew how he felt, what he wanted, or how much he was alone. The silly actor who could never get off-stage long enough to tell the one girl who mattered that he loved her.

But John Lee knew.

John Lee had to have known how much Crystal meant to me, or else he could never have done such a perfect job of destroying me. He was in the street just like I was, and the only thing that kept him going had been Debbie. Even though he probably knew that he was buying her love. Bought love is better than no love at all.

John Lee knew! He must have seen me on the shore with Crys, and he wanted me out there trying to swim next to him. Too far out of reach to swim to safety or be rescued. Two men who could not survive. Two men in a cave-in with no air to breathe. Two men in the desert without water, watching the vultures circle overhead.

'Let's go to bed,' I said.

'What?'

'Let's go to bed,' I repeated.

I thought for a second that I was going to be Humphrey Bogart one more time. Then I realized that I was going to be Spade again. The truth was that Bogart and Spade never battled. It was always Spade and Eddie Shannon who fought for control. Deb followed me into the bedroom, whoever I was.

July 12, 1969 / New York City

I was on my way to work. The only exception was that for the first time I really felt like I knew what my job was. I could no longer be detached. There was nowhere else to look except into the eyes of the junkies and streetwalkers and pimps. They were my people. I felt that I was killing them just as surely as Smoky would if they didn't pay. I felt dead.

It wasn't even the same type of feeling I had before I met Crystal. I hadn't known what love was then. You can never miss something until you have experienced it and have to do without. I was now a man without love.

At about ten o'clock I stood in back of the church on 127th Street and Seventh Avenue in the park, waiting for one of my men to deliver. He would be the first of fifteen. The breeze came in with token force and swirled the charred ashes of a burned newspaper around my feet. When I looked up at the sound of footsteps, it wasn't Kenton, but Smoky.

'Happnin', Smoke?' I asked.

'Nuthin' much. i come tell you they ain' no work t'night. i try to call an' git you at home. zinari give a l'il thing in his crib startin' 'bout twelve.'

'Oh? That sounds pretty good.'

'yeah, man! menny girls, much tas', l'il smoke.'

'I think I'll make that,' I said, nodding.

'want me to pick you up?' Smoky asked.

'No, I'll be getting there a little late. Could you give me a lift home now?'

'sholy, sir. my limazine iz alwaze at yo' service.'

We hopped into the Cadillac, and Smoky burned rubber getting away from the curb at 127th Street. It would be good to do a little partying. Parties do a lot for the nerves.

Phase Two

John Lee died last night
July 13, 1969

The squat captain was speaking into the mesh microphone of his intercom.

'You can send Mr Watts in now, Sergeant,' he said.

'Right, sir,' came the reply.

The captain turned to his partner, who sat directly in front of the whirling, three-blade fan. The office was large and comfortable, but the air-conditioning was on the blink. The working officers, confined to paperwork in the bowels of the station on 18th Street, hurried through the technical chores in order to hit the street and work on unsolved cases that would take them near coffee houses and bars where they could sneak away for a hit.

'This guy is mighty cool,' the captain said. 'If anyone in the area can give us a hand with the case, it's probably him.'

There was a knock, and a shadow was seen crossing the frosted glass that spelled out the captain's name backwards.

'C'mon in, Watts,' the captain yelled. He was ripping the wrapper off a cigar with a mouthpiece.

The man came in. He was short and black, cigarette dangling from chapped lips, and sunglasses in place. He wore a light topcoat in spite of the merciless heat. There was a sport hat with a red feather on his head, and a wedding band on the smallest finger of his left hand.

'Have a seat, Watts,' the captain said, motioning toward the small swivel chair opposite him at the desk. The second officer turned and waved perfunctorily at the visitor but maintained his seat in front of the fan.

'Hot as hell today,' Watts said, sitting down.

The captain merely grunted.

'Watts,' the captain began, 'd'ja ever see this man before?'

Watts studied the enlarged photo of a black teenager. Yes, it was the baked-bean-colored character with a pimply face and large bone structure.

'Yeah,' Watts said.

The second officer turned his profile to the fan.

'Describe him,' Watts was asked.

The police guest removed the sunglasses and wiped a dirty handkerchief across his eyes.

'A guy named John Lee. He was 'bout eighteen. Six feet, maybe less, weigh 'bout two hundred poun's. Make that height closer to five-ten. He wuz fat. Lived somewhere aroun' 15th an' Seventh.'

'You said wuz,' the captain said, flattening his accent.

'I said wuz 'cauz he ain't,' Watts said. 'He's dead.'

The two policemen looked at each other furtively. The conversation skidded to a halt. The only audible sound was the clicking of the fan as it battled to get a breeze together for the perspiring officers.

'Captain Mason said that you might have some help with this one.'

Watts grimaced at the thought and pulled out a package of filter 100's and lit one up.

'What's the word?' the captain asked.

'They tell it like suicide,' Watts began. 'Accidental O. D.'

'I ain' here for no bullshit. We know it wuzn't that!'

The phone rang at the desk, and the captain picked it up. He introduced himself and then sat in silence for about a minute. He hung up and jabbed at the intercom button.

'Yes, sir?'

'Lay out fresh shirts for me an' Lieutenant Thomas. We'll be going out in about twenty minutes. Have the car ready, too.'

'Yes, sir.'

There was a click, and the captain turned his back to Watts.

'We need some information,' Watts was told. 'Some names.'

The black man was already sweating. His eyes fidgeted in their sockets.

'Lee wuz dealin' pills an' a few reefers on the side. You remember a Puerto Rican named Isidro Valsuena?' Watts asked. The captain nodded. 'Well, his brothers always thought that Lee killed Isidro, and they been after Lee for 'bout six months. That's all I know.'

'Was Lee shootin' dope main line?'

'No chance.'

'Did Lee kill Isidro?'

'No chance.' Watts seemed confident of both of his answers.

'All right,' the captain said. 'Keep your eyes open.'

The black informer got up and put both his coat and sunglasses back in place. He and the captain both laughed at the last line.

The intercom buzzed, and the sergeant came on.

'Everything's ready, sir.'

'Good,' the captain said. He and the lieutenant got up to leave.

'Where to now?' the lieutenant asked.

'The woman that found the body called in. She said she was too sick to talk to anyone last night, but she's ready now.'

The two men went through the frosted-glass door of the office and up the stairs that led to the dressing room. They would shower and shave before interrogating the woman who found John Lee's corpse.

'What was that thing you and Watts were laughing about?' the lieutenant asked.

The captain smiled again. 'I told him to keep his eyes open. He's one of those phony blind men you see in the subway. He does it to support his dope habit.'

'I was looking for tracks when he took that coat off, but I didn't see any.'

'The smart junkies nowadays shoot in their thighs and in the veins under their balls. A whole lot of ways to do it.'

They turned into the dressing room, and the conversation was turned off as they faced the heat and steam from the showers.

'I can use a cold shower,' the captain said.

'Yeah. This is a filthy city.'

'Bite yo' tongue.' The captain laughed. 'You s'pose to "give a damn."'

Junior Jones

July 17, 1968

'Anybody get caught?' I asked, dragging on a cigarette.

'Naw,' Cooly reported.

'Good.' I laughed, and so did everyone else.

My laugh was one of relief more than anything else. I knew I had a lot of faint hearts running with me. If anyone had gotten caught, it was a sure thing that the Man would've been knocking on my door.

'You sho save Lee's ass.' Cooly giggled. Cooly was my main man, really the only cat that I could count on. He and I had been hanging together since junior high, when stealing beer and cigarettes was a kick. I was closer to him than any of the other cats, but it still got on my nerves when people commented that he and I were both in charge of the group. I wanted everyone to know that it was me all by myself, just like it was Spade all by himself. I knew that there was really no way to have a gang and be a loner, but cats got over by themselves, like Spade, and then seemed to hold check over an entire area.

'Where'd Lee go?' I asked Cooly.

'I think he wuz headin' fo' Chelsea,' Cooly drawled. 'I seen the Man gainin' on him near the co'ner, but when the cah blew up, the cops hit the brakes an' Lee wuz runnin' jus' that much fastuh.'

'What the Man do?' I asked.

'Well, when the cah went up, they turn aroun' an' try to git back to it, but wudn' no way. The damn thing wuz hot as hell. Dey lookin' sad as hell, boy. Whut dey gon' tell the boss?' Cooly started laughing again.

I scanned the faces of the group. There were a few Puerto Rican cats, but we were primarily Bloods. There were about fifteen of us in all. Spade called us the Junior Jones boys. To call us a gang isn't entirely right, although I say it sometimes. There aren't really any more gangs in the city. It was just a thing where we all generally got high together and made sure that we didn't get bunted by a lot of goofs and old head dealers.

What had happened to Cooly and me in Harlem had been enough to tell us that we weren't as hip as we thought. The two of us got out of the IND train at 125th Street and came upstairs on Morningside Avenue. The directions we had been given were hazy, but we figured we could find our man. We went through the projects between Eighth and Seventh Avenues and came out on 127th Street.

'Nex' block up,' I told Cooly. 'If we don't see nuthin' that looks like whut Tiger said, we got to check somethin' else.'

Cooly nodded agreement. This was about a year ago, I guess. School was still in session, and a guy told us how we could get some really hip pills. Neither Cooly nor I had ever had any before, but it seemed like the next thing to try. I knew that a lot of the cats from the 17th Street park were talking about 'ups' and 'downs' and a lot of other stuff. We had run through wine and beer and cough-syrup. We had put glue down as a bad ride when I damn near fell off a roof after sniffing. So when Tiger put the word on us about pills, we were interested. We told him most of the cats who were trading on the block had gotten busted and asked him where we could cop. He told us to take the A train to 125th Street, walk to 128th and Seventh Avenue, where we would see an old amputee selling pencils and comics. We were to ask him where we could start flying, and he would tell us where to meet the dealer. The dealer met his load in a different spot every day.

As Cooly and I crossed 128th Street, we saw the old man. He was seated under an awning with the pencils and junk. We came up on him warily. As I look back on it anyone who saw us must have read the guilt on our faces.

'Batman! Superman! Archie! School supplies,' the old man said.

'We want to fly,' I said out of the corner of my mouth.

'Oh?' The old man looked at me rather sadly. 'There's the park behind the church one block down. A guy sitting in the swing with a blue straw hat – well, that's the pilot.' He managed a grin. 'Batman?'

Cooly and I turned and headed toward the park, walking south on Seventh. I didn't even look back at the old man. He was nothing but a shell. It looked like some kind of bug had gotten inside of him and eaten all of his bones and everything that had given him structure. He was burned a crisp brown from the sun, and his face was covered with hair, most of it gray. His clothes had only been shreds of torn this and that with suede patches sewn over the open pants legs that would have exposed stumps. He sat there eternally, from the looks of things. The wrinkled funny books and pencils were his only company. At a time like this, when the sun rested and ended the heat, the old man probably praised God.

Cooly and I waded through the little kids as we entered the park. There were the older cats playing ball and girls playing records and doing various dances. The guy we were looking for sat swinging slowly in the shade of a tree. It looked as though he had reserved a section. There was no one near him.

'Whuss happnin'?' he asked as we approached.

'Nuthin' too tough,' I said.

'Whuss the word, fellas? Batman *and* Superman, or choose?'

'Batman.'

He reached into an inside pocket of his lightweight jacket and pulled out a carrying case for his sunglasses. He forked a cellophane packet from the case with his index finger and thumb and replaced the holder.

'Ten dollars,' he said, throwing the filter cigarette he had been smoking to the ground and squashing it with the heel of his shoe.

I handed him a ten-dollar bill, and he passed the pills.

'Have a good flight.' He grinned. I grinned as best I could.

I shoved the packet into my back pocket, and Cooly and I headed back for the park entrance. Before we could get there, we were stopped.

'Thass good right there,' someone said from behind us. 'Now, don' neither a yawl turn 'roun. Jus han' the pills an' yo money. What I got here is a .32-caliber automatic that you can jus' think uv as a gun fo short.'

I reached into my hip pocket and handed the pills back. Out of the corner of my eye I could see a short black with a process palming a gun, with the nose buried in Cooly's back.

'Money. Money too,' he said.

I squeezed a couple of dollars backward, and he snatched them.

'Now, yawl take off walkin' slow. I'm gon' watch till you git to the corner, an' if you turn aroun', you dead.' He paused. 'It's been a business doin' pleasure wit yawl. Come agin.'

We walked with our hands at our sides, and I started counting. Just after we turned the corner I looked back to see if the thief was still in view, but he had vanished. I was sure that someone in the park had noticed, but no one was looking our way. What was even more strange was that the guy who sold us the pills was gone too. The only reminder of him was the swing, still swaying slightly. I ran back to the entrance of the park, but there was no trace of anything. We had been had.

From that time on, any pills that I bought were from cats in the neighborhood. Cooly and I were hanging with a bunch of kids who were as tired of getting bad stuff as we were. Most of the time the pills were flour and the smoke hadn't been cleaned. Because of the group, many times I had been able to get high when I was flat. The fourteen and fifteen-year-olds would do a lot to be tight with me and Cooly, just as I did to be tight with Spade and I.Q. Soon after the group began, however, Isidro, the P.R., started selling stuff. It was the beginning of 1968. Most of the big-time dealers didn't want to be bothered with smoke and pills. The first reason was that the big money was in cocaine and skag. The second reason was that mainly the younger cats smoke and pop pills, and a young cat will blow your cool when the Man applies the heat. When we found out that Isidro was dealing, we figured we were set. There would be a man on the block, and no more paying older guys to go to Fox Avenue and Tinton Avenue in the Bronx.

Isidro proved to be just as bad as everyone else. He sold us smoke that had so much sand in it nobody could get high. He gave us low-count smoke when we did get a decent bag. Maybe you could roll ten joints for a nickel bag. The pills were messed up too, and some were packed with less than others. For over six months we took that. We took it because every time we complained, the stuff would be better for a while. Then we would get beaten for a good night, like Friday, and he would have it all made back.

The end of June was when John Lee came on the scene. I was in the 13th Street park drinking beer at a card table. John walked up and sat down.

'Whuss the word, Lee?' I asked.

'I need to talk to you, man. I think we might be able to help each other out.'

'Howzat?' I asked. 'You want some beer?'

'Naw.' Lee sat and wiped the sweat off his face. 'I'm gonna be dealin' startin' tomorra, an' I thought we might be able to work sum'thin out. I know Seedy been fuckin' wit' you an' yo boys, an I know you don' dig it.'

I took a swig of the beer. 'What's the play?'

'Today is Wednesday the twenty-sixth, right? Well, I got a l'il smoke for t'night, but I rilly won't be togethuh till tomorrow. I wan' to know if I can count on you cats to deal wit' me. I got a good play from the boats, so you won' be cheated. How much you want, and how often?'

'We'll deal with you,' I said. 'Tomorrow night, not much. My boys iz primarily git-high-on-the-weekend men, you know. But the las day a school is tomorrow, so after that we'll be tightnin' up regular . . . What time on Friday, an' where?'

'Early Friday. 'Bout five meet me here. I'm havin' a l'il gig Friday night. You invited.'

'Bring about ten nickels for smoke, ten red devils or purple hearts. Thass a hundred right there.'

'I'll have some smoke tomorra. Cheebo an' Panam Red. Treys, if you want.'

'You already sound like a goddamn commercial, man.' I laughed.

'Whut you say?'

'I'm tight till Friday . . . Hey, wait!' I called Lee back as he drifted across the park. 'How you know Seedy been buntin' my boys?'

'Aw, he wuz high a night or two ago an' started runnin' off at the mouth about blowin' yawl's mind wit' weak shit an' that all yawl had wuz psychological highs.'

'When does he ship?' I asked.

'His shipments hit on Sundays,' Lee said. 'Somewhere near Eleventh Avenue and the pier. Maybe 9th Street.'

'How much?'

'He pulls off about sixteen hundred dollars a week raw,' John said. 'Including the coke an' heroin.'

'He ain' pullin' nuthin' this Sunday, 'cause we gonna hit him for alla his shit,' I said.

'You got a buyer if you come up with it.' Lee smiled.

I didn't say anything else. Lee waddled off across the

park, and I tried to figure out ways to catch Isidro on Sunday night.

'Hey!' I said suddenly. 'Where's Ricky Manning?' In exploring the faces of the group, I had somehow gotten lost in thought. I suddenly realized that someone was missing.

'He's wit' I.Q.,' Cooly reported.

'I.Q. iz aroun'?'

'Yeah. He wuz stannin' by the bar, but you wuz probably too busy to notice when you went by.' Everybody laughed again.

Lee had been true to his word. Friday afternoon we met him in the park at five, and as far as I could see, the pills and the smoke were both good. I ended up with some reefer.

Everything had been running smoothly for three weeks, until tonight. Lee would show up on Mondays, Wednesdays, and Fridays. We met him at a table in the park and got our stuff. Then it was every man for himself.

Tonight when Lee showed up, there was almost an omen of bad luck in the air. There were too many new cats in the way – guys from Chelsea Houses and other men I didn't know. Before anyone could get together and buy their stuff, everything was interrupted by the arrival of the Man, live and in living color from the Tenth Precinct. The prowl car hit the brakes on the corner of 13th Street and Ninth Avenue. The two cops hit the sidewalk, and everybody who had congregated to buy a high found running more interesting. The group meeting broke up and turned into a track meet, with John Lee, bag of dope in hand, leading in the hundred-yard dash. Several of us who hadn't heard the opening gun were caught in the rear of the pack. We ran behind the park maintenance house and back through the same entrance the cops used. When I arrived at the corner where the idling patrol car sat, I turned and saw the two cops directing each other in terms of who they should try to catch. They were at the other end of the softball field with their backs away from me. Parked directly in front of their wagon was a New York City Housing Authority maintenance truck with what looked like the day's refuse from some set of apartments. On the tailgate was a can of gasoline that was leaking onto the street. I pulled the can out and dumped the gas into the front seat of the copmobile, backed off, and lit a match. I heard the dispatcher's voice reach out for me as I threw the match and fled toward the docks. The car ignited with a roar and a lot of crackling like a dead Christmas tree. Just as I turned for the last glimpse of the Man's reaction, there was an explosion. Chips of metal and paint decorated Ninth Avenue. I ran down to Tenth Avenue and lay under a car away from the streetlamps, panting for breath.

Once I grabbed my wind, I took my shirt off and left it under the car. I knew that at least two or three old white checker players had dug on my red Banlon. I doubt if much more than that could be identified. Until the car went up, all the activity was at the other end of the playground.

I circled the neighborhood and turned finally into the park on 17th Street and Eighth Avenue. I knew that eventually the guys would come in. Less than half an hour after the raid, we were all huddled together again.

I lit another cigarette. Cooly and the rest of the guys were still discussing the speed I had when I passed I.Q. and Ricky at the bar.

'I.Q. wuz there, huh?' I asked Cooly.

'He seen it all.'

If I.Q. had seen everything, then I was sure that Spade would hear about it. Spade was the man around the block. The guy in the area who can beat anybody at any time and get any chick he wants. I wanted Spade to hear that I burned the cop machine so that he could tell everybody I was coming to get him. Spade told all the older cats that I was going to be the man. He would come up on us in the park sometimes when we were getting high, and all the guys would ask him about the days when the Berets were running the neighborhood. It was surprising how they talked to him like he was an old man, even though he was just a little older than we were. We all wanted to know about the time when everybody was in a gang. At that time anybody who was anybody was falling off a corner and kicking so much ass that nobody could keep score. It took a whole lot of heart to walk out on the block and get high with nobody to back you up. Everybody knew about Spade, though. He had been his own gang. Now, he said, the block had been turned over to white hippies and young faggots who couldn't tell a gang from a tea party. I always wished I had been on the scene when Spade was taking over. Me and Spade would have been too much to handle.

'You got time, Junior,' Spade would say. 'Jus' lay an' dig whut iz an' whut ain't, an' when you think you time iz here, don't ask no questions, jus make you move. Even if you got to move on me to git whut you're after. It ain't how old you are, it's how well you carry the years you have.'

I was waiting. I was waiting for the days when the older guys on the block who were running things now started to settle back and fade inside the bars. Then the street would belong to me and those who ran with me. There would be no more Spade. There would be no more of the wild rumors like there were now. John Lee was supposed to be the new man since Spade wasn't on the corner anymore. All Spade would have to do would be to snap his fingers, and John would be decoration on the stage again. When Spade walked down the block in the summertime and everybody was on the stoop, you could tell. The look in his eyes, maybe, or the way he dressed. He didn't say much, only nodded to the people he knew, but there was a certain thing happening, and you could tell if you were there. The way he moved said that the Spade was back and still the man, and anybody who didn't dig his thing could settle it in the middle of Ninth Avenue. Very few people stepped out with him, and he was paid his due respect as a man who had come the hard way. I was going to have my respect too.

'You guys gimme yo bread,' I said to the group. 'Me an Cooly gonna fin' Lee an' git the stuff.' I looked at my watch. 'It's 'bout nine-thirty, an' we gon' be back inna hour.' I looked up and down 17th Street. 'I want you cats travlin' light. No more than three cats togethuh. If you see the Man, you jus' came outside. When yawl see Ricky, tell 'im whuss happnin'.'

A hat was passed up with everybody's bills. Cooly took the money and put it in his wallet. The hat was passed back through the crowd.

'Look here,' I said before we broke, 'if the Man stops you, you don't give out no lip. Ansuh whatever he wants to know an' tell 'im you been watchin' TV an' stay on the block. Stay away from the 13th Street park an' stay in the open where a lotta old people can see you. That way the Man can't rough you up an' claim you fell while you tellin' all you know.'

The crowd started out of the park when I finished. Cooly and I strolled down 17th Street toward Ninth Avenue. We acted as though we owned the sidewalk. Even though it was going on ten o'clock, the block was still lit up with domino games, and crapshooting was on full blast. The Puerto Rican boys on the stoops were drinking beer and rapping to their little painted women. When we passed, they waved and whispered. I grinned to myself. I like to see them spreading the word about me. Soon everyone would have to know me. It would be an unwritten law.

The gambling had started right after work, and now only the beer cans and cake wrappers could say for sure how long José, the store owner, had worked to keep the games going. They kept him rich when they gambled all night, and he didn't give a damn if he had to do a little extra sweeping every morning. Most of the storekeepers didn't want the men gambling anywhere near their place, because the old ladies complained and went elsewhere to buy their cat food. José evidently had no concern for old ladies and their cats.

As we moved closer to Ninth Avenue, the sounds of the night took on a Latin beat. Eddie Palmieri and Joe Bataan were the music heroes of the neighborhood. The Met game was coming out of some window or other, and the Mets were getting their asses kicked again. The blasts coming from off the rooftops told us that a few Spanish boys were having a 'love-in' under the sky. The old ladies crowded the sidewalks in folding chairs and sped through Spanish in no time at all. All I could ever catch was Puerto Rico and something-something 'MeeAmi.' They could rap a whole book while I hung back trying to translate the first word they had flown over.

Aretha was coming from a window. She was singing 'Do-Right Woman,' and for a second I thought I heard Isidro's voice. Every time I heard that side I was reminded of Isidro, because I had been sitting in Tommy's Coffee House the day after school listening to it when Seedy barged in. I was surprised when he walked in, because I had only talked to Lee the day before and found out about my new deal.

I was drinking a Coke with a little rum Tommy had thrown in, and there was my girl Aretha building the atmosphere. It was early afternoon, and very few people were up and about. None of the chicks that I wanted to talk to were around the place, so I kept the back table busy and played sides.

'I wanna talk to you, man,' Isidro said, dropping into the seat opposite me.

'Talk,' I said. From the broken English I hadn't had to look up to identify the speaker. I was cursing under my breath for being caught off guard.

'Who you gize gon' buy you stuff from? Me o' dis odder cat?'

'We gonna deal with Lee,' I said.

'Why?'

'You know good and damn well why! You been beatin' the hell outta us for too fuckin' long! Dirty smoke! Bad pills! Fuck you!' I looked around, but there was no one near enough to hear us. Tommy was watching from up front, however.

Isidro made a gesture with the middle finger of his right hand. His eyes widened, and he pulled closer to me across the table. I could smell the wine on his breath and the odor of coffee.

'Look 'ere. I jus' wan you to know somsing. I heard 'bout dis sheet you wan pull on me. It ain' gon work. Oye? I wan you to know I ketch one pussy near my sheepment, I gonna keel 'im. I don give a fuck you got Spade to back you up. A boolet can kill Spade like any man. I'm gon carry a gun from now on. I can kill too!' Isidro leaned back in the chair. I didn't move or change expression, but my mind was working fast. How could Isidro have found out what I was going to do so fast?

I talked to Lee about it yesterday, I was thinking.

Tommy came over and asked if I wanted anything. He was talking directly about Isidro. I told him that everything was all right.

I only mentioned things vaguely to Lee, my mind went on. Then I brought it up yesterday afternoon to Cooly, and we talked about it somewhat last night. Then I told the gang my plan, and we agreed on it. We were going down to the docks about three Sunday morning when Isidro left to pick up his stuff. At least we would follow him. That's where we thought he got it. Then we were going to jump him from behind. How could he know about it the next morning? Who squealed?

'I don' know whut you're talkin' 'bout,' I told Isidro.

'I'm talkin' 'bout you motherfuckuhs tryin' to take my stuff. Eef you think you can make eet, try eet. I'm gon' kill somebody.'

'Look, man. You mad 'cause somebody beat yo' racket. Fuck you! I don' need you.'

'You don' need me now, but eef somsing happens to the fat one, don' come back to me. Comprende?'

'I dig you, amigo,' I said. 'But if Lee gets busted behind some mysterious phone call, you gon' get picked up the same way. Do *you* comprende?'

Isidro left in a hurry, and I sat in the booth trying to figure out who had turned me in. The logical suspect would be one of the Puerto Rican boys who ran with me, but that was too obvious. It had to be a brother – a twentieth-century Uncle Tom. The setup had been good. We could have robbed Seedy and taken the stuff to Lee. He could have kept us high for a while, and we would have had Seedy up Shit Creek! Now it was the other way around. I was in trouble, because I had to figure out who the rat was. If I didn't, something else might happen, and I could get blown away, and we all end up in jail or juvenile court at least.

I met Cooly about six and told him that the hit was off. I didn't tell him why, but I know he got the idea that somebody was onto our setup.

'What if Lee ain' in Chelsea?' I asked Cooly.

'We'll find 'im. He know we lookin' fo' him.' Cooly gave me a thick smile. 'Where yo min' at t'night, man? Clarice ketch you yet?'

'What you mean?'

'You been in yo' own worl' all night. Daydreamin', o' just heavy thinkin'?'

'It ain' no bitch,' I told Cooly. 'Jus' heavy thinkin'.'

We passed the projects on Ninth Avenue, walking up-town. The projects stretch from 15th Street and Ninth to 19th and Ninth. Across the street from the projects, on the northeast corner of 19th Street, I could see that the lights were out in my apartment. It meant that my mother was out somewhere, either with my baby brother and the neighbor's boy, or alone while somebody watched the brat. My older brother was in the Navy.

Across the street under the low-rise apartment buildings, the young whiteys were drinking beer and macking while they listened to WABC radio. It seemed like they drank enough beer to wash out the whole goddamn neighborhood. The way things lined up, God put black people on earth to blow bush and take a lot of shit, and white people were for drinking beer and dying of boredom.

My thoughts changed to John Lee again. Until he started dealing, he had been just another nowhere cat. The black cats had been going to Brooklyn and Harlem or buying their stuff in school. All at once John was on the street with all kinds of stuff. Most of the older cats said that they knew where John got his supply, but I was sure that they didn't know. John was a smart cat. He was seldom early or late. He seldom carried any more than he would deal. He found out in advance what you wanted and disappeared right after he gave you what you ordered.

John carried Red Birds, Yellow Jackets, Purple Hearts, and Blue Heavens in quantity. They were the genuine pops that everybody had heard of. If you wanted, he could get some depressants, or 'downs,' but black people don't dig that too tough. That stuff was for the hippie poets and folk singers who liked to go around singing the blues and talking about the total destruction of mankind and all that wild shit. They liked to feel like they carried the weight of the world on their shoulders. They convinced themselves when they got high that the message in their poems and flimsy melodies were the true salvation of civilization. It was always that nobody would listen to them. I guess that's why they wore their hair long and had freak-out sessions with psychedelic music. They felt that they might as well cram as much of life as possible into their few remaining days on this doomed planet. You could always hear them ranting and screaming when you got out of the subway at West 4th Street. I figured it was a lot of bullshit and another excuse for lazy cats and chicks to get down without getting married, and stay high all the time without ever getting a job.

John's dealing made him a big thing on the block. He arrived during a time when there was basically no man on the avenue. John started dealing at the end of June. Spade hadn't been around for a long time. You heard less and less about him. The arrival of John Lee prompted more talk. The arrival of a new adventurer. When I was twelve, the man had been Hicks, the leader of the Chelsea Berets. Spade was fifteen or sixteen and saved Hicks's life. That meant that the man owed his life. Spade captured the neighborhood. The women dug him because he never said anything to them. The older cats were scared of him because he knew karate. The old people hated him because he didn't have any manners, and his parents couldn't control him. He was so slick, though, that he never gave them any real reason to call the cops.

I thought about how Lee came to fame, and I was almost mad. I made a quick decision that I would be the man soon. I was going to deal. Then I would walk down the block, and all the girls would dig the things I did, and all the cats would stay their distance. I was going to be the 'somebody.'

Just as the word 'somebody' was repeating itself in my head, Cooly spotted Lee. We had passed the projects and all the stores between 19th Street and 25th Street. We were walking through the Chelsea Houses, another group of apartment buildings. Lee was sitting between two other cats in the play area peered down on by two high-rise apartments. He was dressed in the familiar green trench coat. There was a can of beer in his hand and a brown paper bag protruding from his pocket.

'Happnin', Lee?' I asked as Cooly and I approached.

Lee grinned his same moon-faced grin and slapped me five.

'Juneyuh,' he said, as though he still hadn't caught his breath, 'I wuz jus' tellin' these cats whut you did. That was nice as hell.'

'You the one burned the cop car?' one of the cats asked. There was a look of admiration on his face.

'He did it,' Cooly drawled. I said nothing. I just sat back and listened to Cooly and Lee describe the thing. They had to be exaggerating, because both of them were running in the opposite direction. The net result was a picture of me looking like a cross between Napoleon Solo and James Bond. Lee handed me his can of beer, and I lit up a Kool.

'I tol' you,' Lee concluded. 'It wuz jus' like the time Spade put that stretch a wire across the roof and tripped Happy Stick Kinkaid. The sonuvabitch broke his arm in two a three places and wuzn' on the block for months.' Lee stopped and related everything to me. 'Happy Stick was this whitey who tried to ketch me an' Spade allatime when we drank wine and smoked on the roof. That motherfuckuh wuz fixed good!'

There was a pause. Across the park square, teenagers loafed and pretended to wrestle so that they could sneak in a few public feels. The small kids ran around and did whatever they damn well pleased, while the oldsters listened to the Mets and played checkers.

'Can we git our stuff?' I asked Lee. I handed him the can of beer.

'Sure.' He looked around to see who was watching and then took the brown paper bag out of his pocket. He placed it on the bench between us and slid several packets of pills and small manila envelopes to me. Cooly pocketed the pills and the grass and handed John his green. I noticed that he didn't even bother to count it.

'Mañana,' I told Lee as Cooly and I departed.

Lee and the two other cats waved.

'Hey, Junior!' Lee called. 'Anybody get grabbed?'

'Naw, man,' I assured him. 'Rest easy.'

The thought of Lee hung in my mind. His fat face had been a picture of worry, perspiration dripping down his nose. Some of the Juniors called him and Spade the 'Dynamic Duo,' but I really didn't know why. Spade was six feet and muscular. Lee was short and fat. The best thing that could be said for Lee was that he smiled a lot. Spade was a very noncommittal type of cat. He rarely smiled. When he did laugh, it wasn't because everyone saw something that was funny. The older cats said that when Spade smiled, it generally meant that he had thought of another way to give somebody a hard way to go.

Cooly and I slid back into the park and rationed out the stuff we bought. Almost none of the guys had left the park, even though I told them to. I disregarded it because I had so many things on my mind.

'You gittin' high t'night, o' whut?' Cooly asked.

I looked up, and everyone was gone except us.

'Yeah, man. I got some smoke and some wine down in Tommy's cellar. I'm gon' make it down there later. I got some things to think about.'

'I kin dig that,' Cooly said. 'I git that way.'

'I'll ketch you later,' I told him.

Cooly probably knew what was going on. We had been hanging out together long enough for him to have an idea what was on my mind. There was no big issue as I could see. I was just restless. I wanted to be bigger and older and more important. I didn't care about controlling the Juniors, because they didn't really hold a lot of check. We didn't fight. We got high. I kept remembering back to the party. That was when I got jolted into another plan. Lee had invited me to this gig when I told him I would deal with him. It was the end of June, after all the high schools had closed for the summer.

John Lee's Party
June 28, 1968 / 8:30 P.M.

John's party was on the twenty-eighth of June. I remember so well because it was also my older brother's birthday and my mother didn't want me to go out. She figured he might call or something, and she'd want me to be around so that we could get on the phone like one big happy family. Matt took that seriously, because he considered himself the head of the household. I told her that I had some partying to do and not to wait up. I took off with her sitting on the sofa tuning up to cry.

I walked into the liquor store on 18th Street and Eighth Avenue about eight-thirty. The storekeeper looked at me for a second.

'Can I help you?' he asked.

'Bacardi Light in the pint,' I said through a cloud of cigarette smoke.

He reached behind him and plucked a pint of the clear liquid from a lower shelf. He reached for a bag on top of the cash register. I could see the big German shepherd that guarded the place standing at attention at the end of the counter.

'May I see some identification, please,' I was asked.

'Sure.' I went through the ritual of fumbling through my pockets and my wallet before coming up empty-handed. The dog moved closer.

'Gee! Looks like I didn't bring it with me.' I paused for a

second. 'Look, I always buy from the older cat. He don' ask me for nuthin'.'

The man began to chuckle a bit as he handed me the bottle.

'See that you bring your draft card in or something next time.'

'I'll do that,' I said.

I was wearing a lightweight spring jacket, and I hooked the bottle into the inside pocket and strolled to the park on 17th Street and took a seat.

Once inside the park, I felt better. The sun dimly watched everything progress slowly with its one hot eye. Up and down the street the night people were starting their rounds. Career women and just plain laboring hags staggered home from their nine-to-five with bundles cramming their arms and chests. The calls always started around this time. The music and the gambling that the P.R. people dig so much was off and running. A Parks Department maintenance man was picking up pieces of broken bottles and beer cans. Even the breeze seemed to know it was Friday.

I wondered idly what the gang would be into. Friday night, so they were probably somewhere high. The broads were out of school too, so they might have taken the whole thing down to the dock, where they could sip beer and smoke in peace. The broads would go anywhere as long as they could lay all over everybody and get dicks hard without going too far. Maybe there was a dance in Chelsea. I hadn't even bothered to find out the schedule. For a second I wanted to be with them, because I didn't know what John's party would be like. I knew that a lot of the girls would be my age, but they were always looking for cats older than themselves. What the hell? If it was as dark as I figured it would be, all raps would be the same. I opened the rum and took a swig. It burned a bit and left a sour aftertaste on the edge of my tongue. I was tempted to tip into José's and buy a Coke to mix with it.

One of the Puerto Rican boys came over and sat next to me.

'Hey, man! I'm su'prise to see you over here,' he said.

'Why?'

'I been tol' you at war wit' Seedy the smoke man.'

'You musta heard that from Seedy,' I said.

'Whuss wit' you an' him?'

'I ain' in no sweat, man. Seedy got tight jaws 'cause I ain' dealin' wit him no more.'

The Puerto Rican was carrying a bottle of Amigo in a moist paper bag. He took a large swallow and handed it to me. I handed him the rum, and he nodded.

'I heard you wuz gonna hit him an' he got wize.'

I didn't comment on that.

'He started carryin' a gun. 'Zat true?'

'Iz whut true?'

He took another straight shot and handed me the rum.

'Look, man, you wuz dealin' wit' Seedy until two days ago, right? Now you wit' John Lee.'

I nodded both times.

'There mus' be a reason you deal wit' one man an' then another.'

'Whussat gotta do wit' me hittin' Seedy an' him totin' a piece a thunder?'

'Ef you got another dealer, Seedy ain' necessary anymore, an' eef you theenk you wuz cheated, then you might wan' revenge.'

'Jus' like that?' I asked.

'Sure.' He took another swig from the wine bottle and grimaced when he set it back between his feet. 'This iz tough shit.' I nodded.

The thing to do was to play it cool. Seedy was a junky, and

it was his word against mine. The redeeming factor for me was the three Spanish boys I had who hung out with me. That meant I couldn't be all anti-Spic. Any sign I made that hinted that what I was supposed to have done was more than idle chatter would get me a visit from a few razor carriers that I knew.

It was an unwritten law. If a man puts a contract on another man, he really signs one on the whole community, because that's who his new enemies are. I had been caught putting a price on Isidro, and now the shoe was on the other foot. There were bounty hunters looking for me, and the bounty was community commendation. The only real factor was proof. That and my closeness with Spade kept the noose from around my neck. Anything that happened would be traced by him.

'I got to make it, man,' I told the Puerto Rican.

'You take it easy,' he said.

'I got to.'

There was nobody there when I got to John's house. It was about nine-fifteen, and I had stalled as long as I could. Debbie Clark answered the door and let me in. John was in the back filling the bathtub with beer. It appeared that since John's folks were taking a little vacation, John was setting up a real domestic thing. I lit up a cigarette and parked near the record player, shuffling through the sides and putting what I wanted on the turntable.

Already the fan was losing its battle with the heat. The breeze I had detected earlier had evidently thought better of it.

There was a heavy accent on atmosphere. Incense was burning in every corner. The only light in the front of the house was a table lamp with a red bulb, and that was nearly nothing. For a minute I thought we were going to have a psychedelic thing with filtered light and Jimi Hendrix.

Junior Jones | 95

Anybody who walks into one of those things, high or not, gets his mind blown.

At about ten-thirty the party was together. All the names in the neighborhood had shown about ten or so. Spade, Afro, I.Q., Websta, and everybody else had a corner or a seat. They had all brought taste, and for a minute I wished I had brought a bottle to contribute.

Evidently I had done something wrong with my head. Either I had no business mixing rum and wine and beer, or I had no business smoking half a pack of cigarettes in three hours. I had stumbled through the back of the group trying to make it to the john. There were very few people present now who were not partying. At first there had been some standing around and rapping, but that had disintegrated with a few drinks. Spade had disappeared altogether with his girl. I figured if I was going to get myself together to dance once or twice, best I not feel like the last chapter of what's the use. A couple of the younger girls had been giving me that look. I reached the edge of the dance floor and ran head on into Debbie Clark. She was leaning at an odd angle against the bathroom door and smelled like she had just bathed in a bottle of overproof rum. Her eyes lit up when I nudged her.

'Junior,' she slurred. She looked at me wide-eyed and giggled.

'Hi, Debbie,' I said slowly.

'C'mere, Juney. C'mere, baby,' she said.

'I want to get by.'

'Not now, baby, c'mere.'

I was already close enough to take a bite out of her shoulder, but evidently she was having trouble focusing. She was wearing something black and flimsy, the kind of thing with the two straps over the shoulders. Her breasts were half hanging out, and her lipstick was smeared and messy. The eye makeup was mixing with her sweat and running down her chin.

She reached for me, and before I could react, she had pulled my head down to hers, and the smell of her breath was hot as well as foul. Then her lips were on mine, and her tongue was pushing my lips away. I was so surprised that I lurched backward and shoved her against the wall. Her eyes were at first wide with surprise, and then she slid down the wall pointing at me and laughing. I couldn't help but throw my hands to my ears. Her laugh was loud, piercing, hysterically accusing. She kept pointing at me and stammering drunkenly.

'Juney ain' never been kissed,' she shrieked. The thought of that seemed to be more than her mind was ready for.

I dived at the open bathroom door and locked it behind me. The light sparkling off the soaking beer cans in the tub seemed to cool my burning face. I looked in the mirror and saw someone else. All that I could really distinguish through the tears seemed to be a painting of me when I was five and afraid of thunder. The salt from my eyes trickled down my cheeks and into my mouth. The mixture on my tongue was a combination of sweat, beer, rum, wine, and embarrassment. I fell on my knees and vomited into the bowl, while still more tears streaked my face and dried my mind.

I watched Cooly disappear around the corner and lit a cigarette. I could still feel the cold shivers that came every time I remembered the unpleasant party thing. When I came out of the bathroom Debbie was already stretched out on the bed in the bedroom, but even as I managed to smile my way through the crowd and mumble about what a great sense of humor she had, there were some people who looked at me rather oddly. I hadn't done anything wrong, the eyes seemed to admit, but what a hell of an embarrassment.

August 29, 1968

The summer just seemed to fade away. It always seems as though the things you enjoy last no time at all. I widened the gap between myself and the gang. I still went around to get high every now and then, but there was no more to it than that. I didn't feel up to the lies or the highs anymore. Once we had all sat out in the park and told tales about fantastically built chicks that wanted no more from life than to get screwed over and over by us live and in living color. I was no longer able to put myself in those lies, because I had been blown away. I had had a chance with Debbie Clark, one of the finest little asses in the neighborhood, and just because she was high, I pushed her away. I couldn't understand why people got girls high on purpose to screw them, and when my opportunity came, Debbie disgusted me. None of the people at the party had paid any attention to Debbie, because she was drunk, and none of the gang knew about it, because they hadn't been there, but I had been there and I still had my memory.

'Junior, is that you?'

'Yeah. It's me. What'choo doin' up?'

'Just having some coffee. Come in here.'

I walked into the kitchen. My mother sat in her bathrobe at the dinner table. Her hair was in rollers, and there was cream on her face and forehead.

'It's almost two o'clock. Now I told you to come in earlier this evening because you have to start getting back into that routine. There will be school next week, as far as we know. There's no use in you counting on this teacherstrike thing for keeping you up until all hours of the night. Remember, Bobby will be going to school this time.'

I sat down opposite her and lit a cigarette.

'I guess you jus' ain't gonna listen to nothing that I say, is that it?' She got up and went over to the cupboard and found two cups. She placed one in front of me and then poured both cups full.

'How come you can't say anything?' she asked.

'I'm tired.'

'I guess so. Runnin' the streets until all hours of the night like I don't tell you different. Don't half eat the food that's fixed for you. Livin' off beer, and cigarette-smokin' like you grown. Wouldn't do no good for me to tell you to do this or that. You so grown. I done tol' you, though. Don't have the Man knockin' on my door when you get picked up, 'cause I will swear that I never heard of you, you hear?'

'I hear you.' I sipped the steaming coffee. I heard her, and the people in the next block probably heard her. I had heard her before, too. She had no real time or energy to worry about where I was or what I was doing. She didn't know what she would have me do if I told her I would do anything that she wanted.

All she really knew was what she didn't want. She didn't want me in the Navy like Matt. Each day she secretly expected a letter from Uncle Sam so that she could cry some more. The letter would be headed 'We regret to inform you . . .' and she would burst into tears and run across the hall for consolation. I knew that Mrs Boone, our neighbor, must hate to see her coming. Always another tale of woe. My mother was a one-woman soap opera. She cried and cried, always on the brink of tears, but no matter what happened, she would always fall back on that same weak story about God testing her.

She couldn't tell me what to do, because she wasn't doing anything for her own peace of mind. She didn't want me to be like my father, who died when his kidneys and liver rejected his style of life. His heavy drinking had been the cause of his death and had led to a nervous breakdown for my mother. At sixteen, I had been fatherless for almost eight years. The sign on the tombstone said that my father had been forty-three when he died. I remembered a man of sixty, complete with wrinkles and white hair. Alcohol had turned big patches of his skin to a bluish-purple. What the sign in the graveyard did not say was that when my father died he left behind a woman with a third son in her belly, and two older sons who had no reason to respect anything at all. It did not say that my father had been driven to his death by my mother. Matt realized all this and ran away to the Navy. Her whining and complaining had become as much a part of my life as breakfast. I inherited the position of whipping boy. From the day that my brother left, anything that went wrong with her world was my fault. I started to ask to go out more often, and whereas I hadn't cared for the neighborhood when we first moved from Brooklyn, I really started to enjoy leading my own group. I began to return later than I said I would, and instead of correcting me, she seemed to get more and more into her 'Patience of Job' thing. By the time I was fourteen, Matt had been gone for almost a year. I was riding the corner horses every night of the week. By then I didn't even bother to ask to go out; I just went. That was another source of screaming. She had raised me and loved me and given me all that I had in the world, and I had no respect for her. That was her side of the story, and it was always consistent.

'I'm goin' t'bed,' I told her.

'Goodnight,' she said tolerantly.

I wanted to leave and get out of the way of her latest kick. She complained now that I was trying to embarrass her in front of all the parents in the neighborhood. My behavior was not an indication of the way I had been raised. I was turning out to be my father's son.

I passed my little brother's bed and looked down on him. There was no question about whose son she wanted him to be. Draped over the back of the bed was the baseball shirt with the number seven. I could never tell him enough about baseball, and particularly Mickey Mantle. Once or twice he had talked me into going with him to see the Yankees. But his interest was more the thrill of going somewhere with a million people than the game. He was only seven. He had had pneumonia the year before, when it was time to start school, and missed a year. Now all I could hear about lately was starting school. No more Mickey Mantle. I was a Mets fan anyway, if I was anything. The Mets were losers from the word 'go.' The only kinds of records they set were for the most games lost and most people coming to the game. Shea Stadium was a madhouse. The people got more hits than the team did. Somebody would get high and start cursing, and the next thing you knew, whole sections were being kicked out. The Man was ruthless. The Mets were the team that the Negro and Puerto Rican people could identify with. They were the ones with the whipped heads and the kicked asses. They were the underdog on the streets of New York, like the Mets were on the baseball diamond. The fans who got drunk and swung on the Man when he tried to quiet them down were heroes, because they were striking a blow for underdogs everywhere. When they were finally subdued and beat into unconsciousness, it was a sad, proud moment. They had not given up.

Junior's Dream

'First and third, and nobody out here in the bottom of the fourth. There's no score in the ballgame. Both teams had scoring opportunities earlier, but strong defensive plays turned the tide ... Kranepool is the hitter. Eddie's batting .274. He grounded out to Javier in the first ... They'll be pitching away from his power, trying to make him hit the ball to left. Brock shaded toward the line.'

'So what you been into, Junior. I haven't been seein' you.'

'Nothin' much. Been too hot.'

'I heard the guys tellin' you Clarice was lookin' for you. Why don' you give her a play?'

'I ain' got time to be bothered with Clarice.'

'Well, all right. I guess you said that.'

'. . . pitch on the way to Kranepool is outside. Mets baseball is brought to you by Rheingold, the extra-dry lager beer. Also by Winston, America's largest-selling filter cigarette. Winston tastes good, like a cigarette should.'

'First and third, an' nobody out. Bet the bastards don't even score.'

'They gon' get a run,' I said.

We were sitting out on the sidewalk in front of José's store. In the middle of the block between Eighth and Ninth avenues on 17th Street, there are many walk-up apartments that open onto the street. Ricky, the guy I was sitting next to, lived between José's store and Isidro's house. I had been playing dominoes with José and a few of the other men before the game came on. Kids and old ladies had been all over the place. I knew it wasn't late, but everyone had left. Ricky asked me if I wanted some Colt .45, and we had since waded through the last two innings of the first game of a double-header, and almost four innings of the second game. We had also put two six-packs away.

'. . . there's a fly ball to left field. It's deep enough to score the run. Brock makes the catch, and Harrelson scores, with the first run of the second game. The Mets lead one to nothing.'

'I told you they were gonna score,' I said.

'It sure is a nice night. I wish we could get a breeze like this in my place every night. Last night was so goddamn hot I couldn't even move. José is gonna have to do something about that fan. I bought a fan three weeks ago, and that sonuvabitch is busted already. It never did stir up a helluva lotta air, but, damn, now I can't get a thing.'

'One to nothing,' I said. 'I shoulda bet you.'

'You want some more beer? I got more upstairs.'

'Naw, man, I'm fulla beer.'

'I'm gonna get myself another one. Don't you take my fifty-dollar radio.'

'Fifty dollars my ass! Twenty-five on Forty-second. A 42nd Street gyp joint.' I picked up the radio and looked at it closely, but I couldn't make out the name for some reason. A drop of rain hit me on the nose.

'. . . ground ball to Maxvill at short. Over to Javier for one and to Cepeda completes the double play. But the Mets got one run on two hits. There were no Redbird errors, and no one left on base. We go into the top of the fifth with the score: The New York Mets one and the Saint Louis Cardinals nothing. Now for a word about . . .'

I was watching Orlando Cepeda chase a foul ball on the TV screen. The color was great, but there was no sound. I kept getting up to turn the damn thing up, but I could never hear the description. Ricky was in the kitchen talking about something that I couldn't translate either. I kept thinking he and I were on TV too, because everything in the room was the color of something on the screen. I was drinking some Scotch from a glass that reflected my face in the bottom. I kept thinking that as soon as I finished that drink, I was going to leave, rain or no rain, but every time I tried to drain the glass and looked back, there was as much as I started with.

I was getting sleepy. 'Ricky, fix the damn sound.'

I was half-lying back on the couch, and I could hear Ricky singing in the kitchen. I wanted to sleep, but his singing kept me awake. As I hollered for him to shut up, he came through the door saying that he hadn't opened his mouth. I closed my eyes and cursed the silly bastard. Of course he had opened his mouth, or someone was in there opening it for him.

I could feel his hands on me. He was unzipping my fly, and I knew that he couldn't say he wasn't doing it. I kept thinking I was going to raise up and knock the hell out of him. You find out about people when you get high with them. They start to come out from where they really see things. Ricky was a faggot! Just a second, you scroungy bastard, trying to get me high and feel me up like a bitch! That's the only thing I knew for sure. I didn't know you were a faggot, Ricky, because I wouldn't have come up here and had a drink with you or sat outside and rapped with you if I had known you were a faggot. Ricky, you know how everyone looks on faggots, and I'm going to be the man, and I don't want nobody to think that the man is a cootie-loo. I would've drank your stuff outside and told you I was leaving when it started raining, like I didn't know what you were up to, because I *didn't* know what you were up to. You got to string them queers along so you can use them. They got money and fine cribs an' . . .

'You can dig that, can't you, Junior?' Ricky whispered. 'You got a nice long one for such a young man. Ahhhh, the youth of America.'

I could hear the rain beating against the window, but it wasn't cooling anything off. It was hot in Ricky's stuffy little place with all the colors. I didn't even open my eyes, but I could picture the dingy little room. It was dingy and gray with chips of plaster on the floor. Ricky didn't have any clothes on, and his pecker was stiff.

'I want you to touch me, Junior,' Ricky gasped.

'You're crazy!' I said, opening my eyes. 'Ricky, you a fag! I didn't know you wuz a fag! I'm gettin' the hell outta here.' I looked down and reached for my clothes that were scattered all over the rug. All of the color had come back to the room.

'You know you don't really want to go, Junior. Look at you.

You want everything I can give you. You're conditioned by society not to like the thought of a male-to-male relationship, but nobody is entirely heterosexual, because if he was or she was, they couldn't stand to sit down for a minute with a member of their sex. Junior, we're all the same!'

'Then I'm gonna kick our ass instead of just yours,' I shouted. I'm screaming and running down the hall with good old Ricky right behind me grinning.

'You like it, Junior. You like it, and you know you like it, but you think you can run away because of society. I'm gonna run with you, Junior.'

I turned and swung at Ricky and thought I had broken his face into a thousand pieces, but I had slammed into the wall and knocked a hole in the plaster. The hole revealed Ricky's grinning face. He had somehow sneaked away from me. I ran down the stairs three at a time, and when I looked up at the next landing, Ricky was ahead of me going down the stairs backwards. I tumbled down the stoop in a head-long dive and landed in the middle of 17th Street traffic. I thought it was ten o'clock at night, and it's the rush hour. There is a traffic cop. What's he doing on a side street? I think I'll ask him which way I turn to land back at ten o'clock. Everyone knows that the Man is a friend of the people and not a rotten pig like they're made out to be by hippies and militants. They aren't really the kind of men who spread Vaseline on your body and then beat you so that your body won't show any marks. 'Hey, Mr Cop, Man, Fuzz, Sir,' I said, but I felt silly. Now back inside my head the weekend man that gets in my bottle when I drink hammered away at the bass drum and said: 'But who would believe that only minutes ago you were listening to the Mets game in Saint Louis, where they were playing a twi-night double-header? Just because you think some fag is behind you or in front of you. Why don't you turn on the radio?' Okay, I think I will.

'Bottom half of the sixth inning, in case you've just joined us. The Mets are leading one to nothing. They lost the first game in ten innings by a field goal and two free throws by Larry Wilson, the Cardinal free safety.'

Well, that proves that everything I said was true, I guess. There is obviously a night double-header going on in Saint Louis right now, and the time difference is not that great, so there must be something wrong with a lot of things, so I'll talk to the cop who's ... gone. I noticed that I was in the middle of a circle of REA trucks on their way in from a day of delivering whatever it is they deliver. I was screaming because I knew they'd hit me, and they didn't see me. Ricky! What did you put in the Colt .45? I knelt in the middle of 17th Street and yelled at the top of my lungs.

'Hit me, goddamn you! I don' wanna stay here no more,' I screamed.

I peeked through my fingers and saw a truck coming, but it stopped right in front of me. Ricky was driving the truck. The word 'Clarice' was painted across the front bumper of the truck.

'I've got to find Clarice,' I said to myself.

I got to my feet as Ricky stepped on the gas, and I started running toward Ninth Avenue, trying to make it to Clarice before the truck ran over me. I turned one last time to see Ricky closing in on me. I closed my eyes and watched Ricky swerve and hit the policeman, knocking him through the air and over my head, where he bounced on a cloud with springs shooting out of his back and head. I rolled over, and Clarice reached for me. We were in bed naked together. I was throbbing. I moved to her and kissed her. She opened her mouth like Debbie did, but I didn't dodge. I kissed her as I thrust my tongue against hers in the tunnel formed by our mouths. I felt her hands running back and forth on me lightly, teasing me. She was driving me crazy on purpose, and I wanted to pull back so that I could screw her, but she continued to nibble at my lips and tongue. I was frozen and shaking at the same time. All of a sudden I felt myself tumbling and my stomach starting to twitch. I had a feeling in my lower belly like the minute you're through pissing and there seems to be more fluid in your body. It's a shivering, quivering, nervous excitement. I pulled away and rolled onto the floor. I saw the end of my dick shriveling to normal size.

'C'mon, Junior,' Clarice called. 'You got me all hot and bothered.' I heard her giggling, and her toes dug into my back. I started pounding my fist against the floor.

'You and Ricky and Ricky and you and you all set it up because you wanted me to be all fucked up in the head, but it won't work, because I'm hip to what's happening, and any girl I know that sets up a plot with a cat that everybody knows is a fag except the guy they're trying to run this game on, well, that girl has got a lot of nerve going over to all the Junior Jones boys and telling them that she's in love with this cat she's just about to make an ass of, because she's been had by everybody in the neighborhood and everybody knows she's just a slut, so she should be trying to make a good impression instead of teaming up with a faggot!'

'I can't! can't! Clarice, I'm not a faggot. I just can't.'

I woke up!

My eyes were stung with tears, and the memories of the dream closed in on me. I was tangled in the sheet, and my pillow was gone. My body was covered with perspiration, and I had come in my pajama bottoms. They felt sticky and slimy against my thighs. I got up and stumbled over to the chair and got a smoke while I pulled off the pajama pants and rubbed the cream off my thighs. I wondered if I had screamed and whether or not my baby brother had heard. Evidently he hadn't heard a sound. I stubbed the cigarette out in the ashtray and dived back into bed.

November 16, 1968

School was two weeks late getting started because of a strike by the New York City schoolteachers. I couldn't have been happier before school began. I had been hinting that I wanted to quit school altogether, but my mother wouldn't hear of it. Every time I tried to say something about not going to school but working, she'd bring up the neighbors and the jobs their sons had. All of them had been blessed with seventy-five-dollar-a-week slaves because they had their high-school diplomas. I had more of a feeling that Mom was concerned about what the neighbors would say about her if I just decided I'd had it at the beginning of my junior year.

I always drew the line when she started talking about college and that trash. She wanted me to go because she had never had the opportunity. I'd have a chance to meet a lot of intelligent women. I would also be a thing for her to lay on the neighbors for the next forty years, even if I was unhappy about the whole damn thing.

I was sitting in the schoolyard across the street from Charles Evans Hughes on a Thursday evening when Spade walked by, strolling actually, profiling for all the cats who thought they were seeing a ghost.

'Hey, Spade!' I called. 'Whuss happnin'?'

'Nuthin' that I know of,' he admitted. He came over and sat with me and Cooly. 'Could yawl stand a taste?' he asked, indicating a bottle under his arm.

'Not me,' Cooly said.

I took a swig from the bottle. It was some kind of wine.

'Man o man,' Spade said, meaning Manischewitz wine.

The three of us sat and smoked, looking across the Ninth Avenue crush. It was almost six, and the sun was gone. A gray color had taken over the evening and brought the Hawk along as a bodyguard. The children were inside watching cartoons, and I had stayed outside to watch cartoons. Old white ladies running along with TV dinners, and uneducated black soldiers from the docks heading for Eighth Avenue and the A train.

'I'm sick of this shit!' I said.

'What shit!' Spade asked.

'All this shit.' I pointed out the books between my feet. 'I feel like I'm in jail. Read this and write that. Today I do it, and tomorrow I don' remember what I did, an' it don' make no difference.'

'Schoolitis,' Cooly drawled. 'I think I got me a bad case a that too.'

Spade smiled and took another swig from the wine.

'You know what I wanna do?' I asked. 'I wanna start dealin'. I need to make me some money an' git the hell away from home.'

'Schoolitis an' homeitis,' Spade said. 'One uv 'em is named Lee an' the other is named Isidro. If you deal, you got to deal in yo' neighborhood. Thass the only way you got a chance. You got to have contacts, or one cat will try a l'il pressure, an' when he see you ain' leanin', he'll call the Man on you.'

'Those ain' the only problems I got,' I admitted. 'I ain' got no lead. John an' Seedy got a very steady lead, an' thass whut keeps bizness good. They alwaze have their stuff. I ain' got idea the first 'bout where Lee iz gittin' set up.'

'When the Man jump Lee an' beat his ass, you gon' be glad you didn't know nuthin',' Cooly commented.

'The less you know 'bout another man's thing, the better,' Spade declared. 'An' thass his woman, his job, his fam'ly, an' everything else.'

'We got a meetin',' Cooly reminded me.

'Yeah.' I guess I must have grimaced at the thought.

'Whuss the problem?' Spade asked.

'Nuthin',' I lied. 'I'm sleepy.'

'I'll see you later,' Spade said. He took off in one direction, Cooly and I in the other. Cooly and I were heading for the basement of José's store to hold a meeting. The thing that kept puzzling me was that I still had no idea who had turned me over to Isidro. No one had stopped hanging out with the group or acting extraordinary.

There were two reasons that finding the informer was important. The first was that I felt uncomfortable with the group, knowing that we couldn't plot anything significant. We used to hit a little something once or twice a month. In the summertime, more often that that would've been okay. But without knowing who I could depend on, I couldn't do a thing. The second reason was personal. The rat, whoever he was, was blocking my way to being the man. In so doing, he had almost gotten me killed.

'Only way you can be the man iz to prove that you are a man,' Spade said. 'And in order to deal with other people, you got to make sure your own house is straight.'

That was what I had to do. Before I moved in the street, I had to be sure that things were together with my men in José's basement.

January 4, 1969

The Hawk was kicking much ass when I stepped out of José's basement. The three Puerto Rican boys, Cooly, and I had been blowing a few joints, standing in a circle passing the sticks and waving at a small electric heater to keep warm. I had smoked enough to lay out and nod for a week. Somehow I just couldn't get in the mood to cut loose and laugh at all the funny shit that was happening. The guys were all moving in slow motion, and I was listening to what they said five minutes ago as though I was communicating with some little green men from Mars by way of a language disc. I never really heard the meaning, but the sounds were familiar.

It was almost two in the morning when the group broke up and headed home. I shuffled through the snow toward my crib, hoping to God that my mom was in bed so that I wouldn't have to hear no Sermon on the Mount or whatever. I walked over to Eighth Avenue and then uptown. The avenue was still lit up a bit with Christmas lights and big signs about white-elephant sales that the Puerto Ricans loved. All the P.R. and blood women had been running up and down 14th Street and traipsing off with bundles of shit.

Christmas hadn't been bad at my house for the first time in a long time. My baby brother had given up the idea of Santa Claus, but he got a bicycle with the training wheels and a few other *practical* gifts. I had given my mother a clock-radio that I stole from 42nd Street and told her I had been saving for. What I had been doing was giving my money to Lee. My mother fell for what I told her, and enjoyed the holiday in spite of herself. She didn't work because of the nervous breakdown she had had, but with money from Matt plus her check, we managed to have a tree and a big Christmas dinner and the whole family bit. As a special holiday surprise, my big brother, Matt, left Vietnam in one piece. My mother swore that it was an act of God and that the seven years of famine were over.

'Step over here an' don't move.' My thoughts about the season were cut short at that instant. I knew the voice.

'Okay, amigo, I give up. Why me?' The guy's name was Pedro. I had met him at the park the day John gave his summer party. He had had a bottle of wine, and I had given him some rum.

'Jus' step careful.' I could feel the point of the gun jammed into my back. 'What eef I tol' you Seedy wuz dead, man? What would you say?' I half-turned and then halted when I heard him cock the trigger.

'I'd say this was the first I heard,' I said.

'I don' believe you, you bastard!' He pushed me ahead of him. 'Start walkin'.'

'Whut if I say I ain' goin' nowhere?'

'Then I'll shoot you here. But you gonna die anyway.'

Isidro was dead? I had laid a contract on him almost six months ago and hadn't done anything to him now, but by the time Pedro found that out, it would be too late for me.

'What time wuz Seedy killed?' I asked. 'I been with frien's all night.'

'I would be su'prised eef you didn' have a lie worked out. I ain' sellin' time. Yo' time ran out this summer when you plotted on our man. I been jus' waitin' 'cauz I knew you couldn' be trusted. I didn' know you planned to keel 'eem.' The faster Pedro tried to talk, the more pronounced his accent became. I could see his breath coming past my shoulder in long streams.

'Look! I didn' hook Seedy. I don' know who did. I been wit' my boys blowin' bush all night. Why don't you check it out?'

'Whatever I check mean that more than the dead man knows who killed you. I can' check nuthin'. They would lie for you.' He paused. 'Start.'

We started walking slowly toward 18th Street, and then he prodded me into a left turn that pointed us west, toward the river and the docks.

'Look! I wuz wit' my men,' I said. 'I ain' seen Seedy in three months or more. He wuz the las' thing on my mind.'

'That's right,' someone else said. 'He wuz with us.'

Pedro and I turned, to see Ricky Manning right behind us. He was breathing heavily into his hands. He wore no gloves.

'When? Cuando?' Pedro moved at an angle so that he could watch us both at the same time.

'From ten-thirty till about ten minutes ago,' Ricky said.

Ricky, you stupid bastard! I was thinking. You should have come up on him with a gun. You standin' there ain't givin' us a chance. Now he's gotta get both of us out of the way.

There was silence. I watched Pedro. I was looking for a chance to grab the gun from him. He shook his head and then looked at me and gestured with the rod. I nodded that Ricky was telling the truth. Pedro turned and walked away.

'I'm grateful to you, Rick,' I managed. 'You saved my life. I owe you.'

'It was nothing, brother.' Ricky turned, and before I could add anything, he was gone, wheeling around the corner at a trot. I broke into a trot too, even though I don't know why. My nerves were on edge. The cold weather was no factor. The chills I had were goosebumps.

That's a weird cat, I said to myself.

Ricky was the quietest of us all. He hung around with I.Q., like a Siamese twin most of the time. Even when I was with them and they were getting high, they were arguing over the merits of this and that. Ricky was my age, but he had skipped a class because he was smart. That had put him only two years behind I.Q., and he seemed to thrive on the thought that even though he was younger and might not have read as much, he was as smart as the Q. In my mind, and most of the other corner cats', there was no chance of anyone being as heavy as Ivan Quinn. He had been on TV for the High School Bowl, voted to *High School America's Who's Who*. There were very few honors he had not gotten in school. Out of class, he smoked and got high like the rest of us.

There used to be a particular hangout that we don't use much anymore down on Eleventh Avenue. It was an old warehouse that had been abandoned. Whenever we wanted a little privacy, we went up there to smoke and pop pills. It was there that I first saw and heard Ricky and the Q get into their philosophical who-did-what. They were as high as two kites. When I showed up, they had already popped three 'cats' apiece. I wanted to smoke, but they told me that in order to relate to the greater realm and a lot of other shit, I had to be high on what they were with. The only thing about 'cats' that I had ever heard was that they were 'downs.' I avoided all kinds of downs, because I thought they would make me feel like I was at home.

'Look at mankind,' Ricky was saying. 'There is nothing right with the world the way it is. Everywhere you look there are bombs being dropped and people being flooded and diseased. For the advanced state that mankind has reached technologically, he has achieved nothing humanely. Discomfort and discontent. Hippies, yippies, beatniks, anarchists, revolutionists, rebels, communists . . . are there no more just plain people who believe in living life singularly and finding a separate peace?'

'Peace was created by people as a way of describing oneness with God. There are no more Thomas Mores, if that's what you mean,' I.Q. said.

'Then why must I remain in this state? I believe in reincarnation. I think that I would be much better off as another form of animal if this is the highest form. I need to know nothing of all this. Why must I conform?' Ricky turned to me. 'Do you know what the answers are? The purpose of life can't be in preparation for praising God forever. . . . Just as I can't see myself burning in hell throughout eternity, I can't see myself kneeling at the feet of an Almighty God and singing of his glory.' Ricky looked up, and there were tears in his eyes. I was thinking that this was some white-boy action. All of this conversation and these words that sounded like some kind of a book. What kind of a brother got high and ran all of this shit down? 'It simply means that I will be as well off anywhere in the universe as I am here,' Ricky said. 'The brain is made up of electrical impulses that can never be shut off. That means that when death comes it cuts off the transmitting of signals from the brain to the body. It does not mean that the brain itself desists. Electricity does not fade like breath . . . I should not have to live under oppression and something less than the ideal humane conditions when I can end this fiasco . . . I should kill myself.'

'Who, then, is free? The wise man who cannot command his passions, who fears not want, nor death, nor chains, firmly resisting his appetites and despising the honors of the world, who relies wholly on himself, whose angular points of character have all been rounded off and polished.' I.Q. made a long speech and then explained it for my benefit. 'If you have no need of life, then you have no need of death. Who knows what you may someday do to inform others of your unconcern?'

'You're full of shit!' Ricky screamed. 'You talk all that shit tonight when you're high, but what about when you need and want? I have already experienced the pains of a man who has lived twice my age, and not half of the joy that one is supposed to squeeze from life like juice from an orange. I know what you want. You want like the rest of us. The cool of I.Q. is not as notorious and impregnable to me as it might be to others. I reject life in a test tube. I shall leave you to your maker.'

The conversation continued. Ricky would tell about sixteen years of pain. That he had ached for the salvation of mankind since his first realistic look at the system.

I.Q. was the master of the quote. As he supplied quotes to explain to Ricky why life was worth living, he would name the author, the year, and the speech if he felt like it. Ricky screamed about suicide and actually looked like he was trying to jump one time. Q and I managed to control him. The pills that we took kept us up. I nodded as Q and Ricky continued, and finally cried myself to sleep as the sun rose.

June, 1969

'You workin' for John?' Cooly asked.

'Yeah.'

'Whattaya do?'

'I deal.'

'Thass why you don' hang out no mo'?'

'Yeah, I'm too busy.' I lied and exaggerated a bit.

I was working part time for Lee. It started at the end of May, when he went down to take his physical for the service. He had had some appointments to make that couldn't be canceled, so he sent me to deliver the stuff and started to use me as an errand boy after that. To no one's surprise, he didn't pass the physical and beamed on the block about his 4-F.

I spent as much time as I could watching Lee. He had become good at smelling the Man and staying out of trouble for almost a year. The closest he had ever come to getting nailed was the night I burned the car. I was learning all that I could.

'In other words, you ain' gonna be with us no mo'?'

'In other words, brother,' I told Cooly, 'I ain' got no mo' boys on the block. I'm gittin' into a thing where yawl don't fit in. In a year or so, maybe less, yawl gonna all be movin' on yo way, an' there ain' gonna be no big thing. I'm jus' leavin' a l'il early. I'm sorry if it looks bad, but . . .'

'Fuck it,' Cooly said. I watched him closely.

'I'm seventeen, man,' I said.

'That ain' no hundred,' Cooly drawled.

'Spade an' John Lee ain' much older! I got to move!'

Cooly laughed. 'You still wanna be the man?'

I didn't comment. The way he said it made it sound like a comic-book hero.

'Lemme tellya,' he said. 'Lee an' Spade may not be much older than you inna way, but in other ways they ten times yo' age. Can you dig that?'

'The only way to learn iz to find out.'

'The hard way?'

'If thass the quickest way.'

'You ain' comin' to no mo' meetin's an' tell the gize?'

'No.'

Cooly started off across the park. He turned back long enough to shake his head.

'Man, you ain' never gonna be another Spade,' he said.

July 9, 1969

'I got something for you ta do,' Lee said.

'Yeah?'

'If I can trust you . . . This is important.'

'You know you can.'

John was sweating. It seemed as though he was always sweating. Either because he was fat or because he was nervous.

'I got some pills for you to deliver,' he told me.

'Where?'

'Brooklyn.'

John reached into a brown paper bag and came out with the familiar cellophane packets. He rewrapped the packs in cloth and stapled the ends together. He did all of this on the kitchen table. His parents had left the day before to see his mother's sister in Syracuse. I had been practically living there anyway. They weren't due back for a week.

'I want you to go to a place called the Ivy Hall.' He took out a piece of paper and started to jot down directions. 'You take the A train to Hoyt and Schermerhorn and catch the bus on Hoyt, the QL, four stops. You get off on this corner. The place you're looking for has about five entrances. You want the one on the west side in the back. This is a side door that says "Personnel" on it. Ask for a cat named Immies. Tell him you got held up last night and couldn't make it. Anything. You give him the pills and then he 'spose to give you two-fifty . . . You got that?'

I nodded. I picked up the piece of paper, but he stopped me.

'Memorize it,' he said. That was smart. If I got caught, the Man wouldn't have a map of my plans.

'Now,' he said. 'I may not be here when you get back, so jus' cool it. I got bizness elsewhere.'

He handed me a jacket with stitched-in pockets under the armpits. I put the pills in these pockets and took off. John saw me to the door. I almost ran down the back stairs in my eagerness to get started, but I figured John might be looking out of the window, so I took the slow way down on the elevator. I didn't want him to think I was running off to cheat him. He'd make a call, and I wouldn't make it to the corner. I settled in the elevator and lit a Kool. This might well be my big break. I was finally getting a chance to meet the Big Boss.

6:30

I remembered Brooklyn. Brooklyn's Bedford-Stuyvesant was the new Harlem. People were stacked on top of each other, and rats and roaches were the most familiar thing about the buildings. I had lived in Brooklyn until I was almost ten. I had watched my old man drink until he could no longer hit my mother with any kind of accuracy as she screamed and yelled about the lack of this and that and the other. There was the solitude of sharing the bathroom with the families down the hall and sitting on the toilet with your ass out while the

Hawk whistled through the cracks in the wall and turned your balls to ice.

There were the radiators that fizzled and hissed and made noises that were supposed to convince you that they were heating while you watched TV after dinner in your overcoat. I watched my father beat knives out of shape signaling the landlord that we were freezing. Into the night he would sit up with his liquor cursing the white man who owned his forefathers and the white man who owned us.

Even in Brooklyn my mother had been into a fate bag. She was always predicting her own downfall through the Lord's punishment of us for our wicked ways. Our father was being punished because he was a man who wanted his wife to open her legs and close her mouth. Matt and I were doomed because we loved him and he was a wicked man.

When I was almost eight, my father died. He was a stranger to me. He was in the Veterans' Hospital for four months while the white men did this and did that to him. They did not bring back his smile. He was in pain, and I heard my mom praying that he would die. I hated her more than ever until I understood that she really loved him after all and wanted to see him out of his misery. Then I hated her for what she was without him.

When my mother had her breakdown, we moved to Manhattan. Six months after her husband's death, God sent her a third son. The city decided to finance our trip to a lower-rent zone. I noticed the changes in our new house. The street was different, too. The boys' names were Juan and Enrique, and Cuba. The way they talked was funny, and the way they dressed was even more odd. I knew the Beast when I saw him, though. My father always told me on trips to the barber shop, where we saw men leaning almost parallel to the ground, that when the Beast got us we were no longer sons of God or man. The Beast was dope.

Junior Jones | 119

The A train was through with the rush-hour millions that piled into each other at nine in the morning and five at night. Those who had run into the Manhattan shopping districts and Wall Street district and business areas had once again escaped to the Bronx, Brooklyn, and Queens. They were safe in their other cages.

7:10

I knocked at the door marked 'Personnel' at the Ivy Hall.

'Yeah?'

'I want to see Immies,' I said.

'I'm Immies.' It was a fat white man who blocked my way. 'You Lee?'

'Yeah,' I lied.

'Good shit! I thought you'd pull out on me. All goddamn night I'm waitin' an' waitin', ya know? Whut happened?'

'I got held up.'

Immies had on a baggy suit that just seemed to match his baggy face with the overflowing jowls and rubbery lips. He had an unlit stogie in his mouth, clenched between yellow teeth.

There were two other men in the room. Both of them were white. A squat, fireplug-looking cat with a derby on sat propped against the wall with his feet on a battered desk. The other, a short, red-nosed faggot with a casino man's dealing hat on, sat at a desk trying to write in a big ledger under the glare of a no-watt bulb.

'You got dem pills?' Immies asked.

'Yeah.'

'Lemme have 'um.'

I pulled the packets from the pockets under the armpits and tossed them at him. Immies had a small pouch in his hand which he handed me. It felt like a roll of bills.

'Cheg dem dolls,' Fireplug said.

I leaned against the wall and relaxed opposite the three men who gathered around the desk. Immies pulled the staples from the cloth and opened one of the cellophane packs. He spilled the contents onto the desk.

'Whatcha say, Nita?' Immies asked the fag.

Nita picked up a pill daintily and popped it between his index finger and thumb. The white, powdery filling spilled onto his fingers and the desk. He tasted it.

'It's salt,' he purred.

I didn't think I heard him right. I looked from Nita to Immies to Fireplug. The three of them looked at me accusingly. I moved to the desk and ran my finger through the powder. I placed it to my tongue. It *was* salt!

'It's salt!' I said.

'Thass right, you schemin' l'il black motherfuckuh, you. Goddamn salt! All these goddamn capsules iz prob'ly fulla the shit! First I gotta wait, an' then you play me like a dumb bastard, some dumb fuck in the playground!'

I hadn't been watching Fireplug. I was still trying to find out what had happened. Plug hit me across the head, and I stumbled face down on the floor, my head spinning and smacking against the wood. Immies kicked me in the ribs. That's all I know.

1:35

I woke up in a crowd of Juniors. Everything near me was pain. My eyes opened and then quickly closed as the hurt stabbed my head.

'Who done ya, Junior?' Cooly asked. 'The whiteys?'

'How'd I get here?'

'We saw them dumpin' you here. Two men threw you outta car . . . Who wuz it?'

I was getting my mental and physical together. My mind

was in worse shape than my body, because the body can't hurt unless the mind is registering. There was a taste in my mouth that reminded me of blood. My brain was running here and there, never stopping, always running.

There was an echo chamber that kept repeating John Lee's name. I was ashamed to look at Cooly. I felt that he knew what happened somehow, even though *I* didn't really know. John must have known I wanted his job. He set me up to eliminate the competition, just like he might have gotten rid of Isidro. He never cleared himself of that. He had set me up by giving me phony pills and making me think he was trusting me for a big job. Immies thought that *I* was cheating him. John wanted me dead.

I stayed at home the next day. My mother got into a terrible thing when she saw me with my face all kicked in and my ribs crunched, but she was quiet long enough to prod for broken bones and patch me up as well as I would let her. John came to see me about his money. I told him that the pills had been bad and that I had gotten a bad ass kicking and no money. If he wanted anything from Immies, he'd have to go and get it. He said that he didn't know how those pills happened to be bad, since the rest in the shipment were good. I decided that my showing up alive had brought a great performance from the fat man. He was the picture of concern. When I told him I didn't have the money, he looked like he would die.

I hated the very sight of him. Cooly's words kept coming back to me. He had said that I would never be as smart as Spade or Lee. He had said that I would never be the man. John Lee reminded me of those words, and Debbie Clark reminded me of them. I supposed that Spade would make me think when I saw him, too. I didn't want to see him, though. I didn't want to tell anybody what happened. The only reason I told John was because it seemed to be one of the games we were playing.

John Lee is dead.

Phase Three

John Lee died last night
July 13, 1969

'Mrs González,' the captain said, 'I know this hasn't been a very easy thing for you, but your help could be vital. . . . I assume from your call that you are willing to help us.'

'My wife will help all that she can, sir, but she is not a well woman. She is to have another child,' the middle-aged Puerto Rican man said.

Captain O'Malley and Lieutenant Thomas sat in a cramped apartment on West 16th Street. They had refused Mr González' offer of beer or lemonade and now waited patiently for his wife to tell them what had prompted her call about the previous evening.

'Now, last night, what did you see that made you call us?' the captain asked.

'I went for the paper to the corner, and as I am coming home, I walk through this . . .' She asked her husband for the word. '*Como se dice este?* . . . parking lot? Yes. When I come through this parking lot, I see a man bending over this one, and I scream at him . . . He looked back to me and ran away.'

Mrs González was a Puerto Rican woman of about forty. She was plump and short, with long, black hair pulled into a bun. Her husband was older than she by about ten years. He stood at the back of her chair with his hands resting on her shoulders.

The two white policemen sat facing the couple, their light-weight jackets barely concealing the weapons under their left armpits. There was a small fan directly behind them spinning furiously in an effort to battle the ninety-degree New York day.

'About what time was this?'

'About eleven-thirty,' she replied.

'Could you give us a description of the man you saw?' the captain asked.

'Well, it's so fast I canno' really see. An' dark, you see?'

'Was he white, Puerto Rican . . .'

'Not a white man,' she says.

'Well, can you give us anything? Height, weight, dress, that sort of thing?'

Mrs González turned to her husband, who interpreted the question in rapid Spanish.

'Sí. He was about six feet, and very quick for running.' The two policemen smiled vaguely. 'He was wearing a white raincoat with a paper bag.'

'Beg pardon. *Como*?' the captain asks.

'While he runs, he dropped a package, an' she looked, uh, it looked like a pa-per bag. He stopped all his running to get it.' The woman paused. 'But where he was running, there was no light.'

Lieutenant Thomas was jotting down everything in a black note pad. He asked the next question.

'How about a hat? Glasses? *Anteojos?*'

'No. None of this. I wish I could help more for you, but then maybe he could see me too.' Mrs González looks at her husband.

'We were afraid to tell. About the movies, you see? In the movies the ones who see are killed. This is a bad neighborhood for killing, because of the young ones. They kill . . . We went to Mass this morning and asked the father. He told us we should call to talk to you.'

The policemen nodded.

'Well,' the captain said, 'unless you can think of something more, I suppose that will be all.'

'Nothing more,' Mrs González said.

'If you think of anything else, no matter how small, please call us.'

'And thank you,' the lieutenant added.

Mr González showed the two men to the door. Down the hall away from the apartment, they conferred on their information.

'What do you think?'

'Don' know,' the captain said.

'Think some mug shots would help?'

'I doubt it. All she could say was that the man wasn't white. There would be no reason for the mug file.'

The two officers reached ground level on 16th Street and moved to their car, parked near the corner.

'This is fourteen-six to base. Fourteen-six to base. Over.'

'We read you, fourteen-six.'

'This is O'Malley. I want to see Mitchell in Narco when I get back. That should be about four. Tell him that I'd like complete files on our district for a man named Isidro Valsuena. Over.'

'Ten-four.'

The unmarked black sedan pulled away from the curb and swung out into traffic. The kids on the corner had loosened the nozzle on a fireplug, and water banged against scrawny legs and chests and ricocheted to form a small river in the gutter, flowing to the sewer. The policemen drove by, ignoring it.

'Check this address,' the captain said, using his note pad: '357 West 17th Street. I'd like to see where Paco Valsuena was last night.'

Afro: Brother Tommy Hall

July 28, 1968

Applause.

'Thank you, Brother Bishop, for those kind words of introduction ... Brothers and sisters, I'd like to thank each of you for coming out on a night such as this to hear us. As Brother Bishop told you, BAMBU* is a black organization that was founded in New York City almost a year ago. The aim of BAMBU is to develop a collective approach to the specific problems of black people. When we use the word "collective" we mean that black people can only solve their problems when they are unified in terms of thinking and acting.

'Black people have to move to a level where they begin to push toward each other as brothers and sisters. This means that brothers from the Bronx cannot get into a hassle with brothers from Brooklyn. As Brother Malcolm has taught us, "We don't catch hell because we are Baptist or Methodist, Mason or Elks, Democrats or Republicans." In other words, we don't catch hell because we are from Brooklyn or the Bronx. We catch hell because we are black.

'Once you and I understand and accept this, then we may begin to take care of business collectively. Therefore it is necessary for us to do our homework. This means that we must begin to equate and liberate black minds. We in BAMBU have developed a program which speaks to this need. Not only does it speak to this need, but also it provides other means by which black people can deal with the system.

* Black American Men for Black Unity

'We feel that freedom will only be achieved through the *collective* efforts of black people. In other words, that we must develop our own schools and our own cultural values. In this way black people will have a knowledge of self and necessary skills to implement meaningful change for the future.

'Therefore our objectives are: (1) to provide a school system for black children that will replace the present system. (2) To become involved in a politicization of the community to the extent that black people control the governmental offices where they are most directly concerned. (3) To create the necessary means by which people stop the racist police force that brutalizes us, and defend our women and children against the other racists that exist in this country . . .'

Applause.

'(4) To foster a cultural revolution that will create new values for our family. (5) And to develop our own means for economic survival in America.'

Applause.

'What we of BAMBU plan to do is the following. On August 7, that's Monday week, we will open our fourth Community Center in Manhattan. The Community Center will be this very building you have met with us in this evening, and the children will be taught about their blackness. Black history, black literature, Swahili, and African music will be taught. This will be for the children between the ages of six and fifteen. In the evenings there will be cultural classes for the adult and young adults of you who would like to participate. Also, for the men, there will be classes in karate, judo, and riflery in the evenings and on weekends.'

I paused because at that moment I saw I.Q. get up and leave.

'Now,' I continued, 'when we say police brutality and racist police force, just what, exactly, are we saying? We mean that we want to inhibit the molesting of our people. We are talking about the lack of response and the downright indecency we receive when dealing with police. We are also talking about the physical abuse that black people have been known to receive in this city. We have categorized all of this under the heading "Police Responsibility," but it ties in with our desire to politicize black people. Through our program people will realize that the police force is only the racist arm of a racist structure, that of the United States government . . . What other country in the world would have a man such as George Wallace receiving thousands of dollars from thousands of people? What other country would allow a state like Mississippi to exist within its boundaries when the reports of countless shootings, lynchings, burnings, and bombings have been reported with black people the victims of all of these atrocities? Where else but in the United States would a man have to demonstrate to get an opportunity to *buy* a hot dog? . . .'

Laughter and applause. 'Tell it, brother!'

'Where else but the United States is the highest court in the land listening to appeals on laws written two centuries ago, in order to discover whether it's legal or not to go to school where you want to? . . . Brothers and sisters, this is a racist institution you and I live under. We of BAMBU are doing our best to prepare a program that will help black people better understand *who* the enemy is and how we can best attack the system and change it . . . Thank you, very much. If there are any questions, I will be glad to elaborate.'

Applause.

Brother Bishop got up. 'Thank you, Brother Hall,' the older man said to me. 'I appreciate your suggestion that we hold our meeting here this evening. It's not often that I have an opportunity to visit this part of town . . . As Brother Hall mentioned, on August 7 BAMBU will be opening a school here for our people, and he will be in charge of the activities in this area. Brother Hall is a recent graduate of Manhattan

Community College, where he majored in history. He will be teaching the history here for our youngsters ... You know, it's good to see the young brothers and sisters involved so heavily with the freedom of black people. It's a warm feeling to go into our centers in Harlem and see the young brothers and sisters serving as instructors for our children, teaching them what it means to be black ... You know, when I was young I was taught that to be black was to be inferior, to be something undesirable. It seems a shame to me that I would have passed so many years along before I saw the error of all this. I'm hoping that all of our youngsters will see the beauty of their blackness and stand up for it ... That, of course, is the purpose of the group programs we have begun here in New York. We have six centers in Brooklyn, two in the Bronx, and three here in Manhattan. Each one of them full of young black minds. This program has recently acquired a secretary for the Chelsea Center. Sister Mason, will you stand up?' A young girl stood near the back of the meeting room. 'Sister Mason will take the names of the students you brothers and sisters might want to sign up. Our program in this area will be able to facilitate seventy children at least ... Now, if you have any questions for Brother Hall, would you please raise your hands.'

A man to the right of the stage raised his hand and was recognized by the chair.

'Brother Hall,' the man said. 'First of all, I would like to say that I enjoyed whut you had t'say very much ... I wuz wond'rin' if maybe you could go into the types of things you will be teaching our chil'ren.'

'Certainly, brother,' I said, standing. 'We are raised in America under many contradictions and hypocrisies. America has always been known as the land of the free whites and the home of the slave. One of the greatest perpetuators of this type of hypocrisy was the Father of the country, George

Washington. How many of our children are aware of the fact that George Washington was a slaveowner and a criminal being sought by the English authorities? Not very many. And it is important that they know, because a lot of our children grow up idolizing George Washington – wanting to be like him, because he never told a lie! Never told a lie!' I repeated. 'He was living a lie! All George Washington represents in my mind is another Virginia racist who thought black people were ignorant savages. We must be careful not to let our children foster these false examples. All of this is part of the white "brainwashing" that has taken place in this country for so long.

'How many of our children know of Nat Turner? How many know that the slaves were living the lives of miserable cattle in the South? The white man has had a way of depicting things through his use of the media to make things look as though the slaves were happy in the plantation and didn't want the South to lose the war. How many know how badly the slaves were tortured and beaten? In 1831 Nat Turner led a slave rebellion in Virginia which resulted in the death of fifty-seven whites. He was a preacher, a man who walked from plantation to plantation spreading the word of God, and it was a sign from God that prompted him to burn and plunder and kill. There was no contentment for any other than the "house niggers" during this period. The black man in America has always been hounded and hunted, hungry, and abused . . .'

Applause.

'How many of our children know that 400,000 black soldiers died in the War Between the States? Fighting on the side of the Union Army to do in the master that he reputedly loved so dearly? . . . No, my brothers and sisters, we have been brainwashed. We might unify our thoughts and our actions. If two and a half million Jews can demand their freedom and hold enough check to scare the hell out of the rest of the world, surely twenty-two million or more black Americans can fight for their rights. These are the type of things I will try to convey to our children.'

Applause.

'Brother Hall, how old are you?' A young lady of approximately my age was asking the question, and the others in the audience laughed.

'I'm twenty,' I told her.

'I was wondering primarily about your background and qualifications.'

'I graduated in June from Manhattan Community College as a history major. I hold two jobs, the most prominent of which is my work with BAMBU.'

'In other words, you condone a section of the education we receive from white people?'

'I'm glad you asked that,' I told her. 'In every great revolution there have been educated men at the top. Mao went to a university. Ché went to a university. Fidel Castro and Ho Chi Minh were educated men. In this country some of our most eminent men are educated at the university level. Dr King, Ron Karenga, Stokely Carmichael, to name a few. These men were not brainwashed during their stay at their schools. They came out with more ideas about how we as a people may better combat the system. I think that it is necessary for us to learn the white man's skills. That applies to science, math, engineering, all of the major fields where we may profit and grow financially as a people.

'I think that it was important for me to gather facts while discovering how history is taught the wrong way, before I came and offered to teach what is more than history, but truth.'

'Thank you,' she said.

There didn't seem to be any more questions, so Brother Bishop stood up and adjourned the meeting. As the people began to file toward the exits, the young girl who had asked me the last question came up from behind me and touched my shoulder.

'Hello,' I said.

'I'd, uh, like to ask a few more questions, but I didn't think I should try and hold up the group. Do you have a minute?'

I nodded and turned to excuse myself from Brother Bishop and a few of the older brothers, who would probably have discussed issues for hours. They nodded and smiled when they saw the young lady behind me. I put on my raincoat and followed her toward the door.

'I haven't eaten,' I said. 'Would you like something?'

'Maybe a cup of coffee or a Coke,' she said. 'Uh, what I wanted to talk to you about concerned something rather personal. I hope I wouldn't be bothering you.'

'No,' I said. 'No bother.'

We walked from the third floor to the first and then out onto 23rd Street. The rain had stopped, and the dampness left a pleasant smell in the city streets. As we walked toward 23rd and Eighth Avenue, where I usually ate, I took a closer look at the girl. She was about my age and well developed. Her hair was done in a short afro, and it topped about one hundred and ten pounds. Her mind was evidently elsewhere while I was taking inventory.

'By the way, I don't know your name,' I said.

'Natalie . . . and yours is Hall?'

'Tommy Hall,' I said.

'I'm Natalie Walker.' We shook hands.

Natalie and I walked into the coffee shop just as the rain started again. We took a booth in the corner facing the only entrance. I took her coat and coaxed her to look at the menu while I selected a couple of records at the jukebox.

After we had ordered, she began to talk a bit more freely.

'I'm going through a similar situation to what you were discussing,' she said.

'In what respect?'

'In terms of education. I'm a student at CCNY, but I don't want to stay in school here. They're not teaching anything relevant. I told my mother I had to go to a black school and enjoy some of the things that young black people are doing in this country, but she won't listen. She absolutely refuses to let me transfer or stop school.'

'What are her reasons?'

'She says I need to be near home. She thinks all of these student uprisings will get me in trouble if I go to a black school with the type of black curriculum that I'm interested in.'

'I agree with her in a way.'

'What?'

'I agree that she needs you close to home.'

'That's not what I said. That's not what she said!'

'That's what's happening, though. She doesn't want to lose you to beliefs contrary to those of her own. Now, she was a follower of Dr King, is that right?' Natalie nodded. 'And you talk about Rap and Stokely, is this right?' She nodded again. 'In your mother's eyes she's protecting you. She believes that if she can keep you close at home, keep her finger on your pulse, that whenever you start talking a lot of that black stuff, she'll be around to remind you of all the fine things Dr King did in the movement.' I paused. 'Because most of the older black people think that this current trend toward being black and expressing your blackness is only a fad anyway.'

'What do you think?'

'I think that black people are waking up after a long hibernation, and after they do their homework, we'll be ready to make some changes in the system.'

The waitress came up with our food. 'A toasted corn muffin and coffee for the young lady, two hamburgers, French fries, and coffee for the gentleman. Will that be all, sir?'

'That's all, thank you,' I said.

'Well, that's what I wanted to talk to you about,' Natalie said.

'What is?'

'I want you to talk to my mother. I want her to see some of the fine things other young people in our area are doing. All she knows is Spade.'

'Spade? What about Spade?' I asked.

'My mother hates him and Hicks and boys like them.'

'Do you know him?' I asked.

'Who?'

'Spade.'

'Not well.'

There was a pause in the conversation. Natalie offered me a cigarette that I refused.

'Will you come?' she asked.

'I don't think I can do much good. I'm not much of an example of anything. Perhaps after the school is on its feet she will be more receptive to my ideas.'

'But don't you see? The school starts in August, and it's almost August already. I need to get her permission soon to send for transfer applications to other places.'

'You mean you haven't sent for the transfer notices and you want to be accepted for September?'

'I sent for the transfer to Howard, and they accepted me, but if I don't get her permission soon, by the time I convince her that I've written off and gotten everything back, Howard will have assumed I'm not coming. In the meantime, I can't say I am coming until my mother reacts.'

'Whew! Girl, I don't know about this situation. It's almost too confusing to even attempt to figure out. I think I know what's what, but I didn't know women did that kind of thing outside of the movies. Especially not black women.'

'I know it sounds confusing, but that's all I could do. Will you help?'

I was about to answer when I.Q.'s face appeared at the window. I leaped to my feet and ran to the door, but before I could get outside, I had a feeling that he would be gone. He had disappeared.

'What's wrong? Who was it?' Natalie asked.

'Looked like a guy I knew,' I said. 'Guess I was mistaken.'

'Well . . .' she began.

'Look, when do you want me to come and see your mom?'

'Tomorrow night. That is, if it's all right with you.' I nodded that it was all right. 'I'll tell her we're going to a movie and you're my date. Come in about eight, and I won't be ready. You can talk to her while I get dressed. Then I can go to a party they're having at my girl friend's house. Would you like that?'

'No. I'm not much for parties . . . I'm not much for lying either,' I added. 'Why can't you just tell her why I'm coming?'

'She wouldn't talk to you.'

'Okay,' I agreed. I said I would do it just because I wanted to see her one more time, without all the lying involved. I wondered what she was like. She made me realize that I had a lot of homework to do when it came to women.

I walked Natalie home and explained that I had some unfinished business to take care of. My unfinished business was named Ivan Quinn. I wanted to learn why we were playing games around the block. I left Natalie at 18th Street and Ninth Avenue and started toward the 17th Street park. The rain had been a shower, hard for a second and then gone. The streets were damp and seemed to reflect a certain calm that I felt.

All at once I realized why I.Q. was following me. He wanted to know why he received a rejection slip from BAMBU. He wanted to see me alone. I knew he had received the slip because *I* had mailed it to him two days ago. All I had to do was wait, and he would find me.

The whole thing with I.Q. started when John Lee held a

party at the close of the school year. For once I had been as anxious as anyone else to go out and do some partying. The school year had been no problem, but it seems that no matter how close you stay to the work, there are a million things to get together when they start talking about finals.

The Party

I had come in expecting a good time. The music was nice in the back of the Lee apartment. The food was cooking somewhere, and most important of all, nobody was drunk or rowdy. I plucked a can of beer out of the bathtub and slid into a corner chair.

'Congratulations, man,' Websta said, coming over and giving me the handshake. 'I hear you untied the knot today.'

'Yeah, brother. It's all over.'

'Soon as I get a l'il bread, I'm gonna go back an' do that thing. What you plannin' on doin' fo' yo'self?'

'I'm working with the organization, you know. We're gonna open a center near here in August. Up near the Chelsea projects. I start nine to three with N'Bala on Monday.'

'You in the same boat I am,' Websta said. 'Workin' two jobs. Hell, seemed like I wuz gon' need an act a Congress t'git here t'night . . . You got that paper. Seem like you could git some bread with IBM or one a them initials.'

'Yeah, I could, I suppose. The only difference is that I didn't get my education so that I could run off the street to the suburbs. I want to work around here.'

'Yeah, you *wuz* that way. You ain' gonna make much with N'Bala. He ain' gonna ketch on aroun' here like New Breed did uptown. We got too many jitterbugs in the neighborhood.'

'Thass all right,' I told him. 'Nothing changes overnight. I mean, I don't expect miracles.'

'You rilly like them African clothes that N'Bala sells? I mean, the shirts like the one you got on. What'choo call 'um?'

'It's called a dashiki, brother. I think they're better than the white man's shirts. You see the way it's cut?' I stood up so that he could see the way the dashiki is stitched under the arms. 'With a cut like this, you have a measure of freedom in case of attack. In a thing like what you have on, you can be limited physically. I could run a jack on you f'rinstance.' Websta nodded in agreement. Running a jack is the street term for grabbing a man's shirt and pulling it over his head.

'It's pretty. They all are. Lotta colors an' whut have you.' He waved. 'I'm gonna have to talk to you, man. Lemme ketch this slow one.'

'I'm So Proud,' by the Impressions, came on. I touched the arm of the sister next to me, and we stepped to the middle of the dance floor. I was caught up with what Websta had said. My mother and father had been disappointed when I told them what my plans were. I suppose they had been looking forward to seeing me leap out into status-symbol-land. My father had always told my mom that the things I was doing were just a passing fancy, because he had been intent on changing the world and helping the Negro when he was in college. Sooner or later I would be out there for the buck too. I would get a haircut and start wearing white shirts and maybe even go on to a four-year college so that I could teach for the state or the city. Now that I had graduated and moved my stuff to another apartment in the same building, even he was asking questions about how long was I going to stay with N'Bala and what the hell was I doing with the organization, pulling eighty dollars a week.

First of all, I wanted to teach black history. The opportunity that BAMBU gave me to do this could never be touched by the city or state. For any government teaching job I would have to have a diploma from a four-year college, and I wouldn't be able to help shape the curriculum until I had gotten tenure. BAMBU was giving me the curriculum for my area, along with the syllabi from other centers for references. I had almost an unlimited budget in terms of books and materials.

The second job was with N'Bala. I didn't consider that a permanent position. N'Bala was an African brother who had opened an Eighth Avenue clothing shop that featured all of the finest in black wear. He was suffering, however. In opening the store he had spent most of his money and didn't have much for salaries. He had been open for a month, and business hadn't exactly been booming. The answer to that was the area. Most of the Chelsea area is Puerto Rican. From 14th Street to 23rd Street west of Eighth Avenue, the population is seventy percent Puerto Rican. The black people live just outside of this wall, in force.

I had bought the dashiki I was wearing at John's party less than two weeks ago from N'Bala, and even though business wasn't heavy, he had his hands full running up and down and trying to make sure that he wasn't robbed while he stocked his shelves.

'Where's your help?' I asked.

'He quit, brother. Yesterday he came to me and he said, N'Bala, I am very sorry, but I cannot work anymore for you because I will never have money.' I watched the little African wipe away the sweat from his face and neck. 'I told him that we will do better and I will raise him some money, but he wants to know when, as though I am God and can see tomorrow.'

'I know what you mean. Getting a business started is a struggle.'

'You think you know?' N'Bala asked. 'I have to close the door to go to the bathroom. The schoolchildren, the little ones, come here to try to steal from me. Not to mention the large high-school ones. I think I will go crazy.

The air is broken down. The air-conditioner, I mean. You don't know!'

'How much you payin'?' I asked.

'Sixty dollars a week for five days. What can I pay?'

I liked the little man. He was self-made, in a way. He had graduated from Columbia as a business major and returned to Africa. When his country became involved in a revolution that failed, he was forced to flee to the United States. With his life savings he was trying to start a little business. It was exactly what we had been asking for in BAMBU. More black businessmen, therefore more black workers in higher positions, better deals for the black consumer, and more financial stability for the black family.

'Can you last two weeks?' I asked.

'Even the dying man finds courage when he knows that help is near.' N'Bala quoted something, and I smiled at the metaphor.

'In two weeks I'll be your salesman,' I said.

'What?'

'If you can use me.'

'Of course. But you will be a graduate then.'

'Two weeks. I'll start the Monday after graduation.'

I was cut short by the record's end. The sister I was dancing with said something that I didn't catch.

'Beg pardon, sister?'

'I said thank you,' she repeated.

'My pleasure,' I said. 'You'll have to excuse me. I'm not together this evening.'

'Are you drunk?' she asked.

'No. No. I'm just doing a lot of thinking when I should be concentrating on more important things like yourself.' I smiled, and she smiled.

'That was a nice try ... That's a beautiful dashiki,' she commented.

Afro: Brother Tommy Hall | 141

'Thank you.'

'I was looking at them. I made one for my brother, but it didn't turn out very well. No pattern.' She was sipping a drink. 'Did you make that one?'

'No, I bought it.'

'How much are they? Aren't they expensive?'

'They come in all styles, colors, and prices. I got this one at N'Bala's Fashions on 18th Street and Eighth Avenue. It just so happens that I'll be working there starting Monday, and I can see to it that you get a well-made dashiki at a reasonable price.'

'I'll have to come in,' she said.

It was nearing midnight. The crowd was wild, but everything was under control. I didn't blame them for celebrating. School was out. The beaches were in. The weather was warm, and the beer was cold. A lot of people had paired off, but it was my misfortune to get into an intellectual conversation with a few of the brothers. I appreciate their interest and am always proud when they ask me a question that's been on their minds, but sometimes you just do not want to talk. That was how I felt.

From my initial remarks about BAMBU when one of the brothers asked about it, an argument had cropped up between several of us as to the cause of riots and the explanation of what constitutes a riot. The real issue was whether or not riots were helping or hindering the movement.

'A riot is a violent dramatization of black despair in America,' I told them. 'Time comes when you just can't stand no more. A man can have his ass kicked so often figuratively that he doesn't care what happens to him literally. A few brothers are standing on the corner, looking inside the white man's store, and their hands are closing in on the nothing in their pockets. Before you know it, they're taking what they want.'

'It's usually 'cauz somebody got high,' one brother said. 'They're all drunk, and then they start throwin' shit.'

'Drunkenness is the ruin of reason. It is a premature old age. It is temporary death,' I.Q. quoted.

'It's not necessarily due to drunkenness,' I said. 'I believe the primary ingredient is frustration and not alcohol. Combine that with opportunity, and you have a very emotional, explosive situation. What is always necessary is the spark that ignites the fuse, because black people are tired of being exploited and taken advantage of. Also of being underestimated.'

'Only the complacent are true slaves,' I.Q. quoted.

'There are very few happy people in the communities of this country that exploded last summer and that may explode again. Being drunk may pacify for a while; that's why I don't think the rioters were drunk. These were the men who had been denied the right to be men, treated like savages for three hundred years, and they suddenly decided that they may as well take what they want. They have seen the white boys' law. It works for the benefit of the white boys.'

'But if you notice,' one brother pointed out, 'the people who are killed are always black. No whitey get offed. It's really murder.'

'Murder is white justice. Livin' in America has always been murder for black people. There has been three centuries of murder. Either the quick death from a gun or a rope, or the slow death of trying to survive under inhuman conditions.' I looked over the group of naturals and beads. 'Black people aren't as foolish as they used to be, though. They ain't callin' on the Lord like they used to. They realize that God helps those who help themselves. And as for those of us in the great North, we know that a whitey is a whitey and that his bullshit is everywhere. We know we've got just as much of a struggle here as we do in Mississippi ... Maybe even more, because we're supposed to have to pick out the good whiteys from the bad ones. Down there you know who the enemy is.'

As the group began to break up, an even more frenzied dancing thing with the women began. I.Q. stayed near the window with me and continued the conversation.

'We're movin' into a new day, brother,' I told him. 'The younger brothers are talkin' black, thinkin' black, and usin' the white boy to better themselves and their people.'

'Victories that are cheap are cheap. Those only are worth having which come as a result of hard fighting,' I.Q. said.

'Don't you ever say anything that's not a quote?' I asked.

'I'd like to join BAMBU.'

'In what capacity?'

'As a teacher. I can teach practically anything.'

'All you need is a general statement. You know what I mean. A little thing about yourself in terms of biographical material. You send it in to the central office and they send it to the branch you specify if you have a choice.'

'I'll do that,' he said. 'Do you see? Everything I say isn't a quote.' With that he moved off toward the dance floor.

As he walked away, I was reminded of a quote myself. It was something very practical that Buddha had said: 'A man should first direct himself in the way he should go. Only then should he instruct others.'

BAMBU originated in August of 1967 in Harlem. That was the time when I first heard of the residents of Harlem asking for more black people to teach in the high schools. They wanted more black courses in the curriculum. Latin was out, because they thought their children should know Swahili. They wanted their children to know more about their roots and heritage. For a while there was very little response from the people to the program that BAMBU outlined. It began as a cultural organization where black dance groups did African numbers and guest speakers came in. By November, however, four older brothers and I began a tutorial program in black history at BAMBU's 125th Street Liberation School, and the community began to gather interest.

I had been working as a tutor-teacher for four months when the organization decided they were going to expand to all parts of the city. Two buildings were acquired in Brooklyn right away, and then came two more in the lower Bronx. In April Brother Bishop told me that the Chelsea area would be opened because a group of parents known as the Black Community Council was establishing a center for us. When the opening was announced formally to the neighborhood, I was set up as chairman because of my familiarity with the people. I was given April and May to get the building into working condition. Sister Mason worked with me as secretary and accountant. Between the two of us a large number of pamphlets and leaflets were distributed throughout the community and surrounding area.

We gave August 7 as an opening date because I hoped by then I would have a staff of capable workers and teachers. I was learning a lot about trying to organize. I found out how difficult it is to get volunteer help. The brainwashing of black people in America had become more serious than I wanted to believe. As a race we were suffering from taking on the white boy's value of the dollar. The white boy values the dollar over everything else that he comes in contact with, including his fellow beings. He had become triumphant over the Indians in America because he sought land and power and money to such a degree that human life was secondary.

By the end of June I had been advertising the fact that a branch of BAMBU was organizing in the community and would need volunteer help in terms of the teaching and maintenance. The maintenance was taken care of by Sister Mason's brother, who would also run the projector for the films I had ordered. The books that had been sent for were simply shoved into a corner until I got to them, because I didn't have anyone to check them and shelve them. The rest of the people who came by the office were high-school students who were willing to run errands but honestly did not have the real qualifications to do anything in the classroom. That was why I was pleased when I.Q. said that he wanted to join us. He was a high-school graduate with a scholarship to Columbia, and I knew that he was intelligent. All of the applications were handled by the same box number, but after they were screened and a check made by the central office on qualifications, they were sent to the area chairman for approval or rejection on the basis of a personal interview. I.Q.'s application would naturally come to me.

The last week of June I found it impossible to get to the office. I had my final exams and graduation practice and a million other things to do. I took a leave of absence and left things with Sister Mason. I told her that I wanted to be sure and pass the exams and get the hell away from under the white man's structure. I was thinking about that as John's party started to get mellow. The forty-fives were replaced by a few Latin jams. Eddie Palmieri, Tito Puente, Cal Tjader, and Joe Bataan took over for a half-hour, and then came Little Anthony and Smoky and grinding couples. I laid low while the women got their heads together. I don't think I'd ever seen so much rum disappear in my life. I thought of the busy weeks ahead of me. I would start with N'Bala on Monday. I would work there from nine until three and then go to the center from four until ten. This would go on five days a week. I didn't know if I was ready, but that was what was happening.

July 12, 1968

I went straight home from the center on Friday night. Sister Mason and I had painted the lobby and stopped about nine when we decided we wouldn't be able to finish another stroke before collapsing. At times I almost forgot that the sister was working two jobs like I was. She came in punctually every day and worked as long as I asked her to with no complaints, but when I stopped to think about her, she was hurrying on her way home. I got home about nine-thirty and made myself a couple of sandwiches. I had no sooner sat down to eat when the phone rang.

'Brother Hall?' someone asked.

'Yes?'

'Brother Hall, you have a possible teacher in your center by the name of Ivan Quinn.' I said yes. I had just received I.Q.'s application that afternoon. 'I don't think you would appreciate Mr Quinn's services very much if you saw the type of black man he really is. Why don't you follow him tonight? He'll be leaving his house about ten o'clock.'

The words 'ten o'clock' were followed by a click on the other end of the line. I checked my watch and saw that it was already a quarter to ten. I gave Websta a call. The phone rang four times before Websta answered groggily.

'Web, this is Afro,' I said. 'Look, brother, I was wondering if I could borrow your car for an hour or two?'

'Yeah,' he said. 'It's parked right across the street from here. You comin' over?'

'I'm gonna be in a semihurry. I'll be there in about five minutes.'

'Okay. I'll put the key under the mat. I gotta get some sack.'

Afro: Brother Tommy Hall | 147

'Thanks a lot.'

'No sweat. Put the key back under the mat when you're through.'

That was a beautiful brother. He was always willing to give a hand when it was needed, without a whole lot of questions. I ate the sandwich on the run and made it from my place on 22nd Street to Websta's on 15th Street in little or no time. The key was under the mat, and I found the 1962 Oldsmobile parked just as I had been told. I swung it out into traffic and circled north on Tenth Avenue and then east on 20th Street. New York streets are generally set up so that the odd-numbered streets go one-way west and the even numbers are one-way east. The avenues with odd numbers generally go downtown and the even numbers go uptown. I pulled up about five cars behind I.Q.'s parked blue Volkswagen.

I still didn't know what I was doing or why. At ten o'clock I.Q. still hadn't come out of the house. I started to think about the whole situation, and I felt a little embarrassed. Who was I to distrust another brother and follow information given me by a man who wouldn't identify himself? But, I decided, if I.Q. wasn't doing anything, I wouldn't see anything. I sat for another five minutes before he came out.

I.Q. wheeled into the street and pointed toward Ninth Avenue. At Ninth he swung downtown to 18th Street and went back to Eighth Avenue. At Eighth he started uptown. I stayed just far enough back to see him without his noticing me. It was clear now that the call I got was at least partially correct, but what was the significance?

We stayed on Eighth Avenue all the way to 59th Street and Columbus Circle. There we took a right turn and started toward the East Side on Central Park South. I was still about five car lengths behind him. At Lexington Avenue I.Q. turned into a parking space and got out. I parked a few yards back and watched. He stood on the corner of

Lexington Avenue and 59th Street smoking a cigarette. He was clean as a whistle, as usual. He was a little under six feet, dark-complexioned, with a very flat nose and thick bush. He was vined in an open-throated white shirt with olive slacks. There was a string of shark's teeth around his throat. Aside from that, he had on the usual wire-framed sunglasses.

Another five minutes passed before I saw what was going to happen. A blazing red 1968 Firebird pulled up at the corner, and I.Q. got in. I took off in pursuit, but this car would be a whole lot harder to lose than I.Q.'s Volkswagen. At Second Avenue there was a right-hand turn, and the late-evening traffic was light enough to clear a path all the way to Canal Street. I fell almost a block behind, timing things so that I still caught the lights. The Firebird gave a left-hand-turn signal between 32nd Street and 31st and swung off down a parking ramp. I was sure that the two of them would be coming back up the ramp, so I parked across the street and watched. There could be no denying anything now that I had seen things with my own eyes. But who called me and told me what would take place? The two of them came back to ground level and walked arm-in-arm through the door that led to the Festival Motor Inn. I merely nodded and drove off.

I.Q. was screwing a devil!

July 27, 1968 / 11:35 P.M.

'I got to talk to you, Afro. Wait up!'

After walking Natalie home I stopped in the park on 17th Street. I knew that I.Q. had been following me, waiting for an opportunity to see me alone. I had waited for almost half an hour when it started to sprinkle slightly, so I got up to leave.

That was when I.Q. hailed me. He was coming in from the 16th Street side of the park.

After catching him with the chick, I stalled for a couple of days before I sent back the rejection. I hadn't known exactly what I would say when I met him and he asked me about it. I decided that since he didn't know I was the one who would inevitably accept or reject his application, I wouldn't tell him anything at all.

'I got this in the mail today,' he said. He passed me the letter with the rejection notice stamped across his application. I went through the motions of reading it.

'I wonder why?' I asked.

'One cannot know everything,' he quoted. He didn't know anything at all. I had him fooled.

'What were your papers like? I mean, what were the references like?' I continued to play the game.

'I had knowledge of naught but victory, but defeat has shown me only a clearer road. It is only a detour to better things.'

'You don't mind being rejected?'

'Sorrows are like thunderclouds,' I.Q. said. 'In the distance they look black, over our heads scarcely gray.'

One of those thunderclouds opened up just then and sent us scampering for the cover of José's awning.

You're a hard man to deal with, Brother Quinn, I was thinking. It's always hard to help a brother defeat himself.

July 29, 1968

I was sitting in Natalie's room with her mother. We were talking about the 'movement' and about my work in particular.

'BAMBU is the type of organization that black people have

been after in this area for a long time. Our parents have felt it necessary that our children be taught our native language and learn more about the contributions black people have made to the world.' Mrs Walker had asked about the place I thought BAMBU might take in the community.

'And what type of stands will your organization be taking?' she asked. 'Will you be pro-violence?' She had already told me that she was a Howard graduate and read everything she could get her hands on. 'I'm referring to groups like the Black Panthers. I wonder if that's really how our young people feel?'

'What do you mean?'

'I mean, do you really feel as though there is nothing else we can do but go out into the streets with guns strapped to our bodies as though we were living in the Old West and shoot everybody in sight?'

'I didn't realize that that was the policy or program of the Panthers.'

'You've seen them, I'm sure. They carry guns and wear berets. And what do they feel themselves capable of? I mean, let's be realistic, Mr Hall. What can several hundred young blacks do with pistols against the United States Army?'

'I think you're missing the point,' I said as lightly as I could. 'The Panthers, to my knowledge, have never attacked the police force or any group of individuals for any reason. They claim they wear their firearms for protection. You know how difficult it is to defend yourself sometimes in the ghetto.'

'*You* are being very idealistic,' she said. 'Of course that's what the Panthers *say* they are wearing the guns for. But in the meantime, they are constantly baiting the policemen and obstructing their duties.'

'The policemen in most cities and towns are not the servants of black people. If you will remember the reason for the riots in 1964 in Harlem and the riot in Watts, they were because a black youth had died at the hands of a white policeman. Beg pardon, that was here. In Watts a man was taking his wife to the hospital for the deliverance of their child, and the policeman claimed his gun accidentally went off. The police force in this country is only an extension of the government.'

'Let me ask you this,' Mrs Walker began. 'What chance do you think the Negroes in America would have in all-out war?'

'The census says that we are outnumbered ten to one.'

'You know that that does not answer my question,' she said. 'But you can still follow the train of thought . . . What do you feel are the best answers in the racial situation? Is the best method violence or nonviolence?'

'Idealistically, I would say nonviolence, but black people are becoming very impatient as far as that is concerned. Black people have lived the lives of second-class human beings in the past and are simply getting fed up.'

'Is this the way you feel? You know, it's very disheartening to see young people without hopes and dreams for better days ahead.'

I was very relieved to see Natalie step into the room.

'By any means necessary,' I said, quoting Malcolm.

Mrs Walker stood and smiled a bit. In spite of the cross-examination, I felt myself starting to admire her a bit. Most people her age leaned on the crutch they call the 'generation gap' and would not confront young people for their opinions. Many times I felt this was because they thought they might come up short in the knowledge department. She walked with Natalie and me to the door.

'What time may I expect you home, Nat?'

'About two.'

'All right. Have a good time. It was nice to have met you,

Tom.' I turned when I heard her use my first name, but the door was closing. Natalie was smiling.

'She likes you,' was her comment.

'Maybe,' I admitted. 'But that wasn't what you wanted me to do. I was supposed to try to get her to wear a natural and blow up Wall Street, wasn't I?'

'No. I don't even think Martin Luther King could have done that.' We both had a laugh as the elevator opened in front of us.

'You sure you won't come to the party with me?' she asked.

'Positive,' I said.

'What are you going to do?'

'Go home and read, maybe watch a little TV.'

Natalie turned to me and kissed me. I put my arms around her for a second and then put her down gently. She turned away as we landed on the first floor.

'I'm sorry,' she said. 'I act like a fool sometimes. It's a very romantic thing, though. Being saved from the tower by a prince. That's almost what it reminds me of.'

The two of us walked outside and started toward I didn't know what.

'Where are we going?' Nat asked.

'I thought we might go down to the Cobra and have a drink and talk about ogres and princesses and night queens and all that.'

'You think I'm kind of silly, don't you? I mean, you think the kind of things that I do are silly.'

'Yep. I do. But in a way they're beautiful, because they seem very real. I can see a whole lot of beauty in you.' I paused. 'Do you drink?'

'Not a lot,' she said. 'I get drunk kinda quick.'

'Well, then, my dear, we'll order you a dragon in milk.'

'What's that?'

Afro: Brother Tommy Hall | 153

'A large Coke with a scoop of ice cream.'

August, 1968

I started seeing Natalie every weekend. There was nothing serious between us. She was good for my ego, and because of me I think she abandoned her plans for going away to school. Her mother and I still had talks from time to time. Once I sat in their apartment and talked until almost four in the morning. The organization became successful, too. The classes that we held for the first week had only about eight students, but by the third week of August our teachers were holding sessions for twenty-five children per night, three nights a week. I had gotten two of the HAR-YOU summer workers to come in during the evenings and work with math and science problems in the tutorial meetings. Sister Mason and her brother covered just about everything else. I was trying to figure out how I could seat eighty students during the school year. I knew that by then I'd have at least three more capable faculty members who were knowledgeable in black history and literature. The men in Harlem sent down an exchange student who attended Colgate to teach Swahili.

N'Bala's was becoming a hot spot. I had put out the word for my friends that I would be expecting to see them come in and buy something. And when the kids in the neighborhood realized that school was sneaking up on them, they started to get their wardrobes together too. That brought the women in, and pretty colors always fascinate women and make them buy more than they had planned on. Many times N'Bala was too crowded and busy to go to lunch. He was as happy as he could be.

Phase Four

January 1, 1969 / 1:00 A.M.

There was only one light bulb in the room, and it was placed in such a position that Afro never saw who was talking to him. He could only hear the voice and be sure that the man was black. He had been told to show up at the main office on 132nd Street and Lenox Avenue in Harlem at one a.m. for a high-security meeting within the division leaders of BAMBU. There were three other black men seated around the table when he got there, but he didn't recognize any of them.

'Have a seat, Brother Hall,' the voice from the shadows said. 'I'm glad you were so punctual. I realize that this meeting was probably a great inconvenience for you, but there are some things that we as an organization must realize and deal with. Are you ready?'

'I had a little trouble with the Hawk, but I'm all right.'

'A drink, perhaps, to warm your innards?'

'No, thank you.'

'I will tell you, then,' the voice continued, 'that the purpose of BAMBU is good, but we are still allowing ourselves to be defeated even within our own areas by the devil. He is infiltrating in more and more abundance every day and destroying the foundation we need in order to start a rebuilding of the American black man.'

There was a pause in the narrative as the speaker cleared his throat.

'Just how much of a revolutionary are you, Brother Hall?' the voice asked.

'I don't know what you mean,' he said weakly. He felt intimidated, caught off guard. The other three men were looking at him.

'Are you a fair-weather revolutionary? Be aware of the fact

that Brother Malcolm said that there is no such thing as a *bloodless* revolution. Are you willing to sacrifice your life for the black people in America if it will help to free them?'

'Yes I would,' Afro said.

'Fine!' the voice boomed. 'Fine! It may not be necessary, but it's good to know that the movement is that important to you . . . The Man has gotten into our neighborhoods and into the very soul of black people, the very bloodstream, by their use of drugs. I am speaking particularly in terms of our young people. They are the rocks, the foundations upon which all our hopes must be placed. And this must be stopped!'

The voice paused again, and the only sound to be heard whatsoever was the roaring trucks that rolled outside, splashing melted snow and slush against the basement window. Afro sat with his back to the door of the basement room, waiting for the voice to speak to them from the darkness. He was wondering what would happen if he suddenly leaped to his feet and turned on the light switch.

'Already in Harlem BAMBU has started an extensive rehabilitation program for the users of drugs, in hope that their souls may not be lost to us. We have also started a movement to get rid of the pushers and sellers of the various narcotics. It is the sort of thing that had to be done sooner or later to keep our people from the continuous robberies and conning that goes on in the community. We are trying to cleanse ourselves of a disease.' Another pause. 'Brother Hall, you know the geography of the Chelsea area better than any other member of our group. For that reason we are asking you to aid us in our attempt to rid black people for all time from this great plague. I feel it only fair to tell you, however, that once a project like this is begun, your actions will be of interest to the syndicate if they should have any idea that you are behind the events that come to pass. If you feel that you will be taking too much of a personal risk, all you need do is indicate this, and we will think no less of you.'

'I'm prepared,' Afro said quickly.

'Fine, my son. Take a look at this picture,' the voice said. A picture was passed to Afro, and he looked at it for only a second. 'In the Chelsea area this is the largest distributor of heroin, cocaine, marijuana, and pills. It would be a tremendous benefit to your area if he, for some reason, discontinued service.'

'I'm sure this could be arranged. Is it important how it is done?'

'Technique is not important, only results. I am not trying to rush you, Brother Hall, but unless you have more questions, I have some information to pass on to the other brothers here that would only endanger you further if you heard it . . . Pass him the package.'

A small square box was passed to Afro. He took it and put it in his coat pocket.

'That is a .32-caliber automatic pistol and a box of shells. The gun is a hand-load Remington with a range of approximately fifty yards. Six-shell maximum.' The voice rattled off the figures with the same even drone with which he had conducted the entire conversation.

'Thank you,' Afro said, and got up to leave. The men heard his footsteps clicking through the door that led to the basement meeting room. Then his echoes were heard on the stairs leading to the street.

'Do I need give any more instructions to you gentlemen at this time?' the voice asked.

There was no indication from any of the men in the room.

'In that case, when we get the first indications that Brother Hall's mission has been accomplished and the little matter of Mr Valsuena taken care of, I will be in contact with you again. In the meantime, I will tell you only this: we are starting with the smallest possible areas. In this particular case we will handle from 112th Street and Third Avenue to 102nd Street and First Avenue. Our infiltration will begin tomorrow. Our second move will be in the Chelsea area. We are not strong enough to allow any detection of a pattern just yet. That is why I will decide when and where we will take over. Is that understood?'

The other three men in the room nodded.

'Don't worry, gentlemen. With the help of young men like Brother Hall, soon BAMBU will be in control of all drug traffic in New York City.' There was an almost maniacal laugh from the voice in the dark. 'Black Power!'

Afro

I took Natalie home about midnight and started toward the 17th Street park. The weather had been about the same for two weeks. Two days before Christmas it had started snowing, and it hadn't stopped until about eight o'clock Christmas Eve. In the daytime, while the sun was out, the gray-brown slush would melt, but at night the freezing temperatures would harden everything back to ice. I skidded momentarily as I walked by Isidro's house. I had been so busy looking for lights in the building that I hadn't watched where I was going.

There were no lights in the building. On the second floor I knew Isidro's parents lived with younger children. There were six kids in all. Isidro's father was the superintendent of the building. On the third floor Paco, Jessie, and Slothead lived. On the fourth floor Isidro lived by himself. He had been married, but his wife left and took the kid when she found out that he was shooting dope.

I surveyed the scene from the park. Between Eighth and Ninth avenues there is not a lot of cover for anything. On the south side of the street came the park, José's grocery, and then Isidro's. I wanted to get in and out without anyone seeing me, naturally, but the only door that led out emptied into 17th Street. Nervously I fingered the .32 in my pocket. I checked to see if the silencer was in place.

I got through the lobby to the stairs with no trouble. I had taken a look at the door, and it looked as though at one time a buzzer system had been used, but it wasn't there anymore. I walked slowly and carefully, trying not to have the old wood creak beneath my feet. I pulled the coat up around my shoulders. The hallway was cold and damp, like a wine cellar in a castle.

When I got to the top floor, I stopped. There was a melodramatic silence that hung in the air when my hand touched the doorknob. I reached out and started to turn the knob and felt the door give way. The door hadn't even been shut. I pushed in just far enough for me to peek inside, but there was nothing but darkness. The dim bulb from down the hall didn't even penetrate the threshold. I squeezed into the room and closed the door behind me. I was flat against the wall opposite the bed. I took one step forward and heard something swish through the air toward me. I tried to duck, but there was no way to avoid the contact. I felt everything in the room crashing down on me.

I don't know how long I was there. I don't really know if I was knocked out. I could see strange visions creeping past my eyes in slow motion. The sounds of the traffic seemed to play a waltz or something that swung to and fro and swung into my head like a hammer. I expected to see Isidro standing over me with a bat, but the lights were still out. I turned over on my stomach, and the room turned with me. Pain shot through my head, and I wanted to throw up. I moved my hands out in front of me and touched something that felt familiar. I rolled it around in my hand. It was a bullet. I kept feeling in the dark. One, two, three, four, five, six, I counted. I shoved them into my pocket. As I raised to lift myself, my head banged against a foot. Squinting a little, even in the darkness I could see that the foot belonged to a body that was sprawled across the bed.

I jumped for the light switch on the wall, ignoring the pain in my skull. It didn't work. I scrambled through my pockets and came up with a match and lit it. Isidro was lying face up on the bed with a bullethole squarely between his eyes and blood still trickling from the wound. His eyes were open, staring vacantly at the ceiling. I saw that the window that overlooked the back of the park was open and felt the freezing wind rip against my face and chest. I threw the match down and took off for the window. With a slight jump I caught onto the screen that protected the window from foul balls, and I climbed down with as much speed as I could manage. My right glove got caught in the screen halfway down, and I had to take my hand out of it. The wind then took it upon itself to slice my fingers like an ax. I took the last ten feet with a frightened leap and started running down the back alley toward 16th Street. I stopped under the corner light to look at my watch. It was ten minutes until one.

I was walking back uptown on Eighth Avenue when I heard the sirens, screaming and crying. There were more sirens coming from across 18th Street. I heard them answer like some wild animal's mating call. But then I heard something even more clearly. Someone knew that I had been in the room with Isidro! That someone was a killer! That someone had probably done it with my gun! I reached for my gun and found instead only the six bullets. Slowly, as I felt something even more wrong, I pulled out the shells. To my surprise, I saw that there were only five bullets. But I had counted six! The sixth one, I discovered, was a cigarette butt – with a square tip.

March 18, 1969

'Yes, I am glad you remembered,' I said. I was talking to my mother, who was standing over me watching me eat every bite of the dinner she had prepared for me on my birthday.

'You don't look like you had a meal since you left. Look at him, Henry. I don't like you . . .'

'I know, Mom,' I said. 'We've been through this before.

It was time I took a place of my own. I had all of these things to do.'

'And what do you make from it all? Two jobs, and you're losing weight, and you get a hundred and thirty-five dollars a week after taxes!'

'Mildred. Not on the boy's birthday. He's a man today. How does it feel?'

'Just like yesterday, I guess. Only I got some a Mom's fried chicken and potato pie in me,' I said.

'What do you weigh?'

'How is the work coming, son?'

'I bet you lost ten pounds since you left here.'

'Oh, it's coming all right. You know how it is, trying to get something started. But, considering the fact that I had never even taken part in organizing anything before . . .'

'What you need to organize is a wife. How you gonna get married working forty hours a day? I bet you ain't even met no women that looked like wives, with your nose in N'Bala's stocks!'

'Hold it, Mildred!' I knew my father's tone well enough to predict what was coming. 'Tommy is a man. He will make his own decisions from now on. He has a place of his own, and he works. He is in good health, and we have plenty to praise God about. I don't want to hear any more about any of that tonight. Is that clear?'

My mother's reply was to walk back into the kitchen with an armload of dishes and toss them into the sink. My father and I grinned, and he leaned back and lit up his pipe.

'What about this car we were talking about?' he asked.

'I think I'll get it,' I said. 'It's a sixty-four Rambler. The brother wants five hundred dollars for it.'

'Have you seen it?'

'I drove around in it once. I told him I would send a friend to see it.'

'Good. I know that everybody's supposed to be brother this an' that an' the other, but it's one thing to be dealin' with the white man an' quite anothuh when you're dealin' with each other. Have a mechanic look it over real good.'

'I'll do that,' I said.

'Have some more pie,' my mother said, coming out of the kitchen with the pie plate.

'If he's as bad off for food as you say he is, you don't know anything about medicine,' my father said. 'You keep stuffin' him like the fatted calf, an' he'll die of overexposure to good food.'

Everybody had a laugh. 'I'm tryin' to convince him to come an' live with us again,' Dad was told. 'If he eats enough of my cookin', he'll stay ... I don't care 'bout twenty-one years old. He's still my only child.'

I thought we were going to get into another one of those things about I-remember-the-time-when-you-were-only-so-many-years-old.

'I want two things, Tommy,' she said.

'Yes, ma'am,' I said. 'What can I do for you?'

'They're for you,' she said.

'Now, there's a switch,' my father said. 'Something that's good for both of yawl.'

'I want you to get married.' Pause. 'And I want you to get your hair cut.'

My father and I fell out laughing. 'No bet,' I said.

'I heard you in here with Henry talkin' 'bout a car that's gonna cost you five hundred dollars. That won't leave you any money in the bank,' she said.

'I'll still have enough money in the bank to cover any emergency,' I said.

'I think you need a wife an' family,' she said. 'I think that's an emergency.'

I looked around the living room. My father had done well.

He was a book-store owner. I guess my tendency to learn and read everything had been gotten from him. My mother wasn't much of a reader. She had always been after me to get the education she had wanted to have. My father hadn't been a college graduate either. He had been a partner in the book store from the time he graduated from high school. The man he had shared the ownership with had been dead for nearly ten years now.

'She thinks that if you get a wife and some children you'll want to finish those other two years somewhere,' my father said.

'I wouldn't want to support a family on what I make now,' I admitted.

'I think she has a point, though. Right now, you're very idealistic. That's because you haven't got a lot of responsibility. I'm waitin' to see what happens to you when you get out into the real world. Another mouth to feed. More bills to pay. I wonder if your idealism will support you and your family.'

'I wonder if BAMBU and N'Bala will support you,' my mother said.

'It's hard to say,' I told them. 'I'm doing what I like, though. That's very important. To be able to enjoy your work and watch the young black children reach out for the ideas you're trying to give them.'

'N'Bala is no one's young black child,' my mother said.

'N'Bala is a part of my doing what I believe in,' I said. 'We've been through all of this before.'

'I want more for you than that,' she said.

'Maybe someday *I'll* want more. Maybe someday N'Bala will give me a partnership. Like the one Dad had.'

'This is just a fad. Those African clothes are stylish today and gone tomorrow. I want you to have something stable.'

'Do you mean you want to have something you can brag to the neighbors about?'

'Tommy!'

'I'm sorry, Dad. I'm sorry, Mom.' Pause. 'I love you both. I think I better be going.'

'I was heating coffee. I thought you and your father were going to play a game of chess.'

'Some other time, Dad,' I said. 'I don't think I could stand *another* beating tonight.'

I got my own coat, and instead of stopping downstairs, I went back out into the street. I knew that my mother's questions hadn't been what bothered me. I was still bothered about principles and morals and practicing what you preach. Revolution was on my mind.

There have been no bloodless revolutions. The thirteen states fought off the British Army. From the time of Rome and Greece, and probably further back, man had been fighting and killing for what he believed in. All of the brothers in Africa had had to fight bitter battles against the devil's imperialism. That was the part I had played in doing what I would have done to Isidro.

But killing the white man was different. Shooting the oppressor and killing a man the day before you had called 'Brother.' I wasn't sure. It seemed like the same old thing all over again. CORE against SNCC against Charles Kenyatta's Mau Maus. It still seemed like brother against brother.

The voice in my head was arguing with the voice in my conscience. The voices were raging over my soul. There might never be a winner, I was thinking. They might always fight. There must be a winner!

This is only the first step in the revolution. Cleaning house before you go out to face the Man. This is still the preparatory stage, and there must be men who eliminate the ones who stand in the way of our freedom. When it comes to the Beast and the cleanliness of the community, there is no color. There are oppressors, and there are those who must be free. If the people who are not free are not aware of the way that they must cleanse themselves, then it is up to us who think we have found the solution to help them, whatever the cost. And I had been willing to do that. I had been willing to stain my soul with the blood of another *man* in order to free those who needed freedom most.

I felt good. I felt as though I was right. I felt alive.

April 5, 1969

Dr King was killed a year ago today. He was shot down in Memphis by an assassin. I was watching the reruns on the TV and asking myself when it would all be over. Lindsay was walking around uptown telling the brothers and sisters in Harlem not to be angry. It was the act of one crazed man. But so was the death of Medgar Evers. So was the death of Mrs Liuzzo. So were the deaths of the children of Birmingham and of Cheyney, Goodman, and Schwerner. These were all the acts of crazed men. Slavery itself was the act of madmen. Where would it all end? Be cool? Be calm? Don't riot? Don't tear up? Where would it all end? Every time another Mack Parker story hit the world, it slapped America in the face. Every time there was another bombing or another man like James Meredith was shot at, it was another boisterous round of applause for the United States. One by one the men who stood up for black freedom in this country were being slaughtered, and the only answer was 'Be cool'? It was at times like these when I would say, 'Burn it all down, goddamnit! Burn down every goddamn brick and stick and store! Burn down every piece of concrete and cheap house that the white man ever constructed in this hellhole of a country, and shoot to kill! If we should die today, then what have we lost? Nothing comes from living like dogs. Burn it down!'

May 5, 1969

'I've always wanted you, Tommy. I've always loved you. Since the day I met you.'

'Quiet, Princess. You'll wake up the night.'

'You never believe anything I say, do you?'

'I believe everything you say.'

'Why haven't you ever brought me here before? You've known that I was in love with you.'

'I brought you here because I needed a woman.'

'How did you know I'd come?'

'I didn't know.'

'But that's all there is to it?'

'I care about you.'

'But you don't love me.'

'Why do women always ask so many questions after they've made love?'

'I couldn't ask you this before.'

'Why not?'

'Well . . . I didn't know how you felt.'

'Wasn't it more important to know before you slept with me?'

'I couldn't ask.'

'Because if I had told you this, you weren't supposed to get in bed with me.'

'I don't know.'

'But you wanted to be in bed with me.'

'I loved you.'

'And now . . .'

'Now, I still love you, but I know you don't love me.'

'I care about you.'

'Is that supposed to be the next best thing?'

'Meaning that that's all I have.'

'And you won't ever love me.'

'Ever is a long time.'

Pause.

'Will you ever get married?'

'There's that word "ever" again.'

'Have you ever been in love?' Stop. 'Have you been in love before?'

'When I was eight I loved a girl who was sixteen.'

Giggle. 'Did she love you?'

'She didn't know I was alive. I loved her because she wore pretty dresses and had long pony tails that I would've loved to yank.'

'What happened to her?'

'I don't know. Somehow I knew it wouldn't work out for us. But wow! My hands used to itch sometimes because I wanted to pull her pony tails.'

'For attention?'

'Yes, and because that was the only expression of love that I knew. In school, if my friends ever saw you pull a girl's pony tail, she was immediately your girl.'

'And that was all the love you had?'

'That was *the* crisis. I've had women. We always understood each other. We needed each other, and we made love. That was all there was to it. I really wanted to love some of them. Either because . . . It was always gratitude, because they understood the fact that I needed them, and they came with me. Knowing that there would be no wedding bells and knowing everything else about me, I guess.'

'And me?'

'I don't know.'

'Did you think that I would be like that?'

'Like what?'

'Keep coming and coming because I love you, knowing that

all you want to do is sleep with me and then erase me from your mind?'

'I can't erase you from my mind.'

'But, you're not in love with me?'

'I guess I don't really know what love is.'

July 8, 1969

'Good evening, brother,' the voice said. 'So glad you could make it. As you noticed, we were waiting for you.'

I glanced around the room, and the three brothers nodded at me.

'Your work concerning Mr Valsuena was recognized, brother. Believe me, it was a credit to the people of your community and a step forward for black people everywhere in America who are victims of the Beast.'

The voice was coming from the head of the table. I could see that he was seated, but all there was was a silhouette and no more. I wanted to see his face.

'Unfortunately, brother, there was someone else in your area who took up where Mr Valsuena left off, and there must be something done about him. Are you any less willing to help your people now than before?'

'No.'

'Pass the picture to Brother Hall,' the voice commanded. A large blowup the same size as the picture of Isidro was handed to me. The shock on my face must have been plain.

'You know this brother?'

'Yes. I do.' It was John Lee.

'There are two things that we have in mind for you, Brother Hall. One, of course, you have before you. The other is a trip to Detroit. We will discuss the other matter with you later in the week.'

I didn't know if he was through or not. I simply got up and headed for the door.

'I assume, Brother Hall, that everything will be taken care of?'

'Yes,' I said in monotone. 'Everything will be fine.'

I didn't think 'fine' was the word I wanted to use. I climbed the stairs in a hurry. The night air was hot, sweltering, blanketing, smothering me, and choking off the air. I wanted to run. I wanted to run because the air currents go by faster and you feel cooler. I wanted to run because I didn't feel well. I felt like I was going to be sick. I wasn't going to throw up, I was going to be sick in my mind and my heart and my soul. Where are you, other man? Where are you, man who knows all about me? Where are you, man who killed Isidro, because I need you to kill somebody else for me. God knows I don't want to kill John Lee. John Lee! John Lee is a fat boy who lives around my block and used to work at the food market, bringing stuff to my mother on that bicycle with the big tub in front where the food is kept. John Lee is the guy who invited me to his house for a party . . . Why? Why is he so stupid that he has to keep on dealing those goddamn pills and shit? Why is he so crazy? Why can't he just stop?

I think I know all the answers. He's on a merry-go-round, and he can't get off. Now, that's very funny, John, because so am I! Well, in a way I am. The brother asked me if I would do it, but why should anyone else have to do it? You would be just as dead. Well, now that you mention it, I'm not on a merry-go-round at all. I'm out here in this world. That's just about the same thing, because I don't know if this is real. I don't think it is. I think that we are puppets, and someone is pulling the strings on us all. I don't think I can do what I want out here, but I think that there are some things that have to be done. That's what you think? You think that even if you don't see any drugs, let alone sell them, that there will be someone selling them and I'll have to kill anyway. KILL? John, do you know what you just said? You just said the word. Damn! I think I am a dedicated man to the cause of uplifting black people . . . I said I *think*, John, because sometimes I just don't know. Like I just don't know right now. I know I don't want to kill you, but I know you have to die.

Then all at once it hit me. John Lee doesn't have to die! I think I can scare John Lee into stopping. Maybe I can just talk to him. And say what? And say that if he doesn't stop, I have to kill him. And he'll laugh and say that I'm his boy. I'm a friend of his. He'll say I couldn't kill him. He'll be right!

July 9, 1969

I went to see a guy that I knew on the block named Game. He was called Game because he was a con man. I knew that he would be able to help me with the problem I was having.

'Look, I need to talk business,' I said. 'Where can we talk?' For the moment we were in the middle of a crowd of crapshooters in the crap corner at the 17th Street park.

'Business?' he asked. 'Brother, you just said the magic word.' He picked up a five-dollar bill from the center of the pile and walked away with me.

'I need a key to put a thing together. Can you help me?'

'What kind of key?'

'Door key. A master for an apartment.'

'Frame-up?'

'Yeah.'

Game smiled a bit and pulled out a pack of Luckies. 'I didn't know I had competition in the neighborhood.' He laughed.

'It's not really comp,' I said. 'Just a small thing.'

'What's it worth to you?'

'A yard.'

'Whew! Can't be that small if it's worth a yard to you. A hundred dollars ain' no small action. Why don't you cut me in?'

'A yard for the key. Your help I don't need.'

'Where's the place? What kinda joint?'

'Brownstone walkup. Three to a floor. Even corners coming off the stairs.'

'A yard?' Game came out of his pocket with a key ring that must have contained at least a hundred keys. He shuffled through them while we strolled to the shade of the park maintenance house. The New York heat was merciless. I was watching the smaller children run through the afternoon spray from the sprinklers and wishing I could do it without looking like an ass.

'In advance, brother,' Game said.

'Half and half,' I told him. 'You take all, I keep the key.'

'What if it wouldn't work an' you paid for it?'

'I know how to find you.'

He wiped his forearm across his face. 'This is it. She gonna work every time out of a million.' I handed him fifty dollars.

'I'll see you tonight in the Cobra. About eleven bells.'

He nodded and walked away.

I headed toward 15th Street. The way I had things set up, John Lee had left his house near noon and was still gone. It was almost two o'clock. I had called N'Bala and told him I wouldn't be working today.

I had found out from Nissy what John's main play was in terms of pills. He told me, for the price of a bottle, that John dealt more Blue Heavens than anything else. Our conversation also pointed out that John's parents had left the day before for Syracuse or Buffalo or somewhere. That was why I went to Game and borrowed the key, or should I say rented the key?

The key slipped perfectly into the lock and brought a

satisfying click from the middle of the door. I opened it and slid inside. I noticed quickly that the apartment had been recently painted and that the Lees lived well. I passed through the living room to the back bedroom, where I saw John's clothes all over the bed. I was searching for almost ten nervous minutes before I found what I wanted.

Inside his closet was a brown paper bag, stuffed under a tall stack of boxes full of old clothes and games and baseball gloves. Inside the bag was an entire cuff, twenty-four packets of pills. I stopped at the four packs labeled: 'Immies. Ivy Hall. July 9.' That was more or less exactly what I wanted. When John delivered the pills and they were no good, he would be threatened, maybe even beaten. The possibility came up that he might be killed. Anything was better than my having to do it.

I took the four packs that were to go to Immies and substituted my own special Blue Heavens. The ones I fixed up, filled with salt. I was very careful to leave things the way I found them. I didn't want John to know.

Phase Five

'Are you Mitchell?' the captain asked the officer seated at his desk.

'Yes, sir,' was the reply.

'I read your name on the report we had last night about previous narcotic arrests in the district. I thought you might be able to help us if we talked and compared some notes.'

'I understand you went to see Paco Valsuena and his brothers,' Mitchell commented.

'We went to see them, but that's about all,' the captain said, leaning backward in the chair. 'If the info we got is correct, the trip was a definite dead end.'

'Why so?'

Lieutenant Thomas sat across from the captain's desk in his usual chair, right in front of the fan. Mitchell, the young Narcotics detective, sat in the guest chair that had been occupied earlier in the day by a man named Watts. Captain O'Malley got busy on the phone.

'Sergeant, give me Manhattan State Hospital, please. . . . Yes, I'll hold on.' The captain started unbuttoning his jacket and tie while he waited for a reply. 'Hello,' he said. 'Yes. This is Captain O'Malley of the Tenth Precinct. I'd like to have your records on a man named Paco Valsuena. Yes. That's P-a-c-o, Paco; V-a-l-s-u-e-n-a, Valsuena . . . Yes, I'll hold on.'

'Did you bring those things that we asked you for, Mitchell?' Lieutenant Thomas asked.

'They're outside at the desk,' Mitchell said, getting up.

'Yes,' the captain said into the phone. 'He was admitted on May 19, 1969, and has been given no definite release date. Thank you.' The captain wrote down all of his information in a notebook.

'Dead end?' Thomas asked.

'Yeah. Paco has been in Manhattan State ever since May 19.'

'What about Jessie and Slothead?'

'I'll call,' O'Malley said.

Mitchell came back into the room carrying a small leather case. He flattened the case on the captain's desk, opened it, and pulled out several pads and other notes.

'Give me TWA at Kennedy International, please,' Captain O'Malley said into the mouthpiece.

Mitchell looked questioningly at the captain.

'Jessie and Slothead left for San Juan on July 4, according to their mother, and haven't been back yet. We're trying to clear them. If they were on the flight they were supposed to be on, they couldn't have been on 17th Street last night.'

'Right,' Mitchell agreed.

'I'd like to have you check your passenger list for July 4. This is the ten-fifty-five flight to San Juan, Puerto Rico. The two names I'm looking for are Jessie Valsuena and Francisco Valsuena. That's V-a-l-s-u-e-n-a.'

Pause.

'They were on the flight?' Pause. 'Thank you ... I will be sending a man named Conroy to your offices at Kennedy later on during the day. He will be checking all of your return flights since then. Is that okay? ... Thank you.'

Captain O'Malley hung up the phone and turned to the two officers.

'They weren't in the States?' Thomas asked.

'Evidently not. I'm going to have to do some tighter checking, of course. I know that it's possible that they came through without using their proper names. The way I understood it, neither of them would move without receiving the word from Paco. He hasn't been available.' The captain turned and spoke into the intercom. 'Sergeant. I want you to send

Lieutenant Conroy in here as soon as he returns from dinner.'

'Yes, sir.'

The three men looked at each other for a second. It was a time of year when no one likes to just sit and think. They were doing a job that always seemed to have too many loose ends and too many details to check.

'What help can you give us?' Thomas asked Mitchell.

'Not too much on this one,' Mitchell admitted with a sigh.

'What about Isidro?'

'Isidro was killed approximately twelve-thirty A.M. on the morning of January 4, 1969. He was shot once with a .32-caliber automatic pistol. There was a silencer on it . . .' Mitchell continued reading. 'There was no sign of a struggle, and his mother testified that to her knowledge nothing was missing from the room to indicate robbery as a motive . . .'

'Clues?' Thomas asked.

'One .32-caliber automatic bullet was found. According to our reports, the gun it belonged to was sold by order to a Robert Miller, 169 West 113th Street. We looked into it. There was no such person at that address, and according to the landlord, never had been.'

'Had this bullet been fired?'

'No. If you care to look at the photographs that were taken at the time the body was discovered, you see where the bullet is in relation to the body.' Mitchell passed the two officers a blown-up photograph with the bullet outlined in chalk.

'If the bullet hadn't been fired, how did you trace the gun?'

'The gun was found the next day in a trashcan on Eighth Avenue,' Mitchell said.

'Fingerprints?'

'Clean as a whistle.'

'We got the word this morning that John Lee and Isidro

were having some hassle because of territory and this kind of thing,' O'Malley told Mitchell. 'What about that?'

'John Lee's name never entered the conversation before,' Mitchell said.

'When you searched the room, did you find any narcotics in quantity?' O'Malley asked. 'Such that would indicate that Isidro was a pusher?'

'No, sir. We found his works rolled up in a sheet in the bureau ... The one over here.' Mitchell pointed again at the photograph. 'He had the usual needles, eye dropper, syringe, cotton, and alcohol ... Oh, here's something. There were ashes on the floor, and we took them to the lab to determine whether or not they were from marijuana or what, but they were from regular cigarettes ... The only reason I mention it was because Mrs Valsuena said that Isidro had developed a light attack of asthma and didn't smoke cigarettes at all. I asked her who had been in the room with him visiting, and she said that Isidro didn't allow his visitors to smoke either.'

'So you think that the killer smoked a cigarette while he shot Isidro?' Thomas asked sarcastically. 'What brand?'

'We didn't find any cigarette butts in the room,' Mitchell said.

'The killer didn't leave his cigarette butt, either?'

'He left the bullet instead,' Mitchell said.

The intercom hummed for a second, and then the sergeant's voice broke through. 'Lieutenant Conroy is here, sir.'

'Send him in,' O'Malley said.

'What do you have on John Lee?' Thomas asked Mitchell. The younger man shuffled through the papers in the valise and came out with a sheet.

'Practically nothing. All of this is information we started running down since this morning. No arrests. No pickups. Nothing.'

'We're going to go and visit Mr Lee after we talk to

Conroy,' the captain told Lieutenant Thomas. 'We'll see what he knew.'

A young plainclothes detective came in. He was about thirty years old, black, and wore horn-rimmed glasses.

'Lieutenant Conroy,' O'Malley said, 'This is Lieutenant Thomas of Homicide and Lieutenant Mitchell of Narcotics.' The three men shook hands.

'What else do you have on Lee?' O'Malley asked.

'Autopsy says that the time of death was approximately eleven-twenty-five. Lee was first hit on the head at the base of the skull, causing unconsciousness and second-degree concussion. He was then shot with ten c.c.'s of pure heroin. The direct result of the injection was a heart reaction, causing his left ventricle to explode under the pressure.'

'Could the lab boys give anything about the murderer?'

'Whoever it was weighed about one hundred and fifty pounds at least. This, of course, is a very rough approximation. The blow was struck at an angle of forty-three degrees, which means the killer was right-handed, or at least used his right arm to strike the blow. The weapon was a piece of clean wood, like a billy stick or a broom handle. There were no chips of wood implanted in the skull from the contact ... When we went through the assumed murder routine, it took us seven minutes to strike the blow, prepare the injection, and then shoot the victim with the solution.'

'A calm bastard,' O'Malley said.

'We think they were trying to make it look like a suicide. There were no prints on the needle that was taken from the arm.'

'What was the cloth that they used for a tourniquet?'

'An undershirt. Been through about thirty washings. It was shredded, and we couldn't uncover any laundry marks.'

'Damn!' Thomas said. 'This is as thorough a thing as I have

ever seen. A dozen possibilities, and we don't know much more than we knew before.'

'Robbery?' O'Malley asked. He was enjoying Mitchell's in-depth, detailed report, and was adding the facts that he did not have to his own report.

'There was $28.42 found in the victim's wallet. Evidently that was all he had. There was a picture of a girl named Debbie Clark. You can check her. Also some *Bambú*, cigarette rolling paper that the block uses for reefers. A library card for the library on 23rd Street and Seventh Avenue. A card that names the food market on 28th Street as his employer. A ticket to see Peter, Paul, and Mary in Central Park . . . that's about it on that . . . If there was a robbery, it wasn't for money or concert tickets.'

'The brown paper bag,' Thomas said.

'Sounds like a winner,' O'Malley said. 'Probably some dope.'

I.Q. Is Really Ivan Quinn

July 11, 1968

'You were the model for my sketch,' she said.

I took the rough-surfaced art paper she offered and stared at it. And there I was, or so I am to many, sitting on a gray-slate mantel that was formed like a chair, staring out over the small tributary that tumbles from some distant lake within the vast confines of Central Park. Dressed in a dashiki, blue jeans, moccasins, and wire-framed sunglasses – reading *Alcestis*.

'Was I?' I asked. 'You have painted more than me.'

The look she had given me was somehow reminiscent of small children when first they go to the zoo and see the many animals, restless and nervous inside their steel cages. The young mind is alive, and the eyes dart everywhere at once, trying to see the fantastic before it disappears.

'May I sketch you?' I asked.

'Do you sketch?'

'Not nearly so well, nor with charcoal,' I admitted. 'I consider myself a painter with words. Another mere poet. I really think I'm a romanticist. I would have liked to have been around with Tennyson and Byron, but those were the days when black men were mindless vegetables, if you believe the authorities, capable of nothing more than having a plow strapped to their backs like some pointed-eared jackass, and weaving and stumbling, digging a crooked furrow in the earth.'

'You may "sketch" me if you like,' she said.

I took a good look at her. She was blushing, making

a great to-do about brushing the golden hair from across her eyes. This was more than anything else to keep from looking at me.

She was dressed in a billowing cotton blouse that I disliked. The wind had taken hold of it and blown it away from her breasts. The shorts she wore had once been jeans and came nearly to her knees. I was more interested in her face and skin. The face was soft, so much so that for a moment I thought it only an image of her true face. I felt almost as though I must write quickly in order to capture the impression before the breeze swept it away. Eyes, blue and set wide apart. Nose, thin and well formed, like a sculpture of some ancient Greek goddess. Mouth, sensual and tender, with just a trace of rose lipstick.

It seemed that we looked down together at her feet. They were covered with sand and mud from the bottom of the stream she had crossed to deliver my likeness.

'I like to go without shoes,' she said.

'A true form of freedom,' I said.

She stopped blushing, and her eyes read 'danger.'

'You're making fun of me!' she snapped.

'Be not affronted at a joke. If one throw salt at thee, thou wilt receive no harm, unless thou art raw.'

'A quote from whom?'

'Junius.'

'I . . . see the point,' she said.

She sat very still while I wandered over her face and limbs, discovering with my eyes what I would convey with my pen. I picked out a sheet of paper and started to taste her secrets, as she looked first at me and then quickly away when our eyes met.

'Please remember that poets have a license to lie . . . Pliny the Younger,' I said.

'And will you lie?' she asked.

'What purpose of a lie except to fool those who come with
importance?

   Sweet soft something that must be only now, where
were you when I was straight and cast up on the shore for
God's inspection? were you only in my mind, or truly in
my eyes? with lips like fresh rosebuds, eyes like fountains
of mystery, and all of life in your smile that I no longer
can see, where were you when my mind was smashed like
a rag doll atop a sphere of this concrete hell? . . . and
                         where will you be in the morning?

'Did I make you think of this?'
   'You bring a lot of things to mind . . . What's your name?'
   'Margie Davidson.'
   'I'm Ivan Quinn. Some people call me I.Q.'
   'Hi.' She gave me *that* smile again. 'I thought I was the only
one in the world who knew of this spot. It's covered on all sides
by the bushes.'
   'I only found it today. Perhaps for you it's an unlucky
day.'
   'Why?'
   'Thursday the thirteenth.'
   'But isn't it only on Friday . . . ?'
   'The general root of superstition is that people observe when
things hit, and not when they miss; and commit to memory the
one, and forget the other . . . Francis Bacon.'
   'Are you superstitious?'
   'No,' I said. 'But I sometimes like to know things like that.
I read astrology to find out if the sign is right for whatever I
have in mind.'
   'And if the sign isn't right?'
   'It's according to how badly I want to do it.'
   She smiled again.

I.Q. Is Really Ivan Quinn | 187

'Do you smoke?' I asked, offering a cigarette.

'Thank you.'

I lit both cigarettes and took another look. She was about eighteen or nineteen. I noticed a high-school graduation ring on her finger that said 1966. Beneath us and across the stream, I saw her large painting pad, pocketbook, sunglasses, and sandals. She was watching me closely.

'Did you get anything from Euripides?' she asked.

'Only that without gods walking the streets like cops, there would have been nothing for him to write about.'

I reached into the shirt pocket of my dashiki and pulled out a joint. Without looking her way, I lit it, inhaled deeply, and passed it to her. She took it and pulled hard on it once and handed it back.

'I seldom like to read what dead people have written. I don't mean only people who have been buried, but people who were only walking death when they lived . . . There was nothing there in the beginning, I suppose. Their lives were only struggles for the merest existence, not a battle for the difference between fantasy and reality. Where is the reality in Euripides and Aeschylus and Homer? They . . .'

'They related what the people believed at that time,' she said.

'Then where was the reality within the age they lived in?'

'. . . Where do you go to school?' she asked.

I paused for a second. Without answering, I took a drag on the reefer and leaned against the back of my throne.

'I'll be entering Columbia as a sophomore,' I said.

'*Entering* as a sophomore?'

'It's really all very funny,' I said. 'Because I will go on being a hypocrite there as I was in high school and everywhere else. It's a funny thing about hypocrisy. You see . . . it's contagious. You come to a point in your life where you see the inadequacies and even the stupidity of what you are doing, but you are forced by society to do things that cut against your soul. I would rather be dead sometimes than relating to James Joyce and Norman Mailer, but there is actually nothing else that you can do.' I passed her the stick and lit another. Our pedestal was caught in a fog of perfume.

'You could be a hippie,' she said, giggling.

'Yes. I suppose I could. But even the unorthodox has become a sign of conformity. First there were beatniks, and now hippies, and tomorrow whatever ... They say that they're living life the way they please, but watch them. They get high and cry. They get straight and cry. Where is the reality there?'

'What do you want to do?'

'What the hell do *you* want to do? ... I mean, it's your world. Why do white people always ask so many questions?'

'You were the one asking the questions!'

'Rhetoric. Not to be applied personally, I don't guess.'

I passed her another stick. I was almost certain she was going to get up and go. I didn't really want her to. The sun was setting, starting to drift to another quarter of the flatisphere. God's one great jaundiced eye peering into the insanity of our tabletop world.

'I.Q., who quotes quotes,' she said, giggling. I giggled myself.

'And what were you doing here on a Thursday?' I asked.

She laughed even harder.

'I was stood up,' she said.

'By a doubtless fool. Never see him again. One strike and you're out. Imagine the audacity of the ass to leave you stranded within the boundaries of this mini-wilderness with nothing to save you but a piece of charcoal.' We both laughed. 'I think the swine should be hunted down like a mad dog and shot!'

'And who will be the hunter?'

'I will! It was I who first realized his asininity and made my disapproval a matter of public record. I think that at the next board meeting he'll be castrated and his family jewels set in bronze as a lesson to all those who would dare desecrate the privilege of an afternoon alone with you, disconnected from all the mores and folkways that bind us.'

There was more laughter. The marijuana was affecting us both. We watched, near hysterics, as the poem I had written was caught in a breeze and went floating over our jutting station down into the stream.

'I'm really not amused,' she said. 'I've just – oh – lost – haha – a precious gift. I think I shall have to take my painting back.'

'I'll be damned!' I yelled, still laughing. 'I'll write a thousand more, and all of them will come together only halfway between my ineptitude and the glory of your beauty . . . I mean that.'

'Do you?'

'There was a time when a girl as beautiful as you couldn't stay near me for such a time without being kissed. . . . But I keep thinking that perhaps you are an illusion, something that my fading hope has conjured up to keep me sane.'

'And . . .' I didn't let her say anything at all. I reached for her and gently pulled her to me, until I could crush her cotton blouse beneath my palm and feel her pressing her lips to mine.

Her mouth was wet against my neck, and her tongue darted in and out of my ear, flashing a signal to my loins that sent swift shivers up and down my spine. Still, somewhere my mind was outside, cruising objectively along, snickering and taking notes at the funny-looking black-power advocate and skywriting the word h-y-p-o-c-r-i-t-e across my glasses with indelible foam. Where is the reality here, I wondered. What new games will I play now? I knew all along what she had in mind when she came trotting up here with her silly-assed interpretation of a giant penis charcoaled across that goddamn sandpaper. Here was another blow against the establishment. In the arms of a black man equals running through Central Park without shoes equals wearing cut-off blue jeans instead of Wanamaker's Queen Wardrobe at only a million dollars down and a million a month for the rest of your life. I was all caught up in the whole trip. And the winner of the Miss I-had-a-better-nigger-than-you-did contest that will be held in the girls' dormitory at Miss White America University on the day that school opens. And the reason is because my nigger not only had a tremendous dick, but quoted Junius and other famous people that I had not even heard of.

Here we have, ladeez and gentlemen, the main attraction of the ages. The dainty flower of the Western Hemisphere and crowning feat of world femininity – Miss White Woman! Applause. Whistles. And in this corner, wearing only an XL prophylactic – BIG BLACK BUCK! Boos from the white men in the audience. Right before your very eyes, this beauty, pale as snow, will be ripped to shreds by that incredible instrument that you women are feasting your eyes on between our specimen's legs. He will place it right at the mouth of our fair maiden's sexual opening and plunge it into her very bowels. She will at that time scream. Oh, my God! I'm coming! I'm coming!

In my mind I had to deal with the fact that my discovering a flaw in this new relationship, another ulterior motive that made our frantic involvement still synthetic, was nothing new. I had often related to the ideas of Sartre and Genet as to the basically banal nature of women and my lack of realism when near them. After all, the true nature of existence was one of pure independence, if you believe the Bible. There was no Mrs God, who shared all of her husband's problems, trials, and tribulations. There was no Mrs Jesus to wear black when her man was nailed to a cross. Even without my relating myself to the deity, I could see where men of certain natures would not be able to resolve themselves to sharing all of their innermost thoughts with a woman. The basic nature of a woman is emotional, so how could she possibly be able to relate to an intellectual dilemma? This was a part of the reason for my sneering at women in professional positions. If for no other reason than for the fact that once a month they *had* to deal with these internal issues that would make them sick to their stomachs.

On the block I was constantly engaging in the hypocrisy of daily living, simply trying to find an object or a theory that I could say was something I shared with others. The little girls I knew were incredible. They stared at me as though I were a freak, and when I got high I wondered if subconsciously I didn't perpetuate their images, because I couldn't understand them either.

'Let's go down there,' Margie said.

'Right.' I was talking to her and getting up and walking with her, and mad at myself.

Perhaps, I thought, sex is the link between men and women. It's possible that Western civilization has created a monster by giving women the same rights that men have. This way, they relate to each other in all phases of existence, and this exterminates the mystery that was once involved with romance and the word 'love' itself. If this is the case, then American society has prostituted everything by building up artificial sexual boundaries between black and white. The grass is always greener on the other side of the fence. White women wanted black men because they saw them treated like animals and responding like animals. Chained and beaten, living in a shack without even the vaguest of sanitary props. They wanted the black man because they saw no tenderness and gentleness, and their masochistic tendencies were brought vividly in their own minds. The white man had brought civilization into the bedroom, and black men could not afford the luxury of an inhibition.

Margie and I lay out next to each other in the high grass. I lit a reefer, and we smoked in silence, watching the rainbow colors attack each other as the sun sank and the leaves on the trees swayed gently in the wind. The only signs of the life we wanted to leave behind us were the blaring of car horns out in the street and the laughter and chatter of other people that reminded us that we did not exist alone.

I kissed her gently on her lips, and she smiled shyly.

White women must have a patent on shy smiles, I thought. I wonder how thoroughly it hides their desires in their own minds?

I disguised myself among the thousands of souls that clutter the Lower West Side of Manhattan. I was turning myself into a multiple schizophrenic with such clarity that at times I could even swear that I had seen my other selves. I could see the guy who wore my body and spoke in monosyllables in order to get into bed with an empty-headed, full-bosomed bore. I could see the other Mr Quinn who sat at a card table in the middle of midnight and filled the air with profanity. All for the privilege of sitting inside a circle of subintellects and drinking Thunderbird wine.

I found my hands beneath Margie's blouse fondling and squeezing her breasts. Her face was buried in my neck, sucking, biting, and kissing. I looked up, and the sky was covered with stars that only the darkness could truly expose. They were dim and faded in the twilight.

She bit me hard and started to nip at my Adam's apple. I squeezed her knee and parted her thighs to my hand. The fleshy thigh near the juncture between her legs was hot and damp. I pulled away the protective panties and teased her opening with my fingertips.

I.Q. Is Really Ivan Quinn | 193

'Please, Ivan,' she gasped. 'Please, take me.'

I almost laughed out loud. That seemed like a direct quote from every piece of cheap pornography I had ever read. White women with fantastic builds slid in and out of bed with the ease of a mouse running through the Lincoln Tunnel. They would be tossed across a bed by our hero of inordinate staying power, and then yield to him at least through four thousand orgasms in the next six pages.

Where is the reality here? I asked myself.

I pulled my pants off with my right hand while I continued to tease her and scratch her with my left. When my job of manipulation was done with her underthings, I reached under to spread her legs, and started to enter her, slowly and with as much patience as I thought the situation warranted.

'Ohhhhh . . . Ivan! Ivan!' she gasped. 'Please, Ivan.'

Wow! I thought abstractly. This is the thing that black women are aspiring to when they paint their faces and dye their hair? This is what black women are trying to be when they get nose jobs, faces lifted, padded bras, and wigs? . . . Our people are too much impressed by the media. The white man has done a job on our women's minds. You can't tell the whites from the light-brights without a score-card.

The things that were going through my mind were just what Afro was telling everybody in the neighborhood when he talked about BAMBU. He said that the only way we could retrieve our people's minds was to take them away from believing that each and every thing they saw on TV would make them more equal.

Afro is really a guy named Tommy Hall. He had been trying to start a chapter of this organization he belonged to in the Chelsea area. I had heard him talk at a P.T.A. meeting in the school on 17th Street. After his speech I acquired some reading material on the group and approached him at a party given by another guy on the block named John Lee.

I had decided to join because I had been fascinated by the idea of revolution, and all of the material spoke of cultural revolutions, and the intimation was that eventually revolution on a grand scale would be inevitable if the demands of black people were not met.

The whole idea of blackness sent your mind through a fantastic tunnel. When I was young, the biggest insult you could throw at an enemy was 'You black bastard' or 'You black something else,' and now there was a stigma about the word 'Negro' that meant you weren't hip to what was happening. But the word 'black' and the theory about white frigidity and negativity took away the word 'individual' from your vocabulary. Anyone who had made a favorable impression on you who was not black had to somehow be made to look as though he or she was something other than white. There was no room within the movement for the search for yourself, because the theory of black unity takes away all of the unique qualities to be discovered within the individual. That was aside from the fact that total autonomy was completely impossible anyway. But what about the countertheories to that? What about the fact that the whole is only equal to the sum of its parts? What about the fact that a chain is only as strong as its weakest link? Without a black man or woman finding out whether or not they were completely compatible with life itself, what was the point of lending total support to the security of a nation? How could a greater cause be supported when first of all the need that we all have to discover our own separate peace was without fulfillment?

The worth of the state, in the long run, is the worth of the individuals within it ... John Stuart Mill, I thought. And we will have a worthless state *and* nation when we find our own insecurity unfolded after there are no more bridges to cross.

I even wrote a poem once to convey my dissatisfaction with a total commitment to the movement.

> i, the finger on the hand,
>   refuse to roll up with the fist,
>   until someone answers this:
>   How long will this anxiety
>   persist in my mind? Who am I?

'. . . And my number is EN 6–0897,' Margie said.

'Good night, good night! Parting is such sweet sorrow, that I shall say good night until tomorrow.'

Margie blushed a bit, and I kissed her lips. Then she was trotting away through the clearing, looking back occasionally, perhaps to see if I was real. I waved back, and finally she was gone. The only true reminders of her were the charcoal sketch of me tucked in my pocket and the floating relic of a poem, hung up on a rock in the middle of the stream like a paper ship caught on a sand bar.

I looked up while lying flat on my back, and heard the wind whisper to me and the concert of the animals, unleashed and feeling free to sing now that most of the intruders had vanished into yet another wilderness. The stars lit up the sky like so many fireflies dashed upon a black canvas. The moon watched without so much as a glance at earth's confusion, cold and removed.

I had promised to meet Margie the next day on 59th Street. We would go to a motel and spend the night. Now I was wondering if that hadn't been a too spontaneous move, something brought on by the delirium that follows making love, when you swear about love that is not there and whisper sweet thoughts that truly have no direction.

July 12, 1968

It was nearing midnight, and I had gotten Margie to let me out where we met. The entire situation about entering the motel with her and listening to her moan out her pleasure had not been a pleasant experience for me. I felt ill at ease about the surroundings and the whole atmosphere. I felt myself doggedly going through the motions of a man ecstatic with sexual pleasure, but it would have taken little more than an amateur to realize the truth.

Just as I was about to get into the car, a drunk stumbled into me. I turned, and his face was appalling, something that I felt disgusted by. There were scabs along his forehead, and he stank of wine and urine.

'Looky 'ere, Buddy,' he choked. 'I rilly ain' gon' han' you no line, cauz you know sometimes I jus' ain' got the energy to git all hooked up wit' no tale about all this wil' shit. I'm tryin' a git me a bo'tl an' I sho' wisha God you'a gimme some money. You know what I mean 'bout gittin' all tied to a goddam' lie so like you livin' one? You eveh felt you wuz jus' livin' a lie, man? . . . My goddam' stahs in heaven know I useda be livin' a lie, but I rilly like to git drunk. . . . Thass why I ain' got nuthin' again' a young hippie anna no motherfuckin' else cauz why inna hell cain' a man git good an' fucked up, right? I mean, thass on him. What you rilly care . . . Have yah got annythin' I can help git my bo'tl wit'?'

'Yeah,' I said. 'Can life itself be not at some times intoxicating to such a point that you are a drunk no matter what?'

The drunk smiled, perhaps realizing what I said and perhaps not.

'You know, I'm glad you ainna a goddam' Chrishun, you know? I mean, the onny thing I got agains' God iz Chrishuns.

*BE*cause they is lushes onna one day an' a Chrishun on anothuh. I would give a goddam' dollah to the man who can criticize from the pulpit an' sympathize fromma bar stool. You know what I mean?'

'There is very little near us, save hypocrisy.'

'Nigh lemme tell you somethin',' he stammered. 'Nigh you a colored fella an' you done gimme this quarter. I done been askin' white folks to gimme somethin', an' they look at me like I got some kinda somethin' thass gon' kill they chil'ren. I mean thass gonna kill they chil'ren. You know?'

If he had ever been white, he could not now be truly so classified. The dirt from the floor of bars and the scars of living the life of a man with nothing was ingrained in him and as much a part of what I saw as his ragged clothes.

'Thanx, buddy,' he said, staggering away.

'Think nothing of it,' I called.

I got into my car and took off across 59th Street, turning on Second Avenue and mixing with the light midnight traffic that drifted toward lower Manhattan. The drunk and the things that he had to say were still on my mind.

Who, if there is no God, decides who is righteous and who is not? I wondered. Where is the special reward for the high and mighty here on earth who sneer at their fellow beings because of his or her particular station in life? Imagine the confusion that is caused by people aspiring only to be better than someone else so that they can base their successes only on the lack of accomplishment by others. Regardless of all the talk about milk and honey in heaven, you are still dead. Even the Pope, the man closest to God on earth, will one day be dead. Has he really gone on to a greater reward, or is he in the ground? Are you on the right hand of Jesus walking up and down through golden streets, or are your bones turning to ash and maggots and worms chewing at your flesh?

People rap about reaping the harvest of the earth by gaining friendship, and set out as best they can so that they may count up their friends like S & H green stamps at the end of the day. In the meantime, you can never count on friends the way you can count on yourself. When you are pulled from the womb, dripping and bawling, you are all by yourself. And when they throw dirt on top of the box that contains what once represented you, you are all by yourself. Your friends will not be in there with you. Oh, they may reminisce for a week or so, and your name will come up in the conversation now and again, and your woman will wear a black dress. But after a while your friends will forget you, and the neighbors will stop peering around corners to see what your woman is into, and she will start going to bed with other men. The same gap that first you fulfilled with friends will be covered with dirt and disappear while weeds and grass come to cover the tombstone that carries your epitaph. The same warm thighs that you caressed and the same love funnel that you entered in your woman's bed will be caressed by others and enjoyed by the living.

And what will you have to show for your kind heart and good will? A stone marker saying 'Here lies a man with a kind heart and a good will.' Soon even the greatest of things that stood for you on earth are gone. All the nice comments that were whispered about you as you walked down the street were as worthless as the air that transported them from mouth to ear.

The only true definition that a man can put on death would have to be in relationship to his definition of life. The true philosophical questions must primarily be left out of the ghetto. A man is too overcrowded in Harlem to spend the first sixteen or so years of life establishing the proper moral codes that will guide him when he moves to live next door to a white man. There will be no thoughts of clean, wholesome

America as long as sex, dope, and discord are your next-door neighbors.

These are the thoughts that had first given me my inclination toward joining BAMBU. This and the thought and adventure that the word 'revolution' seemed to intimate.

I remembered my establishing a desire to become a part of it when I listened and commented during a discussion with Afro at a party given by John Lee. It just happened to be after I had written a poem about Harlem and poverty.

HARLEM: THE GUIDED TOUR

Claude Brown has made it out!
Let the world stand up and shout!
Forty nights and forty days
Shall we sing the zebra's praise.
                              coming outside and reintroducing
myself to the cold that was inside,
smoking a cigarette on 125th Street.
On this block I see six liquor stores.
White man set a black dummy behind
the counter and wound him up. He
responds much like Galton's dog must have.
You come in and it pulls a string:
'May I help you, sir?' sort of like
digging on one of the white man's talking dolls that
blew your daughter's mind
and blew your fifteen food bucks for Christmas.
You pay him and it pulls a string:
'Will that be all, sir?'
                    . . . and you swear because
that pint is all you *couldn't* afford . . .
take about five swigs and the Hawk ignores
you . . .

next block you encounter the
get-white-quick man selling numbers,
and you laugh 'cause some fool said
that the problem with Harlem is that there
ain't no factories for black people
to work in. . . . hell! They got a misery factory
manufacturing hardship and busted dreams.
                              . . . put a dollar down on 444 an'
cross your eyes for good luck.
                              . . . bye-bye dollar and
dollar's worth of food and
dollar's worth of heat and
dollar's worth of hope.
                              . . . bye-bye dollar and
dollar's worth of clothes and
dollar's worth of unpaid bills and dollar's worth of love
                              . . . cause your wife is gonna
close her legs and open her mouth when she sees
that bottle in *your* pocket.
Hello! to a junky in the next block
standing on the corner scratching the corners
of his mouth and imitating the leaning tower of Pisa.
Hello! to 400,000 New Yorkers who loved
reality so much that they never want to see it again.
Runaways, hideaways, and getaways from one hell to
        another.
                              . . . climb the stairs and listen:
to the joyful noises your neighbors are making and
say hello to the rats that have so long been a part of your
life that they all have names.
                              . . . climb the stairs to:
soul music and soul food and lost souls in Harlem—
no longer even singing about heaven.
                              . . . get a good night's sleep because

I.Q. Is Really Ivan Quinn | 201

you're on the air again tomorrow morning
at six a.m.

June 28, 1968 / The Party

'All the world's a stage.' William Shakespeare.

'May you live all the days of your life.' Jonathan Swift.

John's party was a typical thing. You dance, you smoke, you drink, and you take advantage of everything that is happening in your favor. If the chick you're with is drunk, try to get between her legs. If she's not drunk, try to talk your way between her legs.

I realized what was actually happening after I had come in and sat down for a while, merely watching the things that were going on in the room. White people *and* black people are really psychological disaster areas. The whites, because they have never had any feeling for warmth and rhythm and are basically, sexually, frigid. Black people are becoming lost because they strive to imitate the white man's symbols of coolness and by so doing lose contact with their own emotions.

The truly interesting aspect of the set was Afro and the discussion that came up about riots and their causes and effects. I felt, for some reason, that Afro had convictions and was truly doing what he wanted to and living life for what it really stood for in his mind. I knew that I hung out, not because it was intellectually satisfying, but because I was searching, looking for something to relate to. After I heard Afro talk, I decided that perhaps through helping others to gain perspective about the things around us and the nature of the society we live in, I might gain new insight to what I really wanted to do.

Afro told me how I could become a member of the volunteer

faculty that he would be needing when BAMBU opened a center in our area.

Being as objective as I possibly could, Afro was real. He didn't seem to be trying to impress anybody with the amount of knowledge he had about the movement and the topics that we covered concerning it. I was almost a bit thrown off balance when he asked me whether or not all I did was quote people. There was an undercurrent of the question 'Where are *you?*' in the middle of his inquiry.

I felt even more unreal and false when later in the evening I made a play for this chick from down south and caught myself pretending to be drunk and filling my mouth with all the hip phrases and colloquialisms that I knew of. She was impressed right away with the whole setting, the New York thing, and the city slicker who had fallen head over heels for her.

'Look here, baby,' I said. 'You ain' rilly gon' git into no "Goin'-back-down-South-thing" only a few days after I have discovered you, are you?'

'Well, that's where I live. I have to go back home.'

'But, you don' seem to be relating to how well we could do if you were here an' I could be with you.'

'I understand what you're saying, but you know what is.'

'Iz that really the way the world is? Give a man a taste of a good thing and then snatch it from him. How cruel are you?'

She turned to me in the dim light and placed the palms of her hands on my cheeks. The look in her eyes was all concern and apparent sympathy for the pain she was bringing me.

'I'm sorry,' she said.

'Then let's be together for tonight. Let me take you out an' show you New York. Jus' to have you with me for as long as I can.'

'All right,' she said after a brief hesitation.

I rambled all through our trip down the elevator about how many things I would show her and how many things I would like to show her if only we had more time.

'I have always dug women from the South. Square bizness!' I told her.

'Why?'

'I don' know. I guess I always thought that they knew more about taking care of a man an' tryin' to understand him ... Women up here cain' cook, cain' sew, an' the only reason I can fin' for callin' 'um women is because they have the babies.'

She laughed. 'You probably just haven't met the right one,' she said.

'I met you.'

We walked down through the Village. It was a Friday night, and all of the hippies and other weirdos were out there doing their thing. Ruth Ann was amazed by all of the wild clothes and the ramshackle buildings that decorated Bleecker Street and West 4th Street. I could only imagine that her idea of what the Village would be like had been closer to the Taj Mahal. She filled the air with a million questions that always related to the semipuritanical curtain that black women are veiled with in the South.

'How can people live like that?' she kept asking.

We saw all the long hair and serapes and sunglasses that she would need to see for years to come. I showed her a reefer, and I thought she might literally die. There was no chance of her putting it to her lips and becoming a junky. We ate at one of the many corner hot-dog stands and simply watched the people go by, mainly young whiteys out for a night of excitement.

When it was time to take her home, for some reason I was very sad that the evening was over. I had enjoyed being with her. The thoughts that I had had earlier in the evening about getting in bed with her inside some Bleecker Street flophouse had somehow disappeared when I first saw her in the light. I felt even more like a fool, because she had her reality, but I was still a long away from mine. I kissed her good night passionately. It was passionate, for me, because I hoped to continue the masquerade she had become attached to. I believed at that time that the thoughts of what had been on my mind were revealed to her. She took my spending an evening with her without a hint of sex as a sign of true love. I told her that I would call her the next day and take her somewhere, but I didn't.

July 27, 1968

I finally received my letter from BAMBU. It rejected my application for a position as teacher.

Dear Mr Quinn,

We received your letter of application for position on the faculty at our Chelsea branch. Unfortunately, we are unable to grant you a position at this time. Please feel free, however, to apply again at a later date. Also enclosed are free pamphlets about the program of BAMBU in the greater New York area.

Thank you,
Brother Domingo

I had never expected anything at all like that, but my little affair with Margie Davidson had taught me that I wasn't really ready to dedicate myself entirely to blackness. I felt it necessary that I talk with Afro though and tell him that I had really tried to join, but that things hadn't worked out.

In the back of my mind was a glimmer of possibility that he might want to hire me anyway. I caught up with him after a speech that he made at the Chelsea center and showed him my rejection notice. He said in so many words that it was too bad, but that there was nothing he intended to do about it. I simply left it at that.

July 15, 1968

On the Monday following my trip with Margie to the motel, she had told me to be sure and call her. She told me that we would be able to get a lot straight at that time. I stayed up late the night before and watched television. It was amazing how much you could see about the lives people led and about the truth that they seemed to be attempting to escape from in their everyday lives. Television was the current that turned America on, because the whole country is strangled by routine and tight schedules and the anonymity that comes along with becoming a number and relating to the life of an automaton, programmed only to exist.

I had had the pleasure or discomfort of seeing an adventure flick with spies and bombs and gadgets that brought me back to the view I had been taking of the existence the country has succumbed to. Black people with sunglasses on at three a.m. in the subway. White people by relating to the lives of Ozzie and Harriet. Black people by aspiring to the level of Ozzie and Harriet, when the whole situation was really ten steps backwards. For a minute I wanted to look outside in the middle of the flick and see if I could catch a glimpse of Judy Garland and L. Frank Baum skipping down a yellow-brick replica of Ninth Avenue with singing junkies instead of Munchkins.

It was at that time that I decided that black people were

never going to get together with enough authority to cause a major revolution in America. Their whole thought pattern in terms of what the revolt would consist of was hazy and vague. They didn't know if freedom meant working alongside a white man with the same pay, therefore necessitating a 'white' education, or if they wanted a separate state of all black people, such as Texas or Mississippi. They didn't know if they wanted integration or separation, war or peace, life or death. They didn't know if they wanted to kill the whiteys or save a few. There was not even a clear definition of liberal. Malcolm said that there was no such thing as a liberal, but the Black Panthers worked hand in hand with the white SDS. There were too many goddamn groups doing too little.

I wished at that point for a return to the humanity and the reality that black people must have once represented.

Perhaps I was wasting my time even worrying about the movement. What was I into? In the movement or out of the movement, or out of the question, I didn't know.

I dialed Margie's number.

'Hello.'

'Excuse me, I'd like to speak to Miss Margie Davidson, please.'

'I'm sorry. Miss Davidson isn't in.'

'Do you know when she'll be back?' I asked.

'She'll be back on August 11,' came the reply. 'She's gone for her vacation in Paris.'

'Thank you.'

And I'll just be a monkey's uncle or an ass's ass! I almost laughed about the whole situation. I should start some sort of interracial Hertz Rent-A-Dick, giving privileges for any strung out ofay bitches to get their ashes hauled anytime of the day or night. No wonder she had said we would get things straight!

I.Q. Is Really Ivan Quinn | 207

December 10, 1968

Of all the months that there are, December is the worst one to be alone, out on the corner with the Hawk, drinking wine and thinking prose. The people in the city are frozen under ordinary circumstances. Too busy to pay much attention to a faggot strutting down 42nd Street dressed in a G-string. Too preoccupied to feel sorry for a wino or lush strewn in the gutter on the Lower East Side. Much too dead inside to see the pain around them and inside them.

Life whistles by us. We sit in iron castles and scream an occasional 'Slow down!' realizing only that before we are alive there is someone standing over us whispering in Latin. We know that there should be some way to bring existence under our command, so that we might savor the good things and speed the intolerable sadnesses that blanket us far too often on their way to memory banks without keys. The only true disaster is that the thought of death has become so frightening that the reality of life escapes us.

December came, and many of the things that I had seen as life rafts on a stormy sea had gone hurtling by me. Margie was gone, and though she had played only a small role in relation to my total existence, a big part of my mind had been dedicated to the enigma of her presence. I had severed my position with her from the rest of my mind, and set thoughts of her aside as though my head contained volumes and volumes, each covering a separate subject. My attempt at joining BAMBU had been liquidated, and now only came up when I saw Afro or the Swahili teacher they had employed from Colgate.

There was still one person left in the neighborhood that I felt at ease with, however. His name was Ricky Manning. Ricky was almost two years younger than I, but we stayed with each other much the way wallflowers cluster at a party. Neither of us quite fit in anywhere. The only real problem with Ricky was his overwhelming preoccupation with death and the purposelessness of life.

'What are we going to do when we can't get high anymore?' he asked one night.

I looked down at the empty capsule packets between my feet: Darvon Compound-65/ propoxyphene hydrochloride, aspirin, phenacetin, and caffeine. xs3751 amx.

'The human capacity for being bored, rather than man's social or natural needs, lies at the root of man's cultural advances. Ralph Linton. *The Study of Man*,' I quoted.

'And we will advance when we get bored again? To what?'

'To nirvana.' I laughed.

'Will nirvana get us down there?' Ricky pointed at the street below us. We were standing in the loft of the warehouse E. W. Cook abandoned on Eleventh Avenue when the rats moved in.

'That's really the problem, isn't it? Whether or not we want to be down there? What's stopping us from going down there or going into the Cobra or anywhere else?'

'Are we free down there?' Ricky asked.

'Man is free anywhere his mind is free,' I quoted.

Ricky sighed disgustedly. His breath was making steam in the darkness. The steam bumped the windows like stray clouds and blurred my view of the streetlight that illuminated our position.

'Eastern philosophy?' he asked.

I looked at him severely. This is the problem with the whole world. A boy, seventeen, mentally superior to his playmates, and lost. Not lost because his parents didn't love him or for any other trite sociological reason, but lost because a world full of people still make up an empty world.

'It may be the answer,' I said.

'Will you stop it?'

I was acting again, and I could feel it. I thought for a second that Ricky could sense it too. He was always so critical of everything that I got into, trying to save myself. Maybe that was why I always found myself hanging out in places like this, talking about things with more enthusiasm than I really felt.

'You can really understand this,' I said. 'Stretch your mind a little. Why do you think Americans always shake their heads in stupefaction when they look at movies and things that take a close look at the kamikaze pilots? They simply can't imagine a man being willing to commit suicide for his beliefs. They can envision heroism, but not the giving of life. They can see the risking of a life, but not the deliberate dismissal. They see life as an end.'

'But that's brainwashing. There were no free kamikazes.'

'But it displays the point I'm trying to make. The total commitment to a way of life!'

'So you now suggest that we go out and shoot up Times Square so that we can get killed, but knowing that we have taken a few more idiots out of their misery.' Ricky's sarcasm was thick in the air, as thick as his breath against the window. I clenched and unclenched my hands in my pockets.

'It shows the importance . . .' I began.

'Just knock it,' he said. 'I don't need it! If you're committed to the idea of the mind being the controller of everything, go see one of the whitey hippies an' get yourself some LSD. Take a trip after every meal. What do I care?'

'I may do that,' I said.

'And when you come back with your copies of the *Vatsayana* and the *Kama Sutra*, make sure they have epitaphs somewhere in the back that you can read over my body . . . I think I'll come back as a wine bottle.' He laughed derisively. I headed for the ladder that would take me to the roof and back outside. I was very puzzled by Ricky's whole bag. He would find me to laugh at me and my ideas, and I stood for it, when I could blow his whole bag away with ease and show him just where we were. I never quite knew why I didn't do it. There was a ton of confusion involved with the whole scene. I would stay away, come, go. Ricky would come by my house, laugh, sing, and write epitaphs for himself in my notebooks.

Maybe the answer was the 'cats.' There were certain downs that we took every once in a while, called 'cats' colloquially, and I noticed that Ricky was at his lowest when we took them. What I needed to do was check with the man on the block who was giving out with all the dope. I went to see John Lee.

'Look, John, I ain't askin' you to quit dealing altogether,' I told Lee.

'Shhh! Keep it down. You want my old man to hear you?'

'I just want . . .'

'Okay! Okay! But go see Seedy. I ain't the only cat around here with a deal. I ain' sold Ricky no catnip in a long time, anyway. Most of them go to the whiteys in Chelsea and up near 19th Street.'

'So you think he's been getting them from Seedy?'

'What the hell I know? I jus' wanna make sure you don't hold me responsible if Seedy turns out wrong.'

'Where does Seedy live?' I asked.

'Up on 17th Street, next door to José's. The top floor. You won't catch him now. It's too early. He gets in about twelve onna weekdays. Eleven on Saturdays and Sundays.'

'You know a lot about him,' I commented.

'It pays for number one to keep up with number two,' he said, laughing a little.

'Yeah.'

I left John's, making a mental note to catch up with Isidro and tell him what I told John. I was going to protect Ricky, whether he wanted me to or not.

January, 1969

I had been toying with the idea of taking LSD for some time before Ricky sarcastically suggested it. When our school took its midyear break, I decided that the time was right for me to take the plunge. I had a free weekend with nothing to tie me down in the way of homework, so I took off downtown to a spot on Astor Place where a white classmate of mine told me they were always 'making that scene.'

The room was dark and musty; dust seemed to rise from the rotten floorboards with every step I took. A small, apprehensive whitey with big, bloodshot eyes had asked me for a reference at the door, and I told him my classmate's name.

'Anybody know Allan Rosen?' he called.

'Yeah!' I heard. 'Let him in!'

The door was unlocked with a snap and the chain unhooked.

'It's not him. It's a friend.' The doorman turned back to me. 'You never can tell what kind of package the Man will dress up in.'

He led me back through the narrow, dim corridor to a larger living room where all of the furniture had been discarded and crammed into corners. The floor was used for sitting, sleeping, or whatever the people on it happened to be into. There were about ten teenagers and early-twenty-year-olds lying all over in various stages of dress. The only light was supplied by two giant candles. I peered through the shadows uneasily, and the curious peered back.

'You a friend uv Alley's, huh?'

'Yeah. He told me to come down and check you out.'

'Yeah? Why don't he come down and check me out?'

'Are you Barbara?'

'That's right.'

'Well, he said . . .'

'Save it,' she said, cutting me off. 'Sit here. All this yakkin'
will blow everybody's high. Me an' you can converse softly.'

I sat next to her in front of the candles, looking around
the room now and again. She immediately lost interest in me
and started to toy with the melted wax that dripped along the
candle vase, forming thin and thick red stalactites. Somewhere
behind me there was incense burning, and the aroma twisted
its way through the smell of sweat and funk to my nostrils.

'You come to get high or write an article for TV?' Barbara
was laughing and twisting the ends of her dark hair through
the wax on her fingers. 'That's what some people want to
do, you know. I think I coulda been on TV ten times. Dum-
De-Dum-Dum.' She started humming the 'Dragnet' theme. 'I
mean, like on TV programs about freak-outs and all that . . .
I didn't do it, 'cauz I want my parents to think I'm dead.'

She took her hands out of the wax and started waving them
over the candles like one of those strippers from the Far East
in an Ali Baba movie. I was caught up in watching the patterns
formed on the walls and listening to her voice. She giggled.

'This guy from *Life* magazine comes in, an' he wants to
have my picture in the magazine along with my philosophy
about everybody gettin' high an' doin' their own thing. He
comes in here with his camera and a checkbook, the whole
bit . . . So we're sittin' here rapping about this an' that, an'
this chick Susie I had in here comes outta the john freaked
out of her mind on speed . . . Like, she's havin' a bad time,
an' she goes through her thing, an' I'll be damned if Mr
Life magazine doesn't get the hell up an' run outta here!'
Her laughing became so wild that she gave up her hand
patterns for a second to put her hand over her mouth. 'I
mean, like, imagine a big company like that sendin' a square
to dig on life . . . *Life* can't dig life!' The laughter started all
over again.

I.Q. Is Really Ivan Quinn | 213

'I came to get high,' I said.

'Goddamn magazines anyway!' Barbara coughed. 'D'you have a cigarette? I need to go out an' buy a whole lotta shit, but I don't feel like it.'

I tapped the bottom of the cigarette pack until the filter of a smoke stood out, and Barbara grabbed it. I lit it for her, and she nodded. The guy who had let me in came over to us.

'Barb, if I'm goin' to the store, I better go now.'

'So go! You know where the money is! Did I tell you what to get?'

'Yeah.'

'So what now?'

'I wondered what this cat wanted,' he said, indicating me.

'LSD,' I said.

'Seventeen hours'll cost you four bucks,' Barbara said.

'Okay.'

'Get it, Jimmy,' Barbara ordered. Jimmy disappeared into another back room. 'My doorman. A good strong wind come through this dump, an' I'll need another one.' Jimmy came back with a small round tab.

'I guess you gonna take it here,' he said.

I nodded. Barbara took the tab and dumped ice cubes into a glass of water. Jimmy zipped his coat and went through the corridor toward the front door.

'You ever trip before?' Barbara asked.

'No.'

'I didn't think so. It's wild, man, really wild.'

I was lying flat on my back in an open clearing with no one around for miles and watching clouds play leapfrog. The scene reminded me of Coney Island and the bump cars that you get into and try to knock each other to hell. The tall wires that connect your car with the mesh-wire ceiling zoom to and fro like tight barbed steel as you laugh hysterically in the middle of the chaos.

There was nothing near me save a few strands of haggard corn and wheat stalks. The whole countryside was yellow and pale, with few splotches of green about. The trees were naked against the sky, barren and shivering, branches doing their best to conceal the trunk's privates. Birds flocked on limbs and dotted the scenery, chirping uncontrollably. The whole connection seemed to shake loose in my mind. Corn, wheat, birds, but no leaves. What season is this? The grass seemed to be growing under me, pushing me up toward the clouds that were really only bump-'um cars. I looked down at my rising carpet. Blue grass. I was in Kentucky with a banjo on my knee. I looked at my knee. No banjo.

The word that was tugging at my head for attention was 'photosynthesis.' The grass was germinating, copulating, procreating, multiplying under my eyes. I had a microscope inside my head, or a magnifying glass in my hand. Maybe it was only a monocle. But there was the grass reproducing more grass that spread all over the countryside, six feet high. It covered the scrawny corn and wheat stalks and seemed to rise like a sea of blue grass up around the waists of the wading trees. Inside the hollow sprigs of grass were tiny people, tossing buckets of water into one tunnel while buckets of sunlight were being mixed in the next compartment. These were grass follicles; like hair on a human head, they were hollow, and there were things going on inside. I wondered quickly if I had landed on top of some giant's head. A poor giant with blue hair and tiny men living inside the follicles as slaves. *Slaves!* Tiny men and bigger men, and me not being either. I was not a giant or a lilliputian. I was still outside, watching and reporting to myself. There was no one else around to listen. I think I will call out to see if there are any other people near here like myself.

'Hello!' I called. Echo. Echo. Echo. Echo. No reply.

'I'm Ivan Quinn. Is there anyone else here like me?' Echo. No reply. 'I am a human being from the planet Earth. I don't know how I got here, but I am in no particular hurry to get away. My intentions are friendly . . . Take me to your leader.' I laughed at that last part, because it was obvious that I was still on earth. All of the things I saw were totally recognizable. The little men were shaped like humans. The hair on the giant's head had follicles, and I could relate that back to biology. The fact that there were trees on his head being rapidly covered up by the hair was no concern of mine. Or was it? The trees were up to their necks in blue sea hair. The expressions on their faces were sad but resolute, as though they were only succumbing to the inevitable. Oh, no! I thought. Don't tell me that this is a dream with a hidden message about conservation. The only fact that was disturbing me now was the question of what I would breathe once the trees had been killed. This would eliminate the oxygen and the rest of that silly-assed cycle that's supposed to be going on all the time. Unless, of course, this was really just exceptionally speedy grass. In that case, where were all of the people? I would really just like to see someone and ask them what the hell they thought of all this madness. The birds were definitely not in favor of it. They had flown and taken up new perches on the wires that connected the electric mesh with the bump-'um clouds. They were pointing accusing wings at me.

'Birds!' I screamed. 'Get the hell away from that goddamn electric stuff. Don't you know that as soon as someone pays another quarter to ride, you're going to be electrocuted?' The birds didn't seem to be as interested in their preservation as they went about chirping back and forth and pointing at me.

216 | The Vulture

'Then stay the hell there!' I said, still rising. 'At least one problem will be solved. When I see someone get into one of those clouds, I'll be able to find out what gives around here.'

I came to a theory at that time that I had died and gone to hell. I was very disappointed in the fact that hell was a lot like earth. The real exception so far was that there was no sun. Was it day? It was light. I came to the conclusion that the sun had been only a giant electric bulb that God had at last decided to turn out. In that case, what was I doing here? Maybe I was in hell, after all. According to the Norse legends, the center of the earth was ruled by a giant demon named Satyr, who had been banished to that internal oblivion by Odin for attempting a revolution that would have taken power away from Odin and Thor. But where was the heat? Giant demon? Satyr was rising to the surface. Did he have hair? Evidently. I was caught on top of Satyr's head, and there would soon be another conflict with Odin and Thor. I was going to a battle with a front-row seat.

No sooner had I come to my conclusion when I stopped rising. The trees had only their faces above the surface. The birds flew back to their stations at the trees' topmost branches. Their singing had ceased, along with their gestures toward me. I was surrounded by a wall of silence.

PLASTIC PATTERN PEOPLE

(preface to a poem) like, will you come back to the real?
black people – oh – walking cool – oh – silly woman
crying over *AS THE WORLD TURNS* – like, can't you
dig that you have no tears to spare/like, can't you see that
the chains that bound your limbs now bind your mind?
making you relate to silly, make-believe, fairy-tale-type

shit! like, will you come back to the real and see that
Snow White was just that, and a thousand shades later
won't get it.

THE POEM

glad to get high and see the slow-motion world,
just to reach and touch the half-notes floating.
world spinning (orbit) quicker than 9/8 Dave Brubeck, we
   come now frantically searching for Thomas More
rainbow villages.
   up on suddenly Charlie Mingus and Ahmed Abdul-Malik
to add bass to a bottomless pit of insecurity, you
   may be plastic because
you never meditate about the bottom of glasses,
the third side of your universe.
                      Add on
Alice Coltrane and her cosmic strains, still no vocal
on blue-black horizons/your plasticity is tested
by a formless assault: *THE SUN* can answer questions
in tune to sacrificial silence/but why will our
new jazz age give us no more expanding puzzles?
(Enter John) blow from under always and never so that
the morning (*THE SUN*) may shout of brain-bending
    saxophones.
   the third world arrives with Yusef Lateef and
Pharaoh Sanders with oboes straining to touch the
core of your unknown soul. Ravi Shankar comes
   with strings attached/prepared to stabilize
   your seventh sense (Black Rhythm!)
up and down a silly ladder run the notes without
the words. words are important for the mind/the
notes are for the soul.
                        Miles Davis? SO WHAT?

> *Cannonball/Fiddler/Mercy*
> *Dexter Gordon/ONE flight UP*
> *Donald Byrd/Cristo*
>   but what about words?
> would you like to survive on sadness/call on
>   Ella and José Happiness/
>   drift with
>
> Smoky/Bill Medley/Bobby Taylor/
> Otis/soul music where frustrations are
> washed by drums – come, Nina and Miriam—
> congo/mongo beat me senseless
> bongo/tonto – flash through dream worlds of
>   STP and LSD. SpEeD kIlLs and some/times
> music's call to the Black is confused. our
> speed is our life pace/not safe/not good.
> i beg you to escape
>   and live
>   and hear all of the real. to survive in a
>   sincere second of self-self
> until a call comes for you to try elsewhere.
>   we
>   must all cry, but must the tears be white?

My assignment, that is, my task for the coming spring was to connect myself more closely with the interpretation of the insight I possessed so that I might be able to turn others on to the inequalities and hypocrisy involved with everyday survival. I resigned myself to carry a pen with me everywhere I went in order to paint these word pictures during moments of inspiration. Sometimes the thoughts that I wanted to bring out were pages long and often took on the form of essays, but even more often than this I was attacked by little blasts of feeling and sensitivity that I decided to describe as mind messages, for lack of a better name.

I.Q. Is Really Ivan Quinn | 219

MIND MESSAGE #1 I.Q.

Poet am I seeking a separate peace. (John Knowles)
Knowing no boundaries west or east.
Taking the pulse
 of a dying world

MIND MESSAGE #2 I.Q.

minds, like beds, hard to make up in the morning.
so many things to decide for a new day.
so many things went on between the sheets.

I was so concerned with the compact nature of the poems that I even decided to abbreviate my name during these intervals. The tragedy was that I still felt a bit like a hoax, an almost everything and a not-quite-anything. I told myself that someday when I had compiled these notes and gotten a concrete theory from the loose ends that I now saw, I would start a sort of cult to rescue people from deadening of the emotions – a disease I enjoyed comparing to hardening of the arteries, because the structure of the syllables was so similar. The results being equal in my mind, fatality.

School was tolerated. Not because I was hung up about becoming a status symbol for my folks, but because it was so easy to do acceptably while still not devoting a lot of time and energy to it. Half the time the school was in an uproar anyway, with all the young SDS hippies and Village 'anarchists' helping to stage a quasi-revolution. The purpose was to allow a college student to do his thing while still maintaining this student facade. There were hassles, with heads being beaten in by the City Man while chicks and cats ran around up and down 116th Street with signs about Columbia tearing down the buildings in the community and ruining people's lives and so much wild stuff that I never got involved. My stand was that whiteys didn't need any help getting their heads kicked in, when, in fact, they were the target of my revolution and eventual cult. I was going to intellectualize on the redevelopment of the emotions while they were running around succumbing to a mob-type stimulus that made them emotionally weak.

In the neighborhood things rolled along as before. I was into a rap-when-necessary thing with the women that allowed me to woo them when I felt like it was physically necessary that I recharge my battery. I would get drunk and get into a beg-and-plead, prayers-and-entreaties type of groveling, when we should have been begging each other, praying for a union of the soul also. The last of this was idealistic, but it expressed my sentiments on what type of hypnotic, puritanical veil the American black woman had become destroyed by. There was always an overtone of 'I'm doing you a favor,' until you were both between the sheets.

The only real problem that did not concern the path I was choosing concerned Ricky. He was more of an enigma than ever. He was warm and then cold. He was laughing and then sobbing. I wasn't sure if it was autonomous schizophrenia or drug-induced depression. As far as I could tell, he was still strung out on 'downs.' His attitudes intimated smoke, Darvons, liquor, and cats.

It was the cats that I was most concerned about, because he went through the thing about death. It was at a time like that when I felt closest to him and farthest away. Close because I knew I had an answer, and far away because he didn't really listen to me anymore. He came around when he was lonely and just couldn't express what was on his mind within his clique. There had been a time when John Lee first started dealing when he would come to me and ask about highs he should try and for suggestions about combinations that would give him a good ride. Now, there was just an occasional glimpse at what was going on.

July 3, 1969

At the end of the school year I went through a hell of a thing with my parents. During the year I had assured myself of a job as counselor at Camp Cheyenne for boys near Syracuse. At first it was a nice deal for my parents. I would be in the great outdoors soaking up a lot of sunshine, getting a lot of exercise, and all the other garbage that parents like to read into the comics of your life. But, as the year progressed and I finally broke down to them that I was into drugs, not heavily, but experimenting, they became paranoid about not seeing me for two months. By the end of June, when school was out, we had regressed to the 'We'll think about it' stage, and they offered me a trip to Boston for the Fourth of July weekend as a peace offering in case their decision went against me. I was already wondering what form my retaliation against the bureaucracy would take, and I thought seriously about leaving home, which I'm sure was a factor which delayed my parents' decision.

I wasn't very sure that as a writer I shouldn't be away from home anyway. Out from under the umbrella and away from the maternal umbilical cord and the paternal strap. There were many things that I was unable to experience while living with my folks. Things that would be essential in terms of human relations and depicting reality. There was much more involved with introducing yourself to life than a few excursions into drugs. Upon realizing this, I realized how many things there were to do before a man could say he had lived and had nothing more to live for. The problem had been that I experienced too much, too soon, thereby eliminating much of the adventure that comes along with legal, chronological maturity.

I did decide that leaving home would be a poor move, regardless of how my trial turned out. Being able to live at home had given me a taste of both worlds through my first year of college. I decided that to try to make it on my own would involve a job and college and interfere with my further discoveries within my soul through my writing.

I left for Boston resolute on playing pensive if I could not go to the camp, but remaining at home for a while longer anyway. The plane took off, and I was touched with the reality of *real* flying; how unimaginative it was, and how unlike what flying high was. Being high was a floating, cruising, microscopic drifting through all manmade stops. It was a slowdown for the showdown with your mind. This was nearly nothing after the takeoffs, except a tugging force that kept you erect. I vowed to fly back high.

July 6, 1969 / 7:00 P.M.

'That's all there is to tell,' my mother said. 'Evidently he jumped from the top of the warehouse and killed himself. Lord knows that that's probably the only thing that could have gotten him up there . . . But the poor thing. Ivan. Hating everything so much that he would have to do that! His mother almost died too. Can you imagine? Seventeen years old . . . But you know, Ricky did always seem like an old man. He never knew when to be young and when to be mature. He was always old.'

'Was there an autopsy?' I asked.

'Yes. I think she said there would be an autopsy, but no funeral. Ivan, that woman couldn't stand it! I tell you, it was the most pitiful thing I had ever seen in my life . . . They're going to have the body cremated.'

Sunday night. Went to Boston on Thursday. Said good-bye to Ricky before I left. Said I had some very important developments to tell him about when I got back. I had had in mind a purpose for both of us. The purpose of life being to experience all that you can along the specter of emotions and senses. Then to leave pictures and phrases depicting more beauty in the world than could be noticed when you were born. Death being not an end to life, but another experience, the final one, that you could not relate to people. Death being *the* experience, and the one that Fate would not let you describe to your fellow man.

Sadness overtakes the man who runs after it. Death overtakes the man who pursues him. Yama and Charon are alive and well in New York City! Ricky Manning jumped from a building, and there would be an autopsy and then a cremation. Where is the reality here?

8:00 P.M.

'Yes,' Mrs Manning sniffed. 'Ricky was taking drugs. I knew this. He got mad at me and started talking about being down all the time, and I was the reason . . . I never even dreamed that this was what he meant. I just thought it was angry talk. He swore at me about cocaine and all sorts of pills . . .'

'I know,' I interrupted. 'You know, you really shouldn't be out here talking about all this now. You've gone through quite a thing.'

'But I had to talk to you. You were very important in my son's life. All he ever talked about was I.Q. this and what you and he had discussed. I had to talk to you, knowing what a big part you played in my son's life.'

I wanted to say, 'But not a big enough part in his life. And maybe a part in his death.' Because if what Mrs Manning said was true, Ricky had not been looking forward to me leaving for the summer. But that was absurd. Naturally I had mentioned it. Maybe Ricky was jealous of my having found my answer, an answer which he was afraid he might not be able to relate to.

'Thank you, Mrs Manning,' I said. 'Remember, if there's anything in the world I could do for you, just feel free to call on me. I'll do all that I can.'

'Thank you, son.' She smiled through her tears that nearly made me cry. God! There's your reality! In that woman's eyes was a real piece of life and sadness that I had never experienced. Piece by piece, I saw the picture forming again at the top of my mind.

Fuck you, God! my brain was crying. Fuck all that you stand for, because you never even gave him a chance! I was so close! I was close enough to helping him to see my hopes in his eyes. I needed one more day to get back here and talk to him, and you fixed everything! Fuck you, God! And fuck death, because it's real, and there are certain realities that I know exist now. But I'm not ready for them.

'One more thing, Mrs Manning?' I asked. 'Were you told what kind of drugs Ricky was using?'

'I was given some long chemical term,' she said. 'But the police told me that they were called cats. Ricky had taken at least three of them.'

July 10, 1969

'Look,' John said, 'I ain't had no cats in months. I didn't sell Ricky no cats, an' I didn't see him on the night he died.'

John and I were sitting in my bedroom. I had called him after the ceremonies for Ricky were held on Tuesday and told him to come by my place.

'Look, man,' he continued. 'You keep giving me a hard way to go. I wanna know why! Am I the only man in the world who can spell cat?'

'All right,' I said. 'You want a beer?'

'Yeah,' John barked.

I went out into the kitchen and probed the refrigerator for two beers. I opened them and plucked coasters from the rack and took all the equipment back to my room.

'Where else could he get the stuff?' I asked after John took a big gulp from the can.

'What the hell I know?'

There was a thick wall growing between John and me. With every question that I asked and with each minute he spent in the room with me, the wall was growing. I didn't sense that he was afraid of the questions; I believed him. But nonetheless he was annoyed and irritated and a bit shook up. I could see the dark circles under his eyes. The thing that he was doing to the Junior Jones boys took on new meaning. It was no longer only supplying kicks, but quick deaths.

'What about . . .' I began.

'Cut it, Q. Cut it! I don't know nothing. I ain't seen nothing. And I don't want you talking to me about it anymore.'

I made another analysis. He seemed too uptight. Maybe guilt. Maybe personal guilt, and maybe guilt by association, but John Lee was uptight. His face was a sneer. His eyes were on fire. He gulped the last half of the beer in the can and stumbled to his feet, off balance in his hurry to leave. I heard the door slam out in the hall. He was gone.

July 11, 1969

'Hello?'

'Yeah, Q. This is Lee.' I heard the voice coming over slowly and with a hint of danger. 'Where were you on about the night of January 3 and the morning of January 4?' he asked.

'When? How the hell would I know?'

'Think hard. That was the night Isidro was killed.'

'I don't remember,' I said after a pause.

'Well, suppose I told you that while you were getting the beer last night I was looking around your room a little. And what if I said I found the .32-caliber piece you used to carry on the corner when the times was hot?'

'I'd say "So what?"'

'And what if I told you that out of curiosity I took it to the man who made it. A man from your block named Game; and he ran it through a check or two and told me that it was definitely the gun that was used to kill Isidro. Where would you say you were on the night Isidro was killed?'

I heard John's voice, rolling toward me like a giant boulder that I couldn't get out of the way of. His breath was rasping, heavy in my telephone, as though he had been running. I felt the sweat materialize on my top lip.

'I was downtown in the Village. Lower East Side. Hanging out with a few friends of mine. No, my friends didn't show. I was just sort of wandering around looking for them, because I lost the address. Uh. I was going in and out of dives and clubs, trying to find some tail. You know, uh . . .'

'What do you think the Man would say if he knew what I knew and had what I have?'

'I get the message,' I said. 'What do you want for me to get the gun back?'

'You know what I didn't like about the thing?' John breathed. 'I didn't like the fact that you set me up for a lot of people when you killed him. I didn't give a damn about Seedy. I didn't care if he lived or died. The people who dealt with him when he got shot never came to me. But you set me up.'

'What do you want?'

'I want seven hundred and fifty dollars in cash. I want it by tomorrow night. If I don't see you before midnight, I'm taking the gun to the cops, or I'll see that they get it anonymously.'

'What if I say that. I'll see that they get you?' I asked.

'So what if they get me if I ain't got nothing and my house

is clean? They may watch me, even close down my business, but I will survive ... You won't. Murder is a very serious thing. I remember when we didn't think so. We know better now ... You shouldn't have kept the gun, I.Q. A man of your intelligence should know better.'

'Where will I see you tomorrow night?' I asked.

'I'll be around. I won't give you a particular place to meet me. There's too much risk involved. But I'll be watching you. Be in the streets by eight o'clock with the money. I'll be watching you.'

'Where do you expect me to get that kind of money so quickly?' I yelled into the receiver.

'I don't care.'

The phone clicked shut. I was standing there with my ears burning, my ears stung by sweat, my whole shirt wringing wet. I could see the look on John's face. Seven hundred and fifty dollars for the gun. It was really too late to do anything but hope. I picked up the phone again. Many people can play at blackmail. I was all hung up with the adventure of pitting my mind against other people, while the reality of it all gave me a tight feeling in the pit of my stomach that made me think I might piss on myself.

'Hello, Margie?' I asked.

'Yes. Who is it?'

'This is Ivan Quinn, from the Festival Motor Inn,' I said.

'Who? ... Oh!'

'You didn't pay your bill when you left,' I sneered. 'Not all of it. The fact that I know you have an appendix scar and a birthmark on your right inner thigh was tabulated along with the bill. You owe us seven hundred and fifty dollars. Payable tomorrow afternoon.'

Phase Six

July 13, 1969

'Yes, sir. I'm Captain O'Malley, an' this is Lieutenant Thomas.'

The two policemen were ushered into a neat living room, where their host offered them seats. They sat next to each other on the sofa, and Thomas took out his black note pad.

'Now, Mr Lee, I know you've been through quite a bit today, but we have a few more questions for both you and your wife.'

'My wife is in bed now,' Hamilton Lee said. 'The doctor was in and gave her a shot. She has a bad heart condition. I think the shock almost killed her.'

'Then we'll come back and talk to her,' O'Malley said.

'Are you sure I can't answer everything?'

'Well, how long had your son been dealing drugs?'

'I didn't know anything about it until this morning,' Mr Lee said. 'We were out of town until this morning . . . I thought that I had spoken with every cop in town.'

'Then you're saying that you were informed of the drug situation by the men from the Narcotics Department.'

'That's right,' came the reply. 'A short man, Ramirez, and Sergeant Holder.'

'Did they search John's room?'

'They searched the whole house. Everything was in an uproar. The lady next door was kind enough to come over and straighten up.'

'They must not have found anything,' Thomas commented to the captain.

'What about enemies? Did John have any personal enemies he might have mentioned to you?'

'No. John was never involved too much in the gangs. He's only been out around in the last year and a half or so. . . . He got himself a job at the food market and made himself a few friends.'

'You made no notice of the fact that John was out a lot at night?' O'Malley asked.

Hamilton Lee was very uncomfortable. He was searching the walls of his apartment for something to look at.

'John was eighteen years old. The first sixteen years of his life or so were miserable. He was far overweight. He weighed almost 230 pounds, and then the doctor gave him some medicine for losing all this fat. He started going outside, playing a little ball. He got himself a girl friend. Sure, we noticed that he was out a lot, but we thought it was because he had been embarrassed about his weight for so long that he was just making up for lost time ... My wife and I were so happy to ...'

'Yes, sir,' Thomas cut in. 'You mentioned a girl.' The lieutenant searched back through his notes. 'Would her name be Debbie Clark?'

'That's right.'

'Do you happen to know her address?'

'Well, yes, but she and John weren't together ... They had a little fight of some kind. John said he wasn't seeing her anymore.'

'When was this?'

'In April.'

O'Malley and Thomas looked at each other. 'We'll take the address anyway,' Thomas said. Mr Lee recited it.

'What about close friends? People who might have known what John was doing?'

Mr Lee seemed to be lost in thought.

'Spade,' he said. 'That's a boy who lives in the projects. His name is Eddie Shannon. Junior Jones, who lives on 19th Street.'

'Do you know Shannon's address?'

'No.'

'And Jones?'

'His real name is Theodore. They just call him Junior.'

Thomas wrote hurriedly.

'And Ivan Quinn.'

'Who?'

'Ivan Quinn. He's a student at Columbia.'

O'Malley cut in, 'These three know about . . .'

'I don't know if they knew!' Mr Lee said. 'They were friends of my son.'

Tears were streaking Mr Lee's face. He had tried to wipe them away with his hand, and was now simply crying unashamedly.

'I don't know what to say,' he began softly. 'I knew that John was doing something wrong. He was buying clothes I knew that his job couldn't be paying for. He was buying presents for his girl . . . The things he bought for me and Cassie for Christmas cost almost fifty dollars . . . But what could I say? I told him if there was anything he wanted to talk to me about to come and sit down and we'd discuss it . . . Money. A car. Anything. But he said everything was fine. I thought maybe he was stealing money from his job. Drugs? I never even detected John's being drunk. And now this . . .' The big man sniffed and rubbed his eyes. 'Miss Carter, the woman across the hall, told me when she was here this morning that she had had a dream about John. You know how old people have these visions? John was a nice boy. Everybody told me he was always courteous and ran errands for them. And you want me to tell you something – Lord knows, I wish somebody would tell me – Cassie's heart is broken. When we had John, the doctor told us that she couldn't have any more. You know what that does to a woman who's been plannin' on a big fam'ly? Her only son. Her only son.'

July 5, 1969

'Yeah,' Junior Jones said. 'I been waitin' t'git high an' jus' be high alla time. Ya know?'

'Yeah.'

'I been wantin' t'git high wit' you cauz I wanned t'show you som'thin' that Afro gave me today.' Junior reached into his pocket and pulled out a cigarette with a squared tip. 'Ya know where Afro said he got this? He said he found it in Seedy's room. He said he went to talk t'Seedy, an' somebody flattened the back a hiz head. When he came to, whoever killed Seedy wuz gone, but he left this cigarette . . . You the only one 'roun' here square off the butts like this. Right?'

'Afro came to shoot somebody. He had a gun.'

'Yeah. You took it. But my seein' this butt here made me know everything real perfect. The night Seedy wuz killed, you saved me from Pedro. You came up behind us an' tol' him I had been wit' you smokin' reefers. You said that t'give yourself a alibi. The only thing that bothered me was why Pedro believed you . . . That wuz 'cauz Seedy had tol' all the P.R.'s that you could be trusted 'cauz you tol' him when I wuz gittin' ready t'rob him . . . You damn near got me killed twice. Once when Seedy found out I wuz gonna rob 'im an' started carryin' a gun, an' the other when you shot Seedy an' all the P.R.'s thought it wuz either me or John Lee.'

Ricky Manning smiled sourly.

'Does Afro know that I called to tell him about I.Q. an' that white bitch?' Ricky asked.

'I wuz gittin' t'that. I figgered it when me an' Afro started talkin' 'bout how somebody inna neighborhood wuz a dime dropper. When he tol' me 'bout what happened ta I.Q., I started tryin' t'figger out who me an' Q had in common. The answer wuz you. An' to top it all, you had a motive wit' me, but I thought you an' Q wuz tight.'

'I.Q. fell in love with a white bitch!' Ricky said bitterly. 'He met her at a motel an' screwed her. It wuzn't right!'

'Why not?'

'Ha! You simple bastard. You couldn't understand. I.Q. was mine! . . . How would you know what we had? We related on all levels. But there was no way for us to stay with each other. I.Q. is supposed to have a girl. Junior, did you ever love something that you knew you couldn't have?'

'Yeah. I guess.' Junior spoke through a cloud of cigarette smoke.

'Then you know what I mean. I came lookin' for you that night to tell you that Seedy was dead and to be looking out for Pedro. I knew he would probably try to get you. He hates your guts. I had to do something. I was getting all my cats from Seedy. I.Q. told Lee not to sell me any more. I went to Seedy and told him that I could give him some valuable information if he would keep me supplied with cats. I told him that you were going to make a hit on him and take all of his stuff . . . For a while things went on fine. He supplied me. Then John Lee told I.Q. I was getting my pills from Seedy, and I.Q. told Seedy to stop selling me anything. He thought I was going to commit suicide. Seedy got scared because everyone told him that I.Q. was crazy. When I showed up for my cats, he told me to get lost. He said that if I ever bothered him again he'd tell you how he found out about the attack you planned. I had to kill him.'

'Where'd you get a gun?' Junior asked.

'I took I.Q.'s gun. The .32 he has with the silencer. I killed Seedy, and then I put the gun back in I.Q.'s room. He never missed it.' Junior watched carefully as Ricky seemed caught up with a sudden wild sense of humor. 'I.Q.'ll go to jail for me if the Man ever finds that gun!'

'An' you tol' I.Q.'s secret love life to Afro because he stopped you from getting pills?'

'No. No. No. I told Afro long before that. It was about two weeks after I told Seedy about you. I.Q. wanted to join BAMBU, but I couldn't let him do anything that would keep him from seeing me every day. So I told.'

'So you told,' Junior repeated.

'Ha! Ha! You don't know what it's like to have to admit to yourself that you're a freak. To say to yourself that society does not accept what you want. You do a lot to hold on to what little you have. I knew I.Q. would never love me, but I had to keep him near me if I could.'

'And one thing led to another?'

'I told on you to get cats, Junior. Seedy gave me cats for nothing. They have to be the most beautiful high in the world. I told on I.Q. because I love him. You have to try to get the ones you love. Don't you? . . . And I killed Seedy to keep everything quiet. He was scared of I.Q. He was scared I.Q. would kill him if I got another cat from him. He was going to tell you that I was the traitor you were looking for. I couldn't let him do that to me.'

Junior looked away from Ricky. Tears had been welling up in Ricky's eyes as he confessed the things that he had done. It was all quite a coincidence. A light discussion with Afro about Uncle Toms had put them on the subject of brothers who informed on brothers. Junior had not told I.Q. when it dawned on him that the square-tipped cigarette butt made Ricky Manning the missing link. Junior had called Ricky and told him to join him on the roof of the warehouse where they often got high. Ricky agreed to come and get high, but now that everything was clear and tears were rolling down Ricky's face, Junior realized he still had no total answer. He looked across the New York skyline, a thousand twinkling lights, as though he would receive a coded message from the neon jungle. That was why he didn't see Ricky Manning jump eight flights to his death.

July 12, 1969 / 11:46 P.M.

'It's too bad you had to kill him, but I told him night before last that tonight was the deadline. Nobody can hit me for seven hundred and fifty dollars and then tell me to wait ... How much did you get?'

'he had about a hundred and ten in them blue heaven pills. i ain' riff 'im fo' cash.'

'Wednesday night he call me an' tol' me that he had two hundred and fifty dollars' worth of bad pills in the load I sent him. Anything wrong with the pills?'

'not nuthin' i can see.'

'What else?'

'he had a .32 inna paper bag wit' de pills. he gotta be a stupid cat runnin' aroun' wit' a unloaded gun inna paper bag.'

'But, so far as the five hundred dollars he took Monday and the rest, there were no signs, right?'

''ass right.'

'Yeah ... Well, c'mon in then, Smoky. I guess the party'll start in an hour or so. Did you reach Spade?'

'yeah. i caught 'im onna job.'

'That's a good boy. Look, I got this amazon go-go girl for you.'

'right. i need t'go-go fo' a while.' Smoky laughed. 'twenny minits i be there.'

Behind the twenty-five-story apartment building that faces 17th Street between Ninth and Tenth avenues, the crowd of onlookers stared with eyes wide at the bespectacled photographer who fired flashbulbs at the prone body. They did not notice the vulture flying overhead.